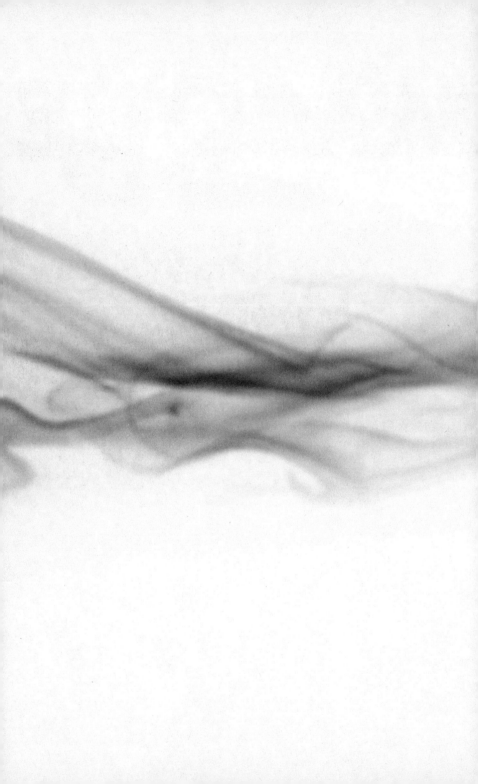

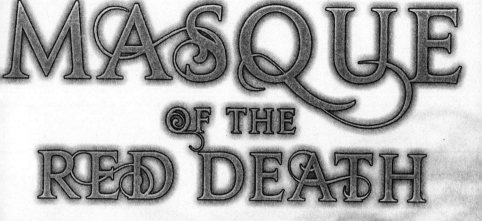

MASQUE OF THE RED DEATH

BETHANY GRIFFIN

GREENWILLOW BOOKS
An Imprint of HarperCollins*Publishers*

Masque of the Red Death
Copyright © 2012 by Bethany Griffin

The text of this book is set in 12-point Venetian 301 BT.
Book design by Paul Zakris

Library of Congress Cataloging-in-Publication Data
Griffin, Bethany.
Masque of the Red Death / Bethany Griffin.
    p. cm.
Summary: In this post-Apocalyptic twist on Edgar Allan Poe's gothic horror story about the wealthy trying to escape a plague, Araby Worth, a privileged seventeen-year-old girl who feels numb after the death of her twin brother, becomes caught up in a conspiracy to overthrow an oppressive government, falls in love, and faces the threat of a new plague.
ISBN 978-0-06-210779-4 (trade ed.)
[1. Plague—Fiction. 2. Love—Fiction. 3. Wealth—Fiction.
4. Adventure and adventurers—Fiction.]
I. Poe, Edgar Allan, 1809-1849. II. Title.
PZ7.G881327Mas 2012   [Fic]—dc23   2011039806
12 13 14 15 16 LP/RRDH 10 9 8 7 6 5 4 3 2 1
First Edition

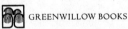 GREENWILLOW BOOKS

TO LEE, WHO IS ALMOST ALWAYS RIGHT,
BUT RARELY SMUG ABOUT IT

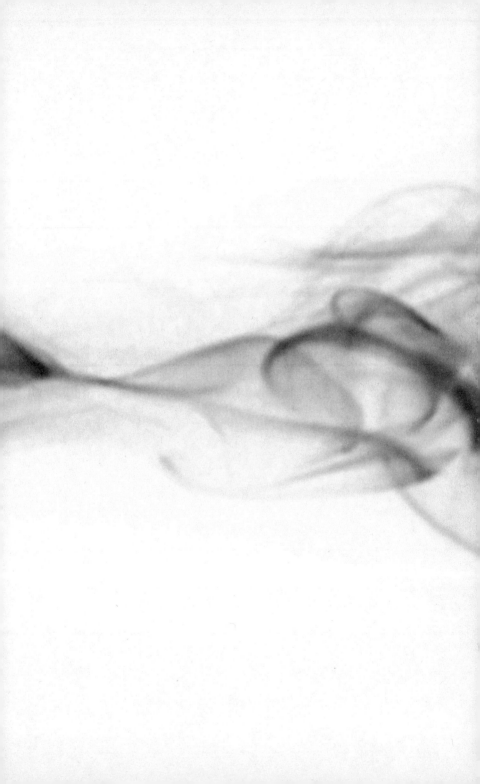

CHAPTER
ONE

THE CHARCOAL SKY SPITS COLD RAIN AS WE rumble to a stop at a crossroad. A black cart blocks the road, and even in an armored carriage we know better than to force our way past.

Burly men stagger to the cart, carrying something between them. Someone. One of the men stumbles, and the body wobbles in a horrifying way.

My friend April gags behind her mask. "Too bad your father didn't design these things to keep out noxious smells as well as noxious diseases."

I wonder whether the people remaining in the houses will be cold tonight. If they've wrapped their dead in their only blankets. They should know better.

The corpse collectors wear cloth masks, flimsy and useless to stop the contagion. They roll their cart forward a scant hundred yards and stop again, unconcerned that they're blocking traffic. They don't care that we have hell-raising and carousing to do in the Debauchery District.

The Debauchery District. The very name makes me shiver.

As I turn to April, prepared to complain about the delay, a girl is pushed through a doorway and into the street.

She is clutching something, and her emergence at the same time that the corpse collectors are making their daily appearance cannot be an accident. Other people appear in the doorway—the inhabitants of the house, perhaps—and I feel afraid for them because not a single one of them wears even a cloth mask.

A corpse collector approaches the girl. Before, I wanted him to hurry, but now each heavy footstep fills me with dread.

The girl is slight, and her ancient dress has been hemmed and stitched so that her arms and legs are visible, but with the rain and the half light, it's impossible to tell if she is blemished or clean. The people in the house want her to give the man the bundle, but she turns away. It doesn't take much imagination to realize that she is cradling a baby.

She raises her face to the rain, her misery palpable.

I can't explain how I know which drops of condensation running down her cheeks are rain and which are tears. But I do.

The girl's eyes catch mine.

I feel something. The first emotion I've felt all day, besides vague anticipation for tonight. This isn't the sort of thing I want to feel. Gnawing and sick, it wells up from my stomach.

She breaks eye contact when a young man comes out of what's left of the building; the roof has been blasted away, probably during some useless riot, and now the structure is covered with canvas. He grips the girl's shoulders and forcibly turns her. I wonder if he is the father, wonder if he cared for the child in the bundle, or if he just wants to get the disease away from him, to keep it from forming a rash that scabs over and sinks through his skin. You don't recover from this contagion. You contract it, and then you die. Quickly, if you are lucky.

I try to guess the age of the mother. From her posture, I'm supposing that she's just a girl.

Maybe that's why I feel connected to her, because we're the same age.

Maybe it's the eye contact she initiated. Usually they don't look at us.

The girl's grief is a mindless, crushing thing, and somehow I feel it, even though I am supposed to be numb. As the men tear the baby away, I feel an aching loss. I want to stretch out my own arms, pleading, but if I do, April might laugh.

My knees begin to shake. What is wrong with me? Soon I will be crying. At least no one is looking closely enough to discern the difference between *my* tears and the rain.

They toss the tiny body into the cart.

I flinch, imagining that it makes a sound, even though I can only hear the rumble of the carriage and April's exasperated sigh.

"You would think they'd be happy," she says. "My uncle is paying a fortune to get rid of the bodies. Otherwise the lower city would be unlivable."

If I pushed April and her sparkling silver eyelids out of the open carriage, the crowd lining this street might kill her. If I ripped the mask from her face, she'd probably be dead in a couple of weeks.

She doesn't understand. She was raised in the Akkadian Towers and has never been on the streets. Not this one, not the one half a block to the west, where I once lived in complete darkness. She doesn't know, and never will.

But I cannot be mad at April. I live for her, for the hours when she makes me forget, for the places where she takes me. Perhaps she's right, and these people should be thankful to have men tear the corpses from their arms.

Out of the corner of my eye, I notice dark shapes creeping from between two buildings. I strain to see, but they never step out of the gloom. All of a sudden I'm afraid. This area can get violent, fast. The corpse collectors stomp toward another door, marked with a roughly painted red scythe, passing through shadows and back into the light. Their disregard accentuates the care the cloaked figures take to cling to the shadows.

April doesn't notice.

Anything could be hidden under a dark cloak. Our driver curses and turns sharply, and we finally lurch past the body cart. When I look over my shoulder, the cloaked men have melted back into the shadows.

At last we can get on with our night.

We turn a corner, and our destination becomes visible. It's in a slight depression, as if the entire city block sank a few feet into the ground after the buildings were erected. There's a hot-air balloon tied to the top of the tallest building in the area. You can't see the lettering, but everyone knows it marks the location of the district.

It is a floating reminder—not that we used to invent things and travel, but that if you can get to the place where the balloon is tethered and if you have enough money, you can forget about death and disease for a few hours.

"You're a million miles away," April says in the small voice she uses when she arrives earlier than expected and finds me gazing out into the falling rain.

I don't know why she seeks out my company. She is animated. I'm barely alive. I stare into space and whimper in my sleep. When I'm awake, I contemplate death, try to read, but never really finish anything. I only have the attention span for poetry, and April hates poetry.

What April and I share are rituals, hours of putting

on makeup, glitter, fake eyelashes glued on one by one. Our lips are painted on with precision; mindless mirror staring isn't that different from gazing out into the toxic slush, if you really think about it. She could share this with anyone.

There's no reason that it has to be me.

"Tonight is going to be insane," she says happily. "You wait and see."

People whisper about the Debauchery Club in the tattered remains of genteel drawing rooms, while they sip a vile substitute for tea from cracked china cups. Real tea was imported; we haven't had anything like that in years.

The first club we pass is the Morgue. It's in an abandoned factory. They made bricks there, back when builders used to construct houses. We won't need to build anything until all the abandoned buildings collapse, if there are any of us left by then.

The line to get into the Morgue stretches around the block. I scan the crowd, imagining that they are hopeful, that they crave admission as if their lives depended on it, but we're too far away to read the expressions on their masked faces.

April and I pass this way frequently but never go inside. We are bound for the Debauchery Club, the place this entire district is named for. Membership is exclusive.

Our driver lets us out in an alley. The door is unmarked and unlocked. When we step into the foyer, it is completely dark except for a succession of throbbing red lights that are part of the floor. No matter how many times we come here, they still fill me with curiosity. I run my foot over the first one in the hallway, looking for some texture, something that differentiates it from the rest of the floor.

"Araby, come on." April rolls her eyes. We remove our masks and place them in velvet bags to keep them safe.

Before the plague, the Debauchery Club was only open to men. But, like everyone else, the majority of the members died.

April and I are probationary members, sponsored by her brother, whom I have never met. We won't be eligible for full membership until we are eighteen.

"This way, ladies."

I catch a glimpse of myself in a mirror and smile. I am not the person I was this morning. I am beautiful, fake, shallow, incognito. My black dress reaches my ankles and flows over the whalebone corset that I appropriated from my mother's closet. It's not an outfit I could wear on the street, but I love it. I look impossibly thin and a little bit mysterious.

For a moment I am reminded of cloaked figures, also swathed in black, and smooth my dress nervously.

"I'll loan you a pair of scissors," April teases as she enters the examination room.

I laugh. Her own skirts are artfully cut above her knees. Our fashions changed when the Weeping Sickness first came to the city. Long skirts could hide oozing sores.

I savor the feel of my skirts around my legs as I turn, watching myself in the mirror.

"Your turn, baby doll."

I follow the velvety voice into the examination room.

If I were honest with myself, I might admit that these few moments are why I come here, week after week. Swirling tattoos cover his arms, climbing up from the collar of his shirt to twist around his throat, the ends hidden by his tousled dark hair. I try not to look at him. He could make me happy. His attention, a hint of admiration in his eyes . . . I don't deserve happiness.

"You know the routine. Breathe in here." He holds out the device. "Are you contagious this week?"

"Not a chance," I whisper.

"Oh, there's always a chance. You should be more careful." He presses the red button so that the handheld device will filter the air expelled from my lungs. There's a needle in his hands now. I shiver.

"You enjoy this more than you should," he says softly.

He puts my blood into some sort of machine. It has clockwork parts and a little brass knob, but I'm fairly certain that it doesn't test anything besides credulity. Yet the serious way he performs his duties always makes me believe that he will know if I've contracted anything, and I breathe faster than normal. Nervous.

What will he do if I'm contaminated? Will he look at me with contempt? Kick me out into the street?

This is the only place in the city where we are safe

without our masks. At home our servants wear masks so they don't bring in contamination from the lower city. Here it would be an insult to suggest you need to filter the air. They only let one of us into this little room at a time, though. How can we be sure that other members aren't secretly fouled by diseases?

"Looks like you're clean this week, sweetheart. Try to stay that way." He dismisses me with a wave of his hand. "Oh, and next time you should wear the silver eye stuff. It'd look better on you than it does on your friend."

As he turns away, I raise my hand toward him without meaning to. If he were standing closer, I would have touched him.

I never touch people.

Not on purpose. Luckily, he doesn't see my traitorous hand or the expression on my face.

I enter the club through a curtain of silver beads. I imagine sometimes that they make a beautiful sound when I move through them, but I have never heard even the tiniest clink. It's like the secrecy of this place has seeped into the furnishings.

April hasn't waited for me. We perpetually lose and find each other in this maze of rooms. She and I enjoy our time here in different ways.

The building is five stories tall, average for this part of town. It was built to house apartments, but now all of the rooms are connected by long hallways and half-open doors.

The only constant, the way that you can tell that you're still in the club and haven't wandered into some other building, is that there is a representation of a dragon in every room. Some of them are carved into furnishings, some are displayed in glass cases, but everywhere we are watched by red eyes.

In some rooms Persian carpets cover the floors, and in other rooms they are affixed to the walls, either to muffle sound or to absorb the scent of tobacco or opium smoke. The upper floors house forbidden libraries; one room is filled with books on the occult, and another has volumes detailing sexual acts that I never dreamed existed. I like books, but I tend to gravitate toward the lower floors, where there is music.

I move from room to room. These spaces are always crowded, filled with bodies, muffled conversation, occasional dancing, and even some kissing in dark corners. April and I are far from the only females who have joined this club.

Hours trickle by, and I wilt. The magic isn't here for me tonight. I can't get away from the heavy feeling of being me. I want to blend in, to be someone besides myself, someone who is part of something secret and subversive and exciting.

A guy is following me. He's thin and blond, wearing a too-formal outfit, dark pants, a blue shirt buttoned to the next-to-last button. He doesn't fit in this room filled with ornate settees, where a girl, accompanied by a violinist, is singing about suicide. He says something to me, but I can't hear him. I keep walking.

He follows me into the women's washroom.

Girls stare at their reflections in a dark room filled with mirrors.

I push past them to the chambers behind. A girl tries to jab a high heel into my foot. I jump back, and don't meet her eyes; don't want her to see how the sneer makes me wince.

He shuts the door behind us. Doors in this club are well oiled and make no sound when they close. So thick that you can't hear what happens behind them.

"What do you want?" he asks in an amused voice. His self-assurance makes him seem older than he looks. I'm guessing that he would be a student at the university, if it were still open.

"Oblivion." It is what I am always looking for.

"What's a pretty girl like you trying to forget?"

A pretty girl like me, with my clean fingernails and my unblemished bill of health.

He doesn't know anything about me.

"Do you have what I want or not?"

He produces a silver syringe.

"I doubt you know what you want," he mutters in a voice that calls me foolish. An amateur. I ignore a sharp burst of anger, determined to get what I need to defeat it and any other emotion that might try to creep in. I'm not an amateur.

I eye the syringe.

"Busy night?" I ask.

"I don't usually share."

I hand him some bills. He barely glances at them before he shoves the money into his pocket. His eyebrows are blond; they make him look perpetually surprised.

I hold out my arm to him. "Do it."

"Don't you want to know what's in this thing?"

"No."

I didn't think he could look more surprised. The blond eyebrows intrigue me.

Whatever is in his syringe, it's cold, and the world blurs around me.

"Where do you want to go?"

"Back to the violinist. I want to hear songs about suicide."

He laughs.

As we leave the room I trip over the threshold. He puts his hand on my arm.

"I hope you find what you need," he says, and sounds like he means it.

CHAPTER
TWO

DARKNESS. WE EAT IN IT, TALK IN IT, WE SLEEP in humid darkness, wrapped in blankets. There is never really enough light in this basement, not if you truly want to see.

"It's your move," my twin brother, Finn, tells me. His voice is soft, no hint of irritation. I know I'm dreaming, but I don't care. I'll stay here as long as I can.

"Sorry." I stare at the squares of the board. There's no sense studying the pieces; they don't speak to me. I have no sense of strategy, but I want badly to keep up with him, to offer some meager entertainment by providing a challenge.

"I'll move the lantern."

He's pretending that my problem is simply a lack of illumination. I touch the ivory knight with my fingertip.

Father comes out of his laboratory and takes off his goggles.

"Is anyone ready for lunch?"

We're always ready for lunch. It breaks up the monotony of our day. We follow him into the kitchen, where cases of preserved goods are stacked to the ceiling. Father pours something into a bowl and puts it into the steam oven.

"I don't think it's—" I try to warn him.

There's a loud crackling explosion, and the gas bulb dangling above us goes dark.

"No point in fixing it, not when I'm so close to a breakthrough." Father says this pretty much every day.

"I'm having peaches," Finn says. "Preserved peaches are good cold." He isn't angry at Father for taking us underground. For not keeping his promises and for disappearing for days on end to work on god knows what. Finn isn't even mad at Mother for not wanting to live here with us.

"I love peaches," I say, because Finn brings out the best in me. Darkness and light, Father calls us.

"I'm so lucky," our father says. "Blessed with patient children." His voice is shaking, and in the murky light I think I see tears in his eyes. He is looking past me, at Finn.

There's a knock at the door, and then it's shoved inward and a man stands above us, silhouetted by the light shining through a front door that we haven't stepped through in ages.

"Dr. Worth," the man says. "My son, he has the contagion, but he hasn't died. . . . It's been over a month."

He must be wrong. If you get sick you die. Everyone knows this.

"Give me your address," Father tells the man. "I'll come later, when their mother is here to mind them." So Mother is coming for a visit. That will please Finn. The man rattles off his address, his voice low and steady. As if he's lived through so much horror that nothing can really bother him anymore.

We return to the chessboard with one jar of peaches and two forks.

"It's still your move," Finn says. "Araby?"

I glance up at him, to see if he's irritated yet. Is he really this inhuman, this eternally patient? But I can't see him. The humidity is so thick, and the lantern is so dim. I strain my eyes. His calm voice resonates, but I can't quite, can't quite see. . . .

And that's when I wake up.

"Oh, God, how'm I supposed to carry you?" April's voice asks. The cold air hits me and I realize that we're outside. It's raining. Out of the club, in open air. I feel myself begin to panic, not because I care, but because I've been programmed to fear the airborne contagions. I put my hand up, feel the ridged porcelain surface of my mask, and sigh with relief. I've worn this thing so long that I no longer feel it.

I try to curl back up. Sleep is difficult for me, and this euphoria is a beautiful thing. Cold rain hits the bottoms of my feet. Where are my shoes?

"You should be careful," someone says. "It isn't safe to be out at night."

"I need to get her home," April says. The tone of her voice reminds me, not exactly of the first time we met, but of the way she tells the story. She thinks she saved my life. "We have guards. We'll be perfectly safe."

If it isn't one of the guards warning her, then who is she speaking to?

I'm lowered onto the plush seat of April's carriage.

"Thanks for your help," she says.

"I doubt it'll be the last time." The velvet voice holds a hint of amusement and a hint of something else. He leans over and looks down into my face. My disorientation intensifies when my eyes focus on his. The tattoos, the dark hair. My heart speeds up. I think . . . I think . . . can a person's heart stop if she is only seventeen years old? I suppose that if I do fall apart, my father can put me back together again.

"You were lucky this time, baby doll. It won't hold out, though. Luck never does."

Yes. I'm the lucky one. It's something I never forget.

CHAPTER THREE

I REST MY CHEEK AGAINST THE COOLNESS OF the glass window. I have been here so long that my cheek is frigid, even when I touch it with my already cold fingers. Curled on the window seat, I gaze through the window. But I'm not looking out, I'm looking in. There are two penthouses at the top of Akkadian Towers. We live in Penthouse B. The team of architects who designed this place created a lush garden between the luxuriously appointed apartments. An indoor Eden.

Sick down to my bones, I stare into the thick tropical plant life. I've been dry heaving all morning.

My mother enters the room, and though I don't turn my head to look at her, I know what she is doing. She is wringing her hands, the slender white hands that she soaks in peppermint oil.

A platter sits in front of me. Four types of crackers,

fanned out like . . . well, a fan. I rub the chilled glass bottle of water against my face, leaving trails of icy condensation across my cheekbones and down my neck.

Then a movement in the garden catches my eye. The guy from last night, the one who gave me the silver syringe, is standing with his hands in his pockets, watching me.

But that's impossible.

When the world got lush and humid and the diseases started multiplying, the Akkadian Towers closed this particular garden, bricked over the doors and sealed everything with mortar.

I sit up, but my stomach doesn't like the sudden movement. I squeeze my eyes shut.

Expensive perfume gags me.

"Araby?"

Mother puts her hand on my forehead. While we hid in the cellar, she stayed here at the Akkadian Towers to play the piano. Her music calmed the rich people while they figured out if they were dying or not. When they identified someone with the Weeping Sickness, they threw them out into the street. I open my eyes.

"Sweetie . . ."

I want to curl up in her arms and cling to her, and that makes me feel worse than the drugs that my body is trying to expel.

The world is spinning.

"Why do you do this to yourself?" she whispers. She blows out the candles on the side table and covers me with a quilt. Light comes in through the windows, both from the outside and from the garden, which is empty now.

Some hours later, my father comes into the room. His hair is wild and his mask is pushed up on top of his head.

"I want you to walk with me, Araby," he says.

He asks me this maybe twice a week. It's the only time he says my name. I like for him to snap out of his daydreams and remember that he still has a child. He puts on his coat and holds out mine. I squeeze my eyes shut for a moment, ignoring the last vestiges of queasiness, and follow him.

As we step out of the elevator, we are approached by one of Prince Prospero's guards, hired to keep my father safe. We all know that our scientists are our greatest assets. And our most dangerous weapons. There was a sort of chaos after the prince opened a factory to mass-produce the masks. No one knew how to respond to hope. People painted slogans on the sides of buildings. SCIENCE HAS TRIUMPHED. SCIENCE HAS FAILED. Always together, the second statement contradicting the first. The same dripping red paint used in drawing scythes on the plague-stricken houses.

The city was a smoldering heap of rubble, and yet people crept out during the night to put messages on the sides of collapsing buildings while the rest of the populace slept peacefully or died quietly.

"It says something about human nature," Father said. But he never shared his interpretation—at least, not with me.

"Where are you going, Dr. Worth?" the guard asks.

"I'm taking a walk with my daughter," he says.

"We'll arrange an escort."

"Just a few men. We aren't going far." Father toys with something in his pocket, resigned.

We wait in the foyer while they are assembled. The fake plants are dusty. The ferns are the worst offenders.

The first guard opens the door and the other three spread out, walking beside us. They carry short swords as well as guns, ready to protect Father from any threat, man or beast. No matter what creatures people fear in the dead of night, in this city, violence is more likely to be carried out by men.

"The shipyard is open again," Father's tone is conversational.

"Is it?" There's a breathless quality to my voice that someone who doesn't know me might interpret as excitement.

When I was a child, when Finn was alive, we loved to walk down to the harbor. This area was busy then, a giant pageant with sailors working on the ships. Father's feet often lead him here; I don't know if he can help himself.

The harbor is different now. Debris litters the shore, and the blackened hulks of ships fill the bay. The mob destroyed most of them. The Weeping Sickness might have been spread from a passenger, or some rodent who arrived via ship.

These days the fishermen use a different port, farther south, to avoid this devastation.

I catch my breath. The afternoon sunlight gleams off the white masks of the sailors, who are outfitting a shiny new steamship.

"She's called the *Discovery*," Father says.

The last time a ship came into the harbor, I was ten years old. Unlike the steam-propelled ship in front of us, it had a tall mast and heavy canvas sails. It might've come from anywhere.

I remember how the passengers hurried ashore, anxious for the feel of solid earth under their feet. They wore modest dresses that reached their ankles, high collars, long sleeves. When I was very young we wore such restrictive clothing, even in the heat of summer.

But the contagion changed all that, and instead it became necessary to show as much skin as possible. Preachers denounced the new fashions, saying we would all be destroyed, even as we wondered what was left to destroy.

I imagine that those who disembarked that day had set out from some distant shore to find hope. What they found was a mob that tore them apart before they knew what was happening. Finn and I watched, horrified.

Mother was the one who came looking for us. We were wandering through back alleys, crying.

The drama pulled Father from his lab. He said that the city had gone mad, and we must not go outside again until the disease had been contained. Hiding wasn't unusual. People quarantined themselves in cellars and attics. Some families fled. Finn and I heard the adults predict, in hushed voices, that they would die in the forests, or the wilderness beyond.

"This is good," Father whispers now, gesturing to the gleaming ship, the *Discovery*. "The first good thing I've seen in a long time." I love hearing the hope in his voice. "We will see what is left in the rest of the world."

The wind that ruffles my hair smells of salt, and white seabirds come and go.

If I don't look over at Father, I can imagine that Finn is standing beside me. I could lose myself to this sort of meditative state that is sometimes better than oblivion. But Father checks his pocket watch and then pulls me along; all of a sudden he's in a hurry. He doesn't ask questions. He stopped being interested in me a long time ago.

We walk back toward the periphery of the old city. This part of town is a little higher than the rest, and the buildings are tall. Fairy-tale towers and spires. Security officers line the sidewalks to keep people without masks out and away. Out of sight and away from our air.

We're heading toward the bookshop. It's the last one in the city, and Father makes a pilgrimage to it at least once a week, to see what treasures people have unearthed in their attics and cellars. The guards are accustomed to coming here. They gather in a circle outside the door, leaning against the wall.

The proprietor greets Father by name while I wander up and down rows of heavy dark tomes. I browse the shelves, but as I turn a corner, I see Father standing between two men. One of them clasps Father's hand, and then puts his own hand quickly in his pocket. I'm sure that something passed between them. The younger man sees me watching and stares back at me through thick eyeglasses, his expression unfriendly.

I step back a few paces, nervous about this meeting.

Suddenly the bookshop feels ominous, with its smells of earth and dampness. I wrinkle my nose in distaste. Boxes of books sit near the proprietor's desk, but some of them are moldy. Newly excavated from some rotting cellar. I pick up a small volume of poetry while I wait for Father.

Without meaning to, I glance back to where he is speaking to the young man. Now he's clapping him on the back. These men have the look of scientists, but all the scientists besides Father are holed up in Prince Prospero's castle, behind thick stone walls and barred windows, for their own protection.

I put down the book and walk to the door. Father

comes to the front of the store and makes a purchase, and then we walk outside. For a moment I'm blinded by the glare from the setting sun; it will soon be evening. This day has passed in a blur, like so many others. As my eyes adjust, I scan the alley. Our guards stand together, leaning against a wall, smoking. Above us, faces peer out of dirty windows. Two children play outside a half-open door. And there are long shadows that my eyes can't penetrate.

Father puts his hand on my arm, as if he can tell that I am ill at ease, but he does nothing else to comfort me. And he makes no effort to explain. I try to think of a way to ask what he's gotten involved with, but it's a short walk back to the Akkadian Towers and my head is aching. We leave the guards in the lobby, and the ride up to our floor is silent. Father reaches into his overcoat.

"I thought you might like this," he says.

It's the leather-bound book of poems. Either he noticed or he knew it was the sort of book I would treasure.

"Father—" I'm standing there with my arm still extended, trying to find a way to ask what is going on without alerting the elevator attendant that Father may be committing treason, when we reach the top floor.

The gilded door slides back, and there's April, tapping her foot. She hates waiting.

"You have to come with me," she says. She's wearing a red corset, and her hair is piled artfully on top of her head and decorated with shiny black feathers.

I turn, ready to tell her that I'm not dressed for going out, that I don't have the energy, and Father slips away. I've lost my chance to question him.

"Elliott will be there." April knows how curious I am about her brother. I owe him for getting me into the club.

"I don't know. . . ." I gesture toward Penthouse B.

"I doubt he'll stay at the club for long. We need to hurry."

The elevator operator is watching us curiously. April holds up my bag, triumphant. "You don't need anything else." I tuck the book into my purse and cross my arms over my chest as we descend. She leads me through the lobby to her ridiculous steam carriage.

The carriage is a marvel as well as a monstrosity, a gift from her uncle. The conveyance has a retractable roof that can be closed when the weather is bad so the rain won't ruin her hair, and it's painted white with gold inlay, like something a fairy princess would travel about in. Except that an armed guard drives it and two guards ride up front. In the back there is a boy who puts coal into the furnace that heats the water for steam.

They say that the scientist who created this thing blew up a turret in Prince Prospero's castle, but I don't know if it's true. Still, we have to have some way to get around since the plague killed off all the horses.

The evening is gray but not rainy. April laughs. "Leave

the top open. I like the wind, and I dare bats to land in my hair."

Bats. They were brought in to try to contain our mosquito problem. The scientists did something, made them bigger, so their bellies would hold more mosquitoes.

The bats caught the virus from the mosquitoes, but they didn't die. They just carry the disease. No one speaks of it—or of the people who carry the disease for weeks or possibly months. Everyone is supposed to kill them on sight. Both the diseased bats and the people. The military gives rewards for bringing the bodies of bats.

April hands me her flask, and I take a long drink.

"I'm not afraid of bats," I say.

We both laugh, but it wouldn't be funny if we weren't drinking and weren't together. We are passing through the ruins of what used to be a bustling city, but now it's really just a monument to our dead.

Someone has painted large black letters on the side of a building. I strain to make them out. LIFE IS SACRED. DEATH IS EVEN MORE SO. I stare at the letters, ugly and lopsided, and then April gasps and shoves me forward into the upholstery.

With a dull thud, a rock slams into the velvet seat where my head was just resting. The guard on my left raises his musket and shoots another, shattering it in midair.

April is more shaken than I've ever seen her. Terrified.

She picks up the first stone, large as her hand and jagged, and drops it to the street. We both wince at the sound it makes. The same sound it would have made if it hit a mask or the bones of my face. If people want to throw stones at us, there is no shortage of them. The city is crumbling to bits that can be used as ammunition, anywhere, anytime.

April's guards scan the area, while her driver adjusts his own mask and accelerates.

"I guess I just saved your life again," she says finally.

I guess she did.

The first time I met April, I was standing with my toes barely over the edge of the roof of the Akkadian Towers. Less than two years ago.

No one ever came to the roof, but she walked up to me and said, "What are you doing?"

I was so surprised that I answered honestly.

"Imagining what it would be like to jump."

She laughed. It was quintessentially April, but at the time I was shocked. I had tried to hide my suicidal thoughts from everyone, and this girl was laughing!

"I like you," she said. "I heard there was a girl living in the prince's old apartment. I need you to help me braid my hair." She took off her hat and showed me her hair, which was half braided and half loose. Her mother had gotten too drunk to finish it. "Don't jump right now, okay?"

The carriage stops in front of the club. April exclaims

over a scratched place on the gold leaf before proceeding to the unmarked door.

In the deathly quiet of the examination room, I wince at my reflection. I'm quiet and mousy, not the sort of girl who belongs in a place like this.

"I wasn't planning to come here tonight," I mutter.

"Yet here you are," he says. He's noncommittal, neither happy nor sad to see me. Not disapproving. Not exactly.

Yet his hand seems to linger at my waist as he helps me stand. I would rather stay and talk to him, but he's already turning to admit another member. It doesn't matter. No matter how much I want to speak to him, I fear I have nothing worthwhile to say.

April has noticed the way I look at him.

"It's too bad you took that vow of celibacy," she says as I leave the examination room.

"It isn't a vow of celibacy."

It is much more than that. It's the way that I have to live my life. I don't have a choice.

"Too bad," she repeats, tapping her foot in her expensive shoes.

We walk through the first floor, peering into room after room. April stops to get a drink, and then we walk back through the same rooms, looking into all the corners and even the stairwell. I scan for fair hair. April has blond hair that she lightens with lemon juice in the summer. So I imagine her brother might favor her.

"Just like Elliott. He probably found someplace more important to be." She's downed one drink and is holding a second one. Her cheeks are very pink.

"Should we look on the other floors? Where do you think he might be?"

"Top floor, maybe. He's more attracted to books than he is to women. He's a disgrace to the family." She slurs the word disgrace. "The reason he won't live with us is that he has this calling. He's a poet, lives in a garret with other artists and writers. They won't wear their masks. They say it's okay to die young as long as they record the human condition, record what has happened to us. He writes day and night and takes drugs to try to make himself more aware."

She rolls her eyes.

Is this why April hates poetry? I'm nervous, suddenly, at the prospect of meeting her brother, because nothing could fascinate me more than what she has just said.

"He said he would be here?"

"You would like him." She looks at me for a moment. "And I suspect he'd like you. But you need eyelashes." She pushes me onto a loveseat beside her and reaches into her bag. "Here." She smears some glittery stuff on my cheeks. I expect it to be gritty, but it's light and foamy. This is what our scientists create while Mother Nature tries to kill us all. Then she opens my bag and begins applying fake eyelashes. I'm surprised that her hands are steady enough.

"Now you're pretty. Even Elliott will notice——" She stops speaking and drops my bag, spilling red lipstick and a bottle of perfume.

Two men have paused in the doorway to this room. I go cold. They are members of the club from before the plague, and we are told to avoid them.

But that's not who April noticed. She's staring across the room at a young man who's leaning against the bar. I know at once that it's not her brother; the look she gives him is too flirtatious. He walks toward us and she stands up.

She doesn't offer to help me pick up the contents of my purse. It isn't something she would ever think to do.

She's smiling, looking up at him from under her eyelashes. When I check, the older gentlemen have passed on.

And then the young man is in front of us. She offers him her hand before saying over her shoulder to me, "We're here. Elliott can't complain. He'll find us if he wants. We might as well have some fun."

Maybe she's right. It's why we come here. To forget. To have fun.

I watch her smile as she pushes back her hair. If our world hadn't imploded, she'd be married by now, possibly a wife and a mother. Instead she's out all night with no chaperone. My mother disapproves of this behavior, but she can't stop April's wildness.

And Mother won't keep me from joining April

because April's family has connections. April claims that her uncle, the prince, is crazy. He lives outside the city in a medieval castle that he had shipped here, stone by stone, from Scotland before the plague hit. He controls everything, including the military. We do what he says. I'm not sure how it happened.

April's father was the mayor before, but he died, and now she and her mother live alone in Akkadian Towers Penthouse A. Her mother drinks brandy all day, and April kisses strangers in the Debauchery District. Her new guy hands her a tall glass and then offers me one. I take it but don't drink. Something about him catches my attention. Not him, exactly, but the way April starts kissing him.

I've never kissed anyone. I made a vow to avoid the things that Finn will never experience. It doesn't usually bother me. April says that's because I don't know what I'm missing, but passion seems very messy.

April's eyelids are purple. His are a blue like a bruise. They are kissing with their eyes closed tight, like this connection means something.

I set my glass on a side table and wander through the club. Restless.

I see April later, sprawled across a velvet chair. She's had someone hack off a few more inches of her skirts with scissors, so it's shorter than when we left the house, and with this ensemble she's finally crossed the line into indecency.

Maybe it doesn't matter. She's made herself so artificial; it's okay to wear next to nothing because we aren't real people any longer.

The ice has melted in my abandoned glass on the side table. I pick it up, and when she doesn't acknowledge me, I drink the contents quickly and walk away, up the stairs to a floor with rowdy card games. But I'm not in the mood to be around happiness. To escape, I duck into a quiet room. When my eyes adjust, I see two people at a table, playing chess by candlelight. They aren't sealed in a humid basement, but my chest constricts anyway.

"Would you like to play?" someone asks. He has blond hair that gleams in the candlelit room.

"No, no, I'm not good at strategy. . . ." Then I recognize him.

CHAPTER
FOUR

COLD AIR MOVES ACROSS MY FACE. IT FEELS
more lived in than the air I'm used to. I'm lying in a bed
that's not my own, shivering.

Cold means outside. But why would a bed be outside?
I snuggle deeper into the blankets. The person beside
me shifts. I freeze. Someone is beside me. I'm caught,
tangled in blankets, in a strange bed, and I can't open
my eyes.

I put my hand up to my face. My eyes are glued shut.
This has happened before, a bad mix of makeup and
eyelash glue. April gave me some cleanser that removes
it, but I know I'm not at home, because Akkadian Tower
penthouses are never uncomfortably cold.

My mask is askew.

And someone is beside me, pressed against me. Closer
than another human being has been since Finn and I

were young. Being this near anyone floods me with loss. I pull away, and then flinch as my bedmate throws an arm over me. The pain of ripping my eyelids open is fierce but momentary.

Nothing in this room is familiar. It's an attic-style dormer with low ceilings and sharp angles. I ease away and realize, with shock, who I am lying next to.

He's even prettier with the muted early afternoon light illuminating his high cheekbones. I stare at his closed eyes. I know that they are dark, but a deep blue? Brown? I will him to open them so that I can see. It's so odd to see him without the club, the lights on the floor, the testing.

His hair is mussed. I move my hand slightly, wondering if I dare to touch him, to run my fingers through his hair and see how far up his tattoos swirl.

My reverie is interrupted by a high-pitched giggle.

The only thing in this room is the bed where we are nestled together and a low couch that looks like it's had better days. On the couch there are two children.

They aren't wearing masks.

But we're inside, so maybe the air is safe? I fidget with my mask. I've been taught better than to trust a strange filter.

The girl giggles again, nervously.

"Are you real?" she asks.

"Yes." I blink at her. "Why do you ask?"

"He's never brought home a girl," the boy says. "Never, and you don't look real. Hair doesn't come in that color."

I put my hand up and try to smooth my hair. April dyed strands of it purple. The color blends beautifully with my dark hair, but I've asked her not to dye it again. Purple is the color of the illness, the bruises that appear before the oozing starts.

The children slip over to the edge of the bed and peer down at me.

"You look like you've been crying." The girl reaches to touch the smeared makeup around my eyes, and I recoil. I'm not used to having someone without a mask so close to me.

I sit up, relieved that I am still fully clothed.

"Don't wake him," the little boy says. "He works hard. He stays up all night."

"Yes, I know," I say, because I often see him, working, in the early morning hours.

I wonder if my parents are worried about me.

"Who are you?" I ask.

"I'm Henry," the little boy says, "and this is Elise."

"And how do you know . . ." I falter, looking down at his sleeping form. "How do you know him?"

The girl notices something in my voice.

"You'd like to be his girlfriend," she says.

"He"—the boy emphasizes the pronoun—"is our older brother."

Their brother chooses this moment to open his eyes and look at me. He's younger than I guessed. I always thought he might be in his mid-twenties, but I see that he's closer to my age. Maybe eighteen.

The little girl leans in and whispers, "His name is Will. It's short for William." This time I don't draw back when she gets close.

He smiles up at me, a smile of unimaginable sweetness, a smile that I would never have expected from him, with his magical hands and shivery whispers.

My heart goes all fluttery.

"You're alive, then?" he says.

"Alive?"

"Deaths are bad for the club. Just a few days ago a girl choked on her own vomit. I didn't want that to happen to you."

My sense of wonder fades. He brought me here for the good of the club. Not to save me. At least, not because he likes me.

"Are you two bothering our . . . guest?" he asks the children. They walk toward the doorway, casting glances over their shoulders, turning to stare back at us until he makes an annoyed gesture and they go, giggling, into the next room.

"Your guest?" I ask as coldly as I can.

"I don't know what else to call you. The person I hoped wouldn't die in my bed? I found you unconscious behind one of the curtains when I was locking up."

My shame is followed by a cold wave of anger.

"You didn't think you should have taken me to the hospital?"

He raises a dark eyebrow. "I didn't have time."

He didn't have time? He found me unconscious, brought me home, but couldn't be bothered to stop at a hospital or to get me to my father, who could have administered appropriate medical care?

I glare at him, furious.

He stares back. I realize that he doesn't use eyeliner after all; his eyes are that dark and that amazing. And angry.

"Listen," he says. "Every second of my day is filled with something that has to be done. Every second. I didn't take drugs last night, and I didn't pass out behind a gold brocade curtain, and I don't have friends who would leave me at a club. Okay?"

"I could've died."

"How does that make last night different from any other night?"

This is unfair, because I rarely go to the club more than twice a week.

The children reappear in the doorway.

"Let's get some breakfast," he says for their benefit, though the words seem to be addressed to me. They scamper away and he climbs out of bed. He's still wearing the same fitted shirt and pants that he wore last night.

"Will," I try his name out tentatively.

"Don't talk about the way you live, not in front of Elise. She doesn't know any women besides our elderly neighbor, so she's bound to be fascinated by you."

He means me at the club. He doesn't know anything else. But maybe that's all there is.

He leads me into the kitchen. Both windows are covered with an array of blankets that appear to have been nailed over the opening. Light still filters in, giving the illusion of a muted stained-glass window. The room feels soft and oddly pleasant. On the table there are six apples. Will unwraps half a loaf of bread and begins to slice it with a large knife. The children pull out a single chair and climb onto it.

"Sit by us," Elise says. I sit gingerly in an empty chair.

"My name is Araby," I tell her. Maybe he really doesn't know my name or who I am.

Will smiles.

"Do you take care of them?"

"Yes. Our mother died three years ago." He picks up one of the apples and then sets it in front of Henry.

"Will, that's all the food we have until tomorrow." Elise's eyes are too big for her face.

I try to calculate how much food that is for each of them, how many bites. It isn't much. He toasts the bread over some sort of burner.

"The air is safe?" I put my hand to my mask; it feels odd being the only person in the room whose face is covered.

"No," Will says. "Keep the mask on. I'd hate to have saved you, just for you to die from unfiltered air."

I glance at the children, their bare faces. The air in

the lower city is said to be thick with disease.

Will cracks an egg into a small pan and holds it over the burner.

"So you live here and raise two children?"

"Yes."

"Is it difficult?"

He laughs. "Yes, it is."

"How did it happen?"

"The usual way. My family survived the plague, so things seemed okay. I was hanging around down in the district when things really started there. I found myself drawn to girls with unusually colored hair who went to clubs wearing black corsets. Girls who stared into their drinks with vacant eyes, mourning the world that they had lost."

"That's sort of poetic," I say.

"It was foolish." He smiles. "But I got a job, started saving money. Then my father died and my mother got sick. I had to pay for the apartment, had to find money for medicine and food. I caught the attention of the prince. He owns the Debauchery Club."

The prince owns almost everything.

Will pushes his hair back from his face.

"Sometimes we had enough for food. Sometimes we didn't. I seem to be well suited to working at the Debauchery Club. A neighbor watches the kids at night while I'm working. She doesn't charge much to have them sleep in her spare bed. I have to be home before sunrise, because she works as a cook for some rich family."

Some rich family. Like mine. For all I know, his neighbor could be our cook.

"I used to leave them, when I was fifteen or sixteen, because I couldn't think what else to do. But I'm more careful now."

Leaving children is dangerous. If the authorities find a child alone, they are required to take that child, and he or she is never given back.

Will hands me a slice of toasted bread. I don't want to eat their food, they have so little of it, but it seems impolite not to accept. So I adjust my mask to the side, the way we do when we are in a place where there might be germs, and nibble at my bread.

Henry is holding a tiny brass toy lovingly.

"Is it a toy steam carriage?" I ask.

"Yes. I have an airship, too," he says proudly.

"I have a friend who makes clever toys for him," Will says.

"You can wind it, and it really works!"

As charming as they are, the children make me nervous with their searching eyes and their rapid movements.

"Do they go to school?"

Will puts a plate with some eggs in front of me.

"I'm hoping they can go next year."

We eat slowly. I tear my bread into three pieces and give most of it to the children. The eggs make me feel much better, more alive. The sun is sneaking in around the window coverings, and Will looks completely exhausted. I want to touch his tousled hair, push it back from his face. He sees me watching him, and his lips do that little half smile. I almost expect him to use an inappropriate endearment like he does at the club.

"Is Araby your girlfriend?" Elise asks.

Will chokes and then says, "No." So quickly that it feels like a slap in the face.

When the little ones aren't looking, he raises one eyebrow at me. He knows that he's insulted me. For just a moment, he's the Debauchery District guy, and not this surprising domestic creature.

When he described the girls who attracted him, he might as well have held a mirror to me. But I don't know if he still likes . . . the sort of girl that he thinks I am. He said it like it was something silly, some childhood fancy that passed. His lips twist again, and I realize that he's amused.

"Here's your bag." He puts the purse on the table and stifles a yawn. The shadows under his eyes only make him more impossibly handsome.

"You look tired."

"I usually sleep later than this. You've disrupted our little household. Luckily I have all afternoon to rest."

All afternoon?

"But how will I get home?" The sharpness to my question comes from fear.

"I've been working out that little problem in my mind

since the moment I rescued you. I'm going to have to walk you home on the way to work this evening."

"But I can't stay here all day." My mother will be wringing her hands, and my father might come out of his lab looking for me.

"This area isn't safe for someone walking alone, especially someone like you."

"I won't be alone. You will be with me."

"I can't leave Henry and Elise."

"Well, bring them along. There's a park near my building. I'll pay for the fare, of course." I reach for my bag.

"There are no paid conveyances in the lower city."

He pushes his chair back from the table. The wood of the chair leg scrapes the wood of the floor, and the noise makes both of us wince.

"Who wants to work a puzzle?"

He chooses a box from a low shelf and dumps the contents onto a table. The children fight for pieces of a colorful jigsaw puzzle. The muted light slipping through layers of blankets over the window has become oppressive rather than comforting.

"You never take them outside, do you?"

Will and I stare across the table, into each other's eyes. "No."

He holds my gaze for longer this time. I look down first.

"Do you want to help with the puzzle?"

"I'd rather lie down."

I go back to his bed. It feels odd, but there's no other place to be alone in this tiny apartment. Pulling the blankets to my chin, I try to disappear. His wardrobe door is slightly ajar. I want to open it, see the shirts that he wears to the club, something more familiar than this place. But instead I curl up and try to sleep.

I dream that I am on a sled, at the top of a hill. My arms are around Finn, but when we reach the bottom of the hill, I'm all alone. It's icy cold, and there's nothing but snow, no other children with sleds, no father, no Finn, even though I can still feel the warmth of him.

I am alone. Crying, in a bed that belongs to a stranger who didn't want me to die on his shift.

"Don't cry," little Henry says. He moves soundlessly over the wood floor to stand beside me, but instead of just staring at me, he presses his cheek against mine, in an effort to actually comfort me. I can't help wrapping my arms around him, this child who has taken the place Finn occupied in my dream. Holding him feels wonderful and comforting, but now I'm sobbing.

"I don't mind if you dry your eyes on my blanket," Will says. "But maybe I'd better remove Henry." He lifts the boy out of my embrace and gives him a gentle push toward the doorway.

Will slides into the chair beside the bed, and I can't get over how different he looks here, even though his clothes are the same, his hair, his tattoos. Maybe it's just that I've never seen him in the daytime before.

"Are you okay?" He sounds genuinely concerned.

"You need to get masks for your brother and sister."

His jaw tightens. "You think I don't know that? Do you have any idea how expensive . . . ? Of course you don't. How many masks do you own?"

I swallow hard. I used to live underground. I don't want to tell him that I have five masks: the regular porcelain one and a black full-face one in case I ever get invited to one of the costume balls that Prince Prospero loves. A purple mask with sequins, and two spares, in case my first mask gets chipped or stained.

I can't give one of mine to the children. Once you breathe through it, it is useless to everyone else. People used to steal masks. But now, even after a murder, you will see the mask, still covering the face of the victim, tossed aside with the bodies of the dead.

"Come here," Will says, leading me back to the kitchen. The children work their puzzle, uninterested in us. Opening a drawer in the china cabinet, he takes out a box. I recognize the heft and shape of it.

The only things that are still manufactured in this city are masks and the boxes to put them in. He opens the lid, and though I've seen a thousand of them, I still let out a tiny awed sound. Nestled in pink velvet, is a small mask.

"This is Elise's. I saved all of my extra money, every penny that didn't go to some essential, for three years to earn enough for this. I just picked it up yesterday." There is something both adorable and frightening about such a small mask.

"Do you have one for Henry?"

"I'm working on it. I decided to go ahead and buy this one so Elise can get used to wearing it. A new school semester begins in two months."

My stomach plummets.

One of the children will have a mask. The other won't.

CHAPTER
FIVE

I WAS THE FIRST PERSON EVER TO BREATHE through a mask. I remember Father coming out of his workshop with it.

"Try this on." Father held out the mask to Finn.

Finn refused to take it. "It looks silly. If I wear that, my face will look like a china doll's." We were thirteen years old, and he refused to play what he considered girl games with me.

"I used one of Araby's dolls. It isn't a perfect design, but it's workable, and it keeps out the germs that cause the Weeping Sickness."

Finn pushed the mask away, and I grabbed it.

The china felt brittle and unpleasant; the scent was upsetting, though I couldn't define it. I didn't see the horror on Father's face, but I often imagine it.

I didn't know that I would be wearing a mask every

day for the rest of my life. They changed the design for mass production, and I don't have the first one anymore. Looking at it would be more than I could bear.

What if Finn had put the mask on first? It was designed for him, after all.

Henry takes a puzzle piece that Elise was reaching for. She tries to retrieve it, but he's too fast. They both laugh.

If Elise wears the mask, then she will be safer, they will both be safer. But imagining him, the little brother with no mask, makes me go cold.

Will returns from his bedroom dressed for work, and I realize that he never got to go back to sleep. He's walking me home—prepared to work all night at the club on just those few hours that we slept. I want to tell him that I'm sorry, or possibly thank him, but I can't find the words.

We escort the children downstairs to stay with their neighbor. Outside the door, he kneels and kisses both of them. There's a lump in my throat, and I have to look away for a moment.

"Be good," he says.

"We'll be sleeping," Elise says seriously.

"Well, sleep successfully, then."

As the door swings open, both children rush to hug me. I'm surprised by the way they cling to me.

"It's time for us to go," Will says.

"Come visit us tomorrow," Elise begs. Will leans in to

disentangle her skinny arms from around my neck and gives her a little shove through the door.

He puts on his mask, and we go outside.

The shadows are lengthening as we begin the walk. I'm not used to seeing him in his mask, and I don't like it.

The building where he lives is brick, and identical to all the buildings around it—four stories tall, wood front door, and quilt-covered windows. A lonely little tree stands right outside the door.

On this street Will and I, walking so close that our arms touch, are an anomaly. I've never been in the lower city on foot before.

"Keep your purse close so no one grabs it," Will says.

"Is it a long way?"

"Yes, but walking with you is much easier than carrying you."

If I were April, I might say something flirtatious. Even the Araby who goes to the club with sparkly lashes and a red smile painted on might come up with something clever to say. I just stare shyly at my feet, and we walk in silence.

His neighborhood has more graffiti and broken windows than I'm accustomed to. The red scythe marks many doors. Some of them have been painted over with white, but the symbol of the contagion bleeds through.

In several windows red banners hang, emblazoned with black scythes. I'm not sure what it means. I try to stay close to Will.

We have to step over dried blood more than once. And yet someone has planted flowers along the edges of the sidewalk, and there are a few trees. We even pass an abandoned open place where a dilapidated sign reads PUBLIC PARK. People used to care about these places, and surely some still do.

I avert my eyes as we pass a black cart. The corpse collectors are out early.

On a building directly before us there is a large, bold message scribbled in enormous letters. DOWN WITH SCIENCE. REMEMBER GOD.

"What nonsense," I say, welcoming the distraction from the reality of the body cart.

"Science *has* failed us," Will says. This shocks me. How has science failed? Science saved us. "Religion failed, too," he says. "But maybe we should try it again. I don't know."

I've seen the graffiti, but I've never heard anyone question the worth of science.

I trip over an uneven spot in the sidewalk. Will steadies me.

"I wish you would be more careful." The lack of teasing is notable. Not like at the club.

Since I can't promise that I will be more careful, I don't answer. After a long silence he says, "I'd appreciate it if you didn't say anything about me, about my life."

"Who would I tell?"

"Your rich friends? Some of the members of the club—they can be aggressive about things."

"What sorts of things?"

"Prying into a person's private life."

So I haven't been the only one to notice how attractive he is. Jealousy burns through me, followed by a touch of excitement. I know things that these other girls don't know, and he wants it to stay that way.

We are close to the border now, where the lower city gives way to the upper city. Armed guards stand along the sidewalk. They turn toward us, but we're both wearing masks, so there is no reason to stop us.

The buildings here are more ornate, but storefronts are mostly closed, with windows boarded and merchandise removed. Couriers rush from place to place, hired by wealthy families to run their errands so they never have to leave their homes.

"That's where I live," I say, pointing up. Mother says the Akkadian Towers were designed to emulate something from a fairy tale. There were supposed to be multiple towers, but the second building was only partially built when the plague hit.

"Of course," he says. "The richer you are, the farther from the ground you want to live, right?" He gives me a long searching look. "But there's something different about you."

I am different. I wasn't always rich. I've been hungry and afraid. But I've never told anyone about those days.

Never spoken of the fear, or the hunger, or the way I still dread the darkness.

I've never told anyone about the day my twin brother died. I think I could tell Will.

We are directly in front of the entrance. The guard watches, frowning at Will. I avoid eye contact, hoping he won't approach us.

Will leans forward, pulls off his mask, and kisses my forehead. "I'm glad I was the one to save you this time," he whispers.

The look in his dark eyes makes me wonder what might happen if this mask weren't covering my mouth. I have to remind myself that I've sworn never to kiss anyone. I break eye contact quickly, and when I look back, he just smiles.

I imagine he's going to say something more, but then he glances up at the building where I live, puts his mask back on, and walks away.

The guard edges closer. "Miss Worth?"

"Yes?" I am still watching Will.

"Allow me to escort you to the elevator."

The Akkadian Towers have the only working elevator in the city. It makes the ascent to my home much too fast. What will I tell my parents? How will I deal with their accusations and worry?

Our courier is noticeably absent in the hallway, but the door is unlocked. When I walk in, no one rushes to greet me or to ask where I've been.

Finally I slide the door of Father's laboratory open. He is bent over one of his experiments. His hair has gone completely white. It seems that last week there were a few strands of gray left. Maybe it's just this light.

"Father?"

"Let me jot this down, one moment." He isn't fully aware of me.

"Can you tell me how to purchase a mask?"

Blinking, he turns toward me. "The factory on Oak Street, the one where they used to make ammunition? They manufacture the masks there."

"How do I order one?"

"Get the money from your mother and send the courier to fetch it." He picks up his notebook and begins to write.

I leave him to his work. He won't be out in a few minutes. He'll forget he ever spoke to me. He doesn't realize that I was out all night, or he doesn't care. Either way, I feel unequivocally sad.

Settling into my favorite chair to wait for Mother, I take the book of poems out of my bag and run my hand over the cover. It smells like Will's house, like warmth and love and freshly baked bread.

I thought, yesterday, that I would enjoy reading these poems, but I'm too unfocused.

Mother enters the apartment with a rush of cool air. I watch the emotions play across her face. Anger. Disgust. Worry? I try not to look at the dark circles under her eyes, try not to let myself feel guilty. Was she worried about me for the two years we lived in a cellar without her?

She crosses the room in three steps and throws her arms around me. I try to return the embrace but feel myself stiffening, pulling away, even as I think how nice her response is after Father's disregard.

"Thank goodness you and April are home safe."

"April? Didn't she come home last night?" Mother shakes her head. "I thought she left me," I say in a whisper. I should have known better.

Mother raises her hand to pat my shoulder but pulls back when I recoil. It was unintentional, but how do I tell her that?

"April never came home?" I ask again, stupid with surprise. My stomach hurts and my chest feels tight.

"Her mother is frantic."

I study my mother's face, but I've forgotten how to read her. Had *she* been frantic?

"Where is her steam carriage?" My voice sounds even smaller. "It isn't like she's never stayed out all night before."

"Araby, they are saying that the carriage was attacked by bats."

I want to laugh.

But not really.

April and I were making jokes about bats last night. It would be too coincidental . . . but then, Father saved humanity and couldn't save his own son. I don't discount coincidence. Or ugly, gut-wrenching irony.

"Mother . . ."

"There were bits of hair in her carriage. You know how people say bats like hair. . . ."

That is what they say, that if you have an elaborate hairdo you will attract the bats. I always envied April's perfect hair.

"At least you weren't with her."

"Yes. I'm pretty lucky." For once Mother hears the implication and flinches. Does she have survivor guilt, too, or just survivor hatred for the daughter who lived?

I steady myself with a hand on the back of the sofa. The hopeless masses watch us as we pass on our way to the Debauchery Club. Sometimes they have the energy to yell at us or shake their fists. Who is to say that they wouldn't attack April, a rich girl in a fancy carriage? She was probably drunk. I remember the dark figures who materialized from between the buildings while the young mother gave up the body of her child. The rock, seemingly thrown out of nowhere.

And there was that boy, the one with the blue eyelids. What was in those glasses that he was handing around? Did he drug April? I feel dizzy. Did he drug me?

"Where was the carriage found?" I ask.

"Near a club owned by her uncle." Mother gives me a look. She's too much of a lady to use a word like debauchery.

I could lose April, like I lost Finn. I'm weak suddenly, and glad I'm holding the back of the sofa.

"You're pale. Should I have the cook make you something?" Mother places her hand on my shoulder. Apparently she'll still touch me if I'm about to collapse onto the floor.

The cook . . . Will and the children ate their last apples before we left. I can do nothing, in this moment, to help April, but I can help Will. Our cook will be happy to prepare something; she doesn't think we appreciate her cooking, since none of us ever has much appetite.

"I'm glad you're home." Mother isn't looking at me. I believe her, but I also know that, like me, she'd be happier if Finn were here.

She'd trade her living child for her dead one in a heartbeat.

"I need money for a mask," I say. "Has the courier returned?"

"Not yet. April's mother borrowed him. She sent her own courier to all the places April usually goes, and our courier to search the carts, just in case." There are too many dead to allow everyone the privilege of identifying their loved ones. People die and are carted away.

She can't look at me. The constant reminders provided by the corpse collectors are one of the reasons she rarely leaves our apartment.

Mother hands me a purse filled with heavy coins.

I sit down because my legs are shaking. I should never

have let myself care about frivolous April with her silver eyelids and her evil sense of humor.

I drop the purse of coins onto the table, and it knocks my poetry book to the floor. A slip of paper falls from between the pages.

Meet me in the garden at midnight.

CHAPTER
SIX

THE GARDEN?

Midnight?

An eye has been sketched at the bottom of the note. I glance through one of the inner windows at the overgrown garden, trying to ignore the uncomfortable feeling of being watched.

I run my hands over the book's scarred leather cover. This book belonged to someone else. Does that mean this message did as well? Did whoever it was meant for already meet whoever wrote it, at midnight in a garden? Perhaps years ago; perhaps both are dead now.

I wish the message could be from Will, but he's always working at midnight.

Would April leave a message for me? I stare at the handwriting, but it is blocky and unrecognizable.

I walk to the interior window. In the mud, I see

something that might be part of a footprint. You wouldn't see it if you weren't expecting to.

Drifting through the penthouse, I run my hands over the glass. The windows don't open. And the door is hidden behind a brick wall.

Hours pass. I wait. Mother taps at my door before she goes to bed.

"They may find her, Araby." The way she says it exacerbates my fear. I touch the scrap of paper, hoping it means something. I hear Mother sigh and walk across the hall to her own room.

I watch the clock impatiently, and then finally slip out of our apartment.

If the entrance to the garden isn't on this level, then it must be above or below us. There is a terrace on the roof, and I've been up there enough, when I was allowed access to the roof, to know that there are no trapdoors.

I have never been on the floor directly below this one, though. The elevator operator, with his smooth white mask, always brings us straight to the top. But there are stairs.

Our hallway is lit by a flickering gas lamp that is too weak to truly penetrate the gloom, and the stairway at the end of the hall is completely dark. I walk gingerly, placing one foot carefully in front of the other and touching the wall with one hand.

The corridor is filled with doors. These apartments must be considerably smaller than the penthouses above.

I try each door gently, so that I don't alert the occupants, but near the end of the hall I crash into a chair, obviously placed in the hallway for a courier, and it grates loudly against the floor before hitting the wall.

From inside the nearest apartment, someone shouts, "Who's there?"

And then a door is opening. I expect to see a servant, maybe, or a family, but instead I see several young men in military uniforms.

"What are you doing on this floor?" one of them asks, reaching for me. I step backward before he can touch me. I don't know if he has mistaken me for someone else, but it is certain that I don't belong here. A second door opens, revealing another, older, soldier.

"Stop her," he says.

More doors are opening. The uniforms proclaim that they work for Prince Prospero. Why has he placed so many of his men on the floor directly below ours? On the older man's lapel, I see a pin. If it weren't for my hours with April, her attention to style and detail, I would never have noticed it. An open eye.

I hold out the note, as if it will somehow save me.

"'Meet me at the garden at midnight,'" he reads.

His uniform has many bright decorations, and I'm guessing he is in charge. None of these soldiers have the closed, cruel look of the men I see turning hungry children away from the perimeter of the upper city— but he's looking at me like he thinks I'm crazy. Then he glances at the slip of paper again, and this time he sees the eye, faint as it is, sketched with pencil at the corner of the sheet.

"Let her through," he says, and bows to me. "Enjoy your time in the garden."

He glares up and down the hallway. "Prepare to move to someplace less luxurious in the morning." Even in the semidarkness the underlings see his expression and slink back into the apartments.

"It's the last door on the right," he says to me when he sees I haven't moved.

The knob on the last door turns easily. I open it and hurry through, glad to be away from the staring men. My mother has warned me repeatedly never to be in a dark corridor, a dark alley, an abandoned room, with even one man. I sigh. Her days of chaperones and fainting females are long gone, but her warnings can still frighten me.

I can tell right away that the room is not large, but I stand in darkness for what feels like hours, waiting for my eyes to adjust. It's a maintenance closet filled with brooms and buckets and a ladder that is attached to the back wall. I catch my breath. It's the right height to reach the garden.

The ceiling is covered with gears and pulleys. Crossing the room, I place one hand on a rung, and then both feet. My elegant shoes have no traction, and by the time I'm halfway up, my hands are starting to sweat.

A large circular brass door covers the top of the ladder.

I push it, and it moves upward with a loud grating sound while a bit of earth trickles down, hitting my cheek. So this Garden of Eden isn't fully sealed after all.

My hands make contact with soil, then grass. The air isn't as thick as I expected from the beads of moisture that pool and roll down the window in my bedroom. It's muggy but bearable.

A slender tree branch slaps me in the face, and I suppress a scream. I've moved from the familiar darkness of the hallway to an unfamiliar darkness that smells of growing things. Vines touch my face and snake around my ankles.

My feet make squelching sounds in the mud, so I stop, straining to listen.

I hear the striking of a match, and my eyes latch on to the sudden flash of orange light. Someone is very near. I smell pungent smoke. Tobacco, perhaps? Taking a tentative step forward, I can make out a shape, long legs, crossed at the ankle. Obviously male.

"Hello?" My voice is embarrassingly tremulous.

"You're early. I like that. "

"This garden is supposed to be sealed."

"I grew up in Penthouse A. It would be cruel to keep me from the garden where I played as a boy."

"You're April's brother, Elliott?"

He puts whatever he is smoking to his lips. I watch the brightness where the paper is burning. His movements are unhurried.

"Yes."

"Do you know where she is?"

He sighs. "I suspect that our uncle got tired of her making a spectacle of herself and has made her an unwilling guest in his castle."

"He can't force her to stay."

He laughs. "The prince *can* make her stay. He can kill her if he wants, but I don't think he will."

"He wouldn't . . . you're sure he won't . . ." I can't say the word kill. "He won't hurt her?" I move closer, listening to the cadence of his voice, trying to be sure of his identity before I make my guess. "You're the guy with the syringe."

"Yes." He might be sticking out his hand for me to shake, but I can't see well enough to be sure.

"Blond eyebrows." I try to remember everything I know about him. He's a year or two older than April, eighteen or nineteen.

He laughs again, but when he speaks, his voice is completely serious.

"April said we could trust you, so I'm going to." He takes another drag from his cigarette, leaving me with an impression of long, aristocratic fingers. "Would you like to sit down?"

I put my hand forward until I can feel the wall and then, awkwardly, sit.

"Those soldiers downstairs. Are they connected with you, somehow?"

He coughs twice. "They didn't bother you? I needed a place to house them, and several floors of this building are abandoned. It seemed a good enough solution."

"They were wearing Prince Prospero's uniform."

"For now."

"Why do you need soldiers?" I ask.

"Rebellion," he says. "April and I are planning a rebellion."

His voice has changed from slightly bored to low and intense. Without meaning to, I lean toward him, too shocked to make even the slightest sound. This is treason.

In this city, people who commit treason are put to death. But he has soldiers.

"A rebellion?" I ask finally. "April is part of this?" How can April be part of a rebellion? She has trouble deciding what dress to wear.

"She has to be a part of it. This rebellion is who we are." He makes a sudden movement, and even in the dark I can tell he's agitated. "April and I hid behind a curtain and watched the worthy Prince Prospero slash our father's throat—"

I gasp.

I can't help it. I actually put my hand up to my own throat. Because I know . . . the gush of warm blood . . . I force the memory away.

"He murdered our father. He claimed lawless citizens broke into the mayor's office. I was a boy then, and my father wanted peace, so I didn't fight. I waited. And now we're going to destroy the prince. I'm going to save the city."

I try to see his expression, but it's too dark. Odd that he chose this place for our meeting.

"But other forces have begun to move in the city, and we can't afford to let anyone else take control. We have to act soon. I asked April to bring you to meet me so I could see for myself how fearless you are."

I nearly fall off the stone wall. Did April tell him that? He is wrong. I have so much fear. And since last night I've become more interested in the future. I'm not the person Elliott thinks I am.

"We couldn't find you at the club," I say.

"I was detained."

"And you didn't tell me who you were. You left me passed out behind a curtain."

"I did not. I left to speak to . . . a friend. And you made it home, while my sister did not."

"I'm not sure either of us was meant to make it home. There was a boy who gave us drinks. . . ."

"What did he look like? I'll find him." Something about the way he says this, with complete confidence, speaks to me. He's so different from my father, who is quiet and always afraid.

I describe the boy as best I can.

"Probably working for our uncle," Elliott says. "But if he hurt April, I'll kill him. So . . . here we are in this dark, forbidding garden. Will you help me, Araby Worth? I need someone like you. Willing to take risks."

I stare into the darkness. He can't see my expression, but I try to keep my face impassive anyway.

"I don't think I can help you."

"I can give you drugs," he says. "Good ones."

I want to laugh. Yesterday I wanted drugs. Yesterday I needed . . . my hands are trembling. Maybe I still need them. But his offer eases the pressure. Maybe it's his voice, disembodied in the humid darkness, or maybe it's how easy he thinks I am. I think of Henry and Elise, and of course I think about Finn. Can anyone overthrow the prince? Even with an army? Elliott is quiet as he waits for my response.

"I have an idea," I say. "A suggestion for your new government."

"Oh?"

"Free masks," I say. "For the children."

He coughs and chokes. On smoke from his cigarette or on his surprise?

"That is an excellent idea."

Elliott stubs out his cigarette and then lights a match. In the moment of illumination I can see that he isn't wearing a mask. I'm not as shocked as I might have been a few days ago. He holds the match between his fingers and watches it burn.

"There is one problem," he says. "Very few people know how to make the masks."

He drops the match to the ground. It sizzles in the mud, and then we sit in silence for what feels like a long time. Suddenly I know why he agreed so easily, what he's going to ask, that this is why he truly wanted to meet me. This was a game of chess, and he understands strategy.

"Whoever can make the masks can defeat the disease. There is great power in that." Elliott shifts, and a couple of stones fall from the low wall. "I've spoken to the workers at the factory. The filters are manufactured secretly, within the prince's palace."

But I know where Father keeps the blueprints.

I think of the young girl putting her baby's body into the black cart. Her anguish. A mask might have saved her child. Isn't it worth any price, any risk, to save someone from watching the contagion ravage their family? I wish I could see his face.

I move my foot in a half circle, testing the resistance of the unseen mud.

"I know where the plans are," I admit quietly.

He doesn't waste any time.

"I have clever friends. If you can get the blueprints, we can start production in just a matter of weeks. Days. We can distribute them secretly to people without money, for their children. I'd thought of making the masks more readily available, of course. But it would be genius to have you, the scientist's tragic daughter, distributing them. People would love that."

Is that who I am? A tragedy? Is that what Will sees when he looks at me?

"I will get the information," I tell him.

"Be careful. Your father is surrounded by spies."

Now it's my turn to laugh. "We know that." We've always known.

"I'll contact you soon. Now that April has disappeared, I need you." I like that he sounds less self-assured when he says this. It makes me think that maybe we could be friends.

I ask, because I have to know. "Was April lying, or is it true that you write poetry?"

A moment of silence. "It's true." His voice is barely audible. "My father nearly despaired of me ever amounting to anything."

He takes my elbow, guides me back to the ladder. "Descend carefully, Miss Araby Worth."

CHAPTER
SEVEN

WINCING AT THE BITTER TASTE, I SWALLOW MY sleeping draft. Father mixes it for me, tired of being kept awake by my screams. Thanks to the medication, I can sleep a dreamless sleep. Most nights.

I try not to think about anything. Not matches lit in dark gardens, or small children who are unprotected from the Weeping Sickness, or April imprisoned. Not rooms upon rooms of soldiers directly below me. I breathe carefully, fighting the panic that threatens to overwhelm me.

After what seems like an entire night's worth of sleeplessness, I dream of faces obscured by shadows.

I wake with a scream and sit up. My bed is wobbling. I shouldn't be awake before the sun is up; shouldn't open my eyes to darkness. I'm groggy, so the medicine is still in my system. Glass breaks, and something crashes to the floor. For a moment the room is bright as day. Then my bed shakes again.

I press my hands against the mattress and pray for the room to stop moving. Am I hallucinating?

I hear Mother and Father's voices from the next room. They aren't bothering to whisper.

Another explosion rocks my bedroom.

Bombings have happened before. Once, twice, never two so close together. This is bad.

Swinging my legs over the side of the bed, I press my feet against the floor. It doesn't move, so I dare to stand.

Through my window I see flames against a backdrop of darkness.

I'm going to my parents. My door opens soundlessly, but they must feel a draft flowing in from my room, because they both turn to face me.

A third explosion shakes the penthouse. More glass shatters in the kitchen. Mother whimpers.

I won't succumb to fear. I clench my teeth. Mother is ridiculous. I won't be like her.

Smoke billows outside. "Is the entire city burning?" I want to run to the window and look out, as if there is some way that I could see whether Will and the children are safe. Instead I stand, frozen.

"Idiots," Father mutters. "Burning, looting. They will make their situation worse."

"The people who are burning the city, what do they want?" I ask. I'm thinking of cloaked men and Elliott's concern that someone would take over the city before he does.

Father chooses to interpret my question as if I am completely shallow. As ignorant as I was a week ago.

"They want to change their lives. The poverty, their desperation, the state in which they are forced to live. Desperation and apathy are all we have left—" Father is interrupted by a series of staccato explosions. "Sometimes I wish gunpowder had never been invented," he says.

I stare at him, shocked. This is the man who lives by science. Who exists for discoveries.

I collapse onto the couch between my parents, and we sit in miserable silence until the sun comes up. Mother gasps each time the floor shakes. I keep my feet flat on the ground and my hands flat against the sofa cushions.

"What would our lives have been like if the plague hadn't happened?" As soon as I say the words, I wish I could take them back.

Mother answers quickly. "You would have gone to school. We would have traveled. Your father had a good job at the university. You and—"

"There is no 'what if the plague never happened,'" Father interrupts. "It happened. That's all."

We sit, silent and afraid.

"Father," I finally choke out, "can you tell me about the masks? How you made them?"

He gives me a long look. He could be thinking that

all I need to know is that the masks can't be shared, not even between twins. But Father isn't cruel. If that's what's going through his head, he'll keep it to himself.

"I'm not supposed to speak of it," he says. "The prince threatened to cut out my tongue. . . ."

Mother whimpers and Father turns away. As if he's ashamed of upsetting her. Or maybe he's seen the shock on my face.

I know that my father lives in a precarious place, that he used his popularity with the people to keep us here, away from the prince's prison, while ignoring the prince's anger at being outmaneuvered. But I never heard about the prince's threats. Stealing the plans for Elliott could upset this balance that keeps us free.

At breakfast time, the servants arrive, frightened, smelling of smoke. They risked themselves to come to work. Jobs are difficult to come by. Our courier is later than the others, and his mask is askew. When Father takes him into the lab to fix it, I follow them and listen.

"When did it happen?" Father asks as he examines the mask.

"Men were burning and looting." The courier's voice drops, and I have to strain to hear him. "If I contract the disease, please look in on my daughter." His voice trails away.

"You have nothing to worry about," Father says kindly, handing back his mask. But he keeps his own firmly in place.

With the sunrise, the flames are no longer visible. From my window I trace the path of the river. We didn't cross any bridges when we walked home, so Will lives on this side of the river. I scan the lower city for smoke, telling myself that he must be fine.

The city is laid out simply. The upper city is elevated, and the harbor is close. The lower city is bordered by a marshy inlet where the ocean meets a swamp. The river curls around the lowest part of the city, and the remnants of streets frame everything, creating a grid that I can see as I look down, though there are trees and grass growing in places that used to be streets.

Today I don't recognize the world from up here, and the room I inhabit in this sterile apartment seems completely unfamiliar, too. If April were here, she would laugh and offer me a drink. We would toast to something banal. We wouldn't talk about what our lives were supposed to be. But we would know.

I turn away from the window, pace back and forth. Without April and her steam carriage, I am trapped.

The hours trickle by. At lunchtime the cook assures me that she sent my packet of food to the address I gave her in the lower city. After lunch Mother plays piano. That's how she seeks her oblivion.

Instead of working in his laboratory, Father sits on the couch, staring out the window. If he doesn't leave the apartment, I won't be able to search his lab.

This conviction that I won't be able to steal from

Father fills me with relief. But relief is quickly followed by guilt at my cowardice.

"Mother gave me money," I tell him. "I want to buy a child-sized mask."

Father writes instructions on a slip of paper and then signs it.

Our courier is back at his post in the hallway. Like most people of our social status, we never really have to leave the building. We pay him to brave the germs and the violence. Except that I want to get out. The walls are closing in on me. Without April, I'm only allowed to leave the building with Father. And if I can't go to the club, I won't see Will.

I instruct the courier carefully. He is an older man, balding and thin. I remember what Mother told me yesterday, that they sent him to search through the bodies. I shudder, because he was looking for April, and because he had to look, had to touch . . . I force that thought away.

"Do you have children?" I ask, remembering the half-overheard conversation he had with Father.

"A daughter," he says.

"Does she own a mask?"

"Not yet. She isn't old enough for school. We're saving . . ."

I scratch out what Father wrote and carefully rewrite the order for two child-sized masks, instead of one.

"Ma'am?" He stares at the note.

"My parents can afford it," I say.

He folds the paper carefully and puts it in an inner pocket before he walks toward the stairway; couriers aren't allowed to use the elevator. I consider running after him, going with him to the factory. But as a woman on the street . . . he doesn't get paid as much as a guard. It wouldn't be fair to him. I go back into the apartment.

I nearly collide with Father in the foyer. He pats my arm.

"You're so grown up. I always meant to have a portrait made. It's one of my greatest regrets, waiting until it was too late."

I don't ask whether it's too late because I'm too old now, or because what he wanted was a portrait of both of his children.

"I'm going downstairs to inquire about the damage," he says. His voice is pleasant and vague. Perhaps he thinks Mother is listening.

As soon as he's gone, I slip into his laboratory. Beakers filled with bright bubbling liquid simmer above a controlled flame that is not so different from the one Will used to cook breakfast for Henry and Elise. The right side of the room is lined with shelves filled with jars of dead insects, mostly crickets.

Father's notes are scattered everywhere, except for a large wooden desk, which is completely bare. I take one step over the threshold, and then another. Father won't stay downstairs long. I cross the room, drawn to the desk. The first drawer is empty. No ink, no quill, none of the implements that one would keep in a desk. The next drawer is empty as well.

The third drawer is filled with papers. I grab a folded sheet from the back. It appears to be a schematic for some sort of . . . airship? At the top Father has written *Impossible.*

Tell the boy this will never fly.

I hear a noise and jump before I realize it is the cook, padding into the sitting room to ask Mother a question.

In the next drawer I find a stack of carefully labeled papers. Drawings, diagrams, directions. Everything a person might need for making a mask.

"Araby?" Mother calls from the sitting room.

I shut the drawer too hard. Mother must certainly have heard it; I slide the papers up into my sleeve, thankful that I wore this modest dress.

"Araby?" Mother says from the doorway. "What are you doing?" She sounds confused rather than accusatory, and that makes me feel guiltier than ever.

"I was looking for Father."

"He's downstairs, talking to the guards. Didn't you see him leave?" Now she's suspicious. "Come into the hallway. He won't want you in here."

I follow Mother, but before I can smooth the bulge of folded papers in my sleeve, the front door opens and Father steps back into the apartment.

I wait, heart pounding, but Mother doesn't accuse me of anything.

Father stops and waits, obviously wondering why we are standing there.

"I may work in the laboratory before dinner," he says finally, eyeing the door that I neglected to close all the way.

"Dinner will be served in an hour," Mother says. "Cook got some mushrooms—"

She is interrupted by a heavy knock at the door.

I catch my breath. The only person who knocks is April. Everyone else has to go through security at the front desk. A servant opens the door, and we all stare.

A young man is standing on the threshold with a bouquet of very red roses. I almost don't recognize him because I've never seen him in a mask, but he's wearing one now. The arrogant way he stands and his quizzical eyebrows give him away. They have even more impact, somehow, now that his face is obscured. I like the mask on him.

One of his eyebrows looks darker, slightly singed. I remember him sitting in the darkness, lighting matches. Maybe he burned himself. Or maybe he was out in the city last night.

Either way, I'm thrilled to see him.

Elliott saunters in, shakes Father's hand, nods to Mother, and hands the flowers to me. I hold them awkwardly; a thorn scrapes my hand, leaving a thin trail of blood.

"I'm Elliott," he says to my parents. "The . . ." He hesitates. "April's brother. I was hoping your daughter could walk up to the rooftop with me."

The rooftop. I'm not allowed to go there, though I haven't considered jumping in a long time. I deposit the flowers unceremoniously on a side table. Mother stares at Elliott, her face white. She goes to the sideboard and pours a drink. Whether it's for her or for Elliott is unclear.

"The roof?" Before Mother can go on, our courier walks into the room. Tears course down his face. This man who sits outside our door, impassively waiting to run our errands, is weeping. "The bombing last night . . ." he whispers. "It destroyed the factory where they manufacture the masks."

I gasp and put my hand up to the mouthpiece of my own mask, and as I do so, the papers in my sleeve make a loud crinkling sound.

Elliott's eyes meet mine.

"Surely they will rebuild," Mother says.

"People on the street say that even if they do, the workers will have to make each mask by hand again. Only the very rich will be able to afford them." The courier collapses onto our couch.

Mother serves the drink to him instead of our guest.

"Are people saying who did it?" Elliott asks.

My eyes go back to his singed eyebrow. What does he know?

"Black scythes were painted on the walls that were still standing," the courier says.

Elliott nods. "Malcontent." The way he says the word makes it sound more like a name than a mood. Mother and Father seem unaware, but the courier looks up sharply.

Father rests his hands against the windowsill and gazes out. "They will regret this when the next wave of illness hits," he says. He wipes his brow furiously, leaving a residue of ink on his forehead, and puts the handkerchief back into his pocket. "They've destroyed the very thing that gave them hope."

This room is stiflingly hot.

Elliott is staring at Father. Father speaks of the possibility of new diseases, of our vulnerability, often enough that I'm used to it.

"Many people still have masks," Mother says.

But not little Henry. And not the courier's daughter.

Father clears his throat. "Perhaps I will go tomorrow and offer my assistance. One more person might speed up the process. I gave them the knowledge—"

"You helped, sir. No one can question that. But you didn't give *them* the knowledge," Elliott says.

Mother and Father turn to stare at Elliott, the prince's nephew. Elliott isn't intimidated by their anger.

"You gave the knowledge to my uncle, and he kept it," he says.

"If you don't require anything else, I'll go back to my

post." The courier is nervous. As he leaves, he picks up a rose that dropped from Elliott's bouquet and hands it to me. "Thank you," he whispers. "My daughter . . . it was kind of you to try."

We are silent as he hurries across the tile floor and back to his chair in the hallway.

"You could still help the people, sir," Elliott says. "You could pass the plans along to me. I would find a way to share them."

"You know I can't do that," Father says sharply. "And you know why."

I look back and forth between them. The papers scratch my arm. I'm preparing to do what Father won't. And I know it's wrong.

"I do what I can," Father says. "Your inventor friends can attest to that."

Elliott nods. Father turns away as if he does not want to acknowledge Elliott's understanding. His voice is bitter. "There isn't anything we can really do, ever. Not when people destroy . . ." Father's shoulders slump forward. He stumbles into his laboratory. The door doesn't slam. Doors in the Akkadian Towers never do.

"We should go," Elliott says to me, smiling sadly. "None of us can do anything to save humanity this evening." His hand, gently squeezing my wrist, says otherwise.

I offer the rose I am holding to Mother. She's already placed the others in a vase. I want to say something to her. "Good-bye," or "It will be all right," or maybe even "I love you," but she's intent on the flowers.

Elliott leans close to her as we take the three steps to the door. "It was good to see you again, Catherine," he says in a soft voice.

Mother's eyes flit from me to Elliott and back to me. She shakes her head, like she's saying it isn't good to see him again, but she can't mean that. She's flustered. Obviously they have met before.

"Your parents disapprove of me," Elliott says as we walk down the hall. I try to think of something nice to say, but he doesn't give me a chance. "I'm used to it. Parents often disapprove of me."

I could ask him if he calls on many girls. But then he might think I care. So instead I ask, "Are your men still downstairs?"

"For a few more days. I'll leave a few to look after you and my mother. And April, when she returns."

We've reached the locked door that leads to the roof. I used to go up these stairs every day, before April came. She thought she was protecting me by having the heavy silver lock placed on the door.

Elliott unlocks the door and gives me a little bow, indicating that I should proceed.

"Why the flowers?" I ask over my shoulder.

"I had to have some reason to visit you."

"To give me roses?"

"Because I am passionately in love with you," he says.

I snort.

He laughs.

"The more I'm around, the less your parents will question my visits."

"I see." I'm glad I didn't ask him about other girls.

The narrow stairway ends with another door.

I hesitate with my hand on the doorknob. The rooftop holds many memories. Lonely ones from when we first moved here. I had never been so alone. Occasionally, as a child, I would wish for a few moments by myself, but not like that. Not forever.

Then April returned from the prince's palace to her childhood home.

I open the door at the top of the staircase and stop on the landing. Wind whips around us.

I remember the sensation well. I was crushed when April took this away from me. I wasn't going to jump, but she believed I might. That day she insisted on dyeing my hair, trying to make me forgive her for meddling. When it was done, she pushed me in front of the mirror.

"Look how pretty you are," she said.

I kept staring at the bright hair. I didn't recognize myself.

"It's the first time you've looked in the mirror for more than half a second," she said softly. "The first time you've looked in the mirror without seeing him."

Now the cold wind blows my unnaturally bright hair into my face.

"It's disheartening, isn't it?" Elliott thinks my pained expression is caused by the state of the city.

"Terrible," I say.

"With the destruction of the factory, the plans for producing masks are even more important. The quicker you get the information, the quicker we can get masks to the children."

He takes a flask from his pocket, reminding me so completely of April that it hurts.

If I trust him, maybe we can find April. I can have a mask made for Henry. And maybe he really will overthrow the prince. I'm going to betray my father, and I hate myself for it.

"I already have the blueprints," I say.

"You do?"

I love his surprise.

I had wanted to copy the plans before I gave them to him. But his hand is out, and I pull the papers from my sleeve, trading that opportunity for his approval.

"You are amazing." He scans the documents, holding them like they are the most precious papers in the world. At least he appreciates their worth. "Amazing," he repeats. I hold his gaze. He takes a drink from the flask and then offers it to me. The liquor burns going down, but I don't grimace.

"Good girl." His admiration warms me. "You aren't what I expected."

I'm not sure if this is a good or a bad thing.

"I have to go," he says abruptly. "But this is most helpful."

"Please copy the plans and get them back to me," I say. "They were the only papers in the drawer. If Father opens it, he'll know."

Elliott nods. "Of course." But I don't think he's really listening. He's staring out across the city. "It's dismal right now," he says. "But it will change."

I like the idea of making the world better, instead of hiding from all the ugliness. I don't know if Elliott can keep any of his promises, but the prospect of finding out is the first thing that has given me hope in a long time.

CHAPTER
EIGHT

ELLIOTT WALKS ME DOWN TO PENTHOUSE B. After he leaves, I pace back and forth in my bedroom. Without him, my excitement gives way to a sort of despair, and I collapse onto my bed and cry.

At bedtime, I gulp down my sleeping draft. There are no explosions in the night, but I still sleep poorly. I don't tell Father that his medicine is no longer working for me. The dreams that I am not supposed to have are dark.

The next morning is long and uneventful. I empty my makeup bag, spreading bottles and vials over the vanity table.

Mother comes into my room without knocking.

"I know why you were in your father's laboratory," she says.

I freeze. My guilty response proves her suspicions. I can see disgust in her eyes.

"Prospero's nephew sent you there. He wants you to betray your family. I used to know him . . . when you and Finn lived underground with Father. He's troubled. Araby, stay away from him."

I calculate quickly. "He couldn't have been more than a boy."

"Old enough that I could see him for what he was, what he is." She pauses, waiting for me to ask what she means. Waiting for me to turn and look her in the face. I toy with a makeup brush. She puts her hand on my shoulder.

"There are people who are honorable and good, like Finn. There are people like you and me, who try our best. And there are people who scorn everything that is good in this world."

Does she not see that leaving her children for a life of luxury was scorning something good?

"He's April's brother." I open a bottle of glitter. At the least I can hide my red eyes.

"April was spared most of . . . what their uncle put him through."

We hear Father in the parlor, pacing back and forth. Our floors must be wearing thin from all the pacing. I put down the bottle and wait to see if Mother will tell me more, but she shakes her head and leaves my doorway.

Father is still pacing an hour later when I emerge from my room. I want to slip over to the sideboard and pour myself a drink. But I don't.

"We might walk together later," Father suggests. He starts to say something more, his face serious and sad, and I lean forward in anticipation, but then a chord from the piano startles both of us. Mother is playing—not one of her tinkling pleasant melodies, but something dramatic and harsh.

It ruins everything. Father looks upset, heartbroken, like the music reminds him of something terrible. Whatever it is, the moment is over.

Mother continues playing, the same song over and over. Is she playing something wrong? Trying to correct some error? There is no place in the apartment where I can escape from the sound.

Father seems to feel the same way.

"Maybe I should get my coat," he says. "Do you think it's cold outside?"

The music stops.

"Don't go outside," Mother says. "It's dangerous."

Father turns to reassure her, but he's interrupted by a steady rap at the front door.

A dozen white roses nearly hide Elliott's face.

"Oh, how lovely," Mother says before she can stop herself.

He hands half the flowers to Mother and holds out the rest to me.

"I was hoping Araby would do me the pleasure of joining me at the . . . er, at my club. Will you?" Elliott asks. The question is for me rather than my parents.

Mother is shaking her head.

I raise my gaze to meet his. He gestures to the flowers and shrugs, embarrassed. I can't help smiling.

"With pleasure," I say.

As if I would say no. My need to get out of this apartment borders on desperation.

Mother steps forward, preparing to say something, but I hand her the rest of the roses and turn away. Elliott grips my arm, and with a quick, guilty wave to Father, I walk away from them.

Elliott whisks me down the corridor to the elevator.

In the mirrored wall of the elevator I see, not some exotic creature transformed by makeup and sequins, but myself. I hate seeing myself.

If April were here, she would put glitter on my cheeks to make me feel better.

"Next time, send a message." I touch my hair. "I'm unprepared for going out."

"I don't have a courier to send with a message," Elliott says. "Expect me to arrive at any time, and then you'll always be ready."

I give him a dirty look, and I can tell by the crinkling of his forehead that he's amused by my annoyance.

In the years since we adopted the masks, we've become adept at reading the expressions behind them. Eyes and eyebrows are the best indicators. To know when someone is smiling, I rarely have to see his mouth.

Before I can respond to Elliott's smirk, the elevator

begins to shake. The attendant pushes buttons frantically. Elliott reaches for me, as if to offer some sort of protection. I step away from him, and he drops his arms with a shrug, still amused.

The elevator tilts, and I'm thrown into Elliott, hard. He doesn't have his arms outstretched now, so my cheek hits his shoulder, and it hurts. Without looking at me, he wraps one arm around me—the other steadies us, pressed against the side of the elevator.

He seems completely calm, but his hand, against my bare skin, is slightly sweaty. I keep my eyes on the operator's pale face.

The elevator rumbles and I gasp.

"So you *are* afraid of dying." Elliott leans in to whisper in my ear.

As we lurch down to the lobby, I try to emulate Elliott's calm. Finally the elevator stops with a sudden jerk that almost knocks me off my feet.

The attendant's face is white as he opens the door. "I'm sorry, Miss Worth. The explosions must have damaged the cable; your apartment is so far from the ground."

I need to feel the solid marble floor under my feet. Elliott takes his time, smiling. I remind myself that his hand was clammy. He worries about dying, too.

Elliott has a small steam carriage, faster and less elaborate than April's. The seats are close together, and I'm aware of him beside me, that my bare knee is touching his leg, but as we navigate the streets, I forget him and stare out at the rubble. The city blurs in the light rain, and gray buildings merge with the hulks of blackened ones. This was far worse than the single acts of vandalism that happen occasionally. This was organized mayhem. To our left are the remains of a beautiful cathedral, the roof gone, walls blackened.

"What else did they burn?"

"They focused on churches."

I'm surprised, as we drive past the blackened structures, just how many churches there are in our city. Blending in between taller buildings or standing tall at the corners. You see one on nearly every block in the upper city.

Churches make me think of bats, and bats, of April.

"Have you heard anything? Is she with your uncle?"

He knows I mean April. "It's my uncle's style to take her, to prove that he can. If someone else, like these rebels who are burning and bombing, had taken her, we would know. They would ask for something, ransom."

"I'm worried," I say softly.

We drive past the rubble of what used to be an apartment building, and I wonder if any people were inside when it blew up. It must have been vacant. I don't want to consider the alternative.

"When we get to the club, I need you to fetch something for me." He glances over at me, and he looks very serious. "It's too risky to do myself."

My heart speeds up a little as he explains. He wants me to get a specific book with a green cover from the upper floor of the club, then bring it to him There are whispers about the men who inhabit that floor. I've heard odd noises from up there, a scream once, though April says she didn't hear anything. I agree to everything he asks. I won't show him any weakness now.

"Be sure to hide the book," he says. "Don't let anyone see it. And if anyone speaks to you, pretend to be lost."

If they speak to me, I'm not sure I'll have the wits to pretend anything.

We are driving in the shadow of a tall building when the carriage hits something. Elliott swerves, working the controls furiously. I fall into him, and he puts his arm around me, shielding me from impact, and then his face hits the side of the carriage, hard.

I catch my breath, afraid that he has broken his mask.

I look over my shoulder. "Did we run over someone?"

"I don't think so," he says. "It was too flat. I mean, I don't think it was a person." His voice is shaky. "We shouldn't stop.

"We should see what we hit," I say. "We should make sure it's not a person and we'll go," I say.

"Fine."

The thing in the street could be a shadow, except that we both felt the impact as we rolled over it. Elliott pulls the steam carriage closer, takes a sword from behind his seat, and leans out of the carriage to prod the dark mass.

I suppress a scream as he lifts a sleeve with the blade.

"An empty cloak," he says flatly. Something falls from the fabric and clatters to the street. He climbs down and hands me two objects. The first is a crucifix. When he hands it to me, I marvel at how heavy it is. The second item is a reptilian skull. As I reach for it, a tooth grazes my finger.

A thin line of blood appears on my hand.

"Crocodile teeth in a crocodile jaw." He climbs back into the carriage. "The cross is valuable. I wonder if whoever lost it will be coming for it."

I hold up the skull, staring into the deeply set eye sockets.

"What good is a message if we can't interpret it?" he mutters.

"Maybe it isn't a message. Does it have to have a sinister meaning?"

"It doesn't have to," Elliott says. "But I think it does."

He grabs at his mask, trying to readjust it.

"I hate these things."

"April told me that you refused to wear a mask." She called him a revolutionary poet. So far I've only seen the revolutionary part.

"I hate the control they give my uncle. I protested by not wearing one for over a year. But what we're doing now is too important for that type of risk."

He starts the carriage again, and we continue on.

"Risking contagion is a stupid way to live," I say. I don't like the masks. Nobody likes the masks. But we need them. They work.

"It was what I chose." He stares out over the city. "You do believe that people deserve to make their own choices?"

We've passed into the lower city, and the landscape is grim. Windows are protected with planks from the outsides and quilts from the inside. The quilts, visible through the boarded windows, remind me that in just moments I'm going to see Will.

My heart beats a little bit faster.

"Of course I believe in making choices."

"Good."

Elliott parks, and we step out of the carriage and into the alley. He opens the door and ushers me into the club. As soon as the door swings shut behind him, he rips the mask from his face and gasps for air. I'm certain that his near panic is genuine.

I put my hand up to his face. "You will get used to it. Everyone does." His cheek is warm. I would pull my hand back, shocked that I'm standing here touching him, but he looks so vulnerable.

"I don't think I will, but it's nice that you care." His voice is overly warm, but not smooth like the one from the doorway behind us.

"If this can wait until you're inside the club, I need to conduct your examinations."

And now I feel guilty for standing so close to Elliott, with my hand still touching his face.

There are so many things I want to say to Will, questions to ask. Were the bombings close to his home? Were the children afraid? Are they healthy? No coughing? No rashes? Did they get the food I sent? But being near him makes me tongue-tied and awkward. I can't tell him that I was going to get a mask for his brother, because the gesture is meaninglessness now, and my intentions will remain useless until Elliott and I succeed with our plan.

I'm shocked when Elliott follows me into the examination room. I want a few seconds alone with Will, but Elliott dominates the room with his arrogance, and Will barely looks at me as he gestures for me to roll up my sleeve.

"Who moved my sister's steam carriage?" Elliott asks.

"You'd have to ask one of the doormen. They take care of vehicular matters." Will's fingers are cool against my forearm. He might not be looking at me, but his fingers linger on my arm.

"Find out."

Will gestures for me to breathe into the clockwork mechanism, his hand on my shoulder. The dial on the clockwork device twists and turns.

"Is she clean?" Elliott asks.

"Of course she is."

Elliott's eyebrows go up.

They stand looking at each other. I'm supposed to go in now. To hurry to the top floor alone. For Elliott. But Will is gripping my arm.

"I'll need my private rooms unlocked," Elliott says. "I seem to have misplaced the key."

I try to catch Will's eyes, but he won't look away from Elliott. I pull my arm out of his grip. He steps closer to Elliott, presumably to test him, as I slip out of the examination room. I imagine I hear a faint clicking sound as I pass through the dangling beads. I miss April laughing on the other side. The Debauchery Club feels different tonight.

Instead of wandering through downstairs rooms, I go directly to the stairway and climb away from the crowded areas, through the libraries where men whisper secret things to giggling girls.

After seven or eight steps down a long corridor, I stumble over an uneven place in the floor and have to take two steps down. The hallway looks the same, same carpet, same dark paneling, but I'm pretty sure I've entered a different building that has been connected to the original. Following Elliott's directions, I find a doorway. Inside are the same heavy, ornate furnishings that are found throughout the club.

On the far wall, there is a tapestry. Bright red birds nest in a tree with withered purple leaves. Behind the tapestry I find a door, and behind the door is an exceedingly dim stairway. I want to go back to the lower floors, where there is laughter and drinking. The darkness here feels oppressive and stale.

I square my shoulders and tiptoe up the stairs, entering a silent hallway lined with doors. Some are open. Inside the rooms I see older club members playing cards. In one, a man looks directly at me. He has the coldest eyes I've ever seen.

Elliott says that the plague claimed their families and fortunes. They know everything that goes on in the club and are fanatically loyal to the prince, who has given them this refuge.

"They are supposed to stay on their own floor," Elliott told me. "My uncle knows that they could be bad for business, but he also knows the value of ruthless men who live in a state of desperation."

"Who were they, before?" I asked.

"People who did his dirty work. Criminals, assassins. It's unfortunate that the book I want is in their domain. They cannot find out that I have taken it."

Finally I come to a corridor lined with bookshelves, exactly as Elliott described it. I'm supposed to find a book with a green spine, a book filled with maps of the city, but searching for a single book while maintaining the illusion of glancing casually at these volumes makes my head throb.

I am so nervous that I almost don't see it. An open eye stares at me from the spine. In the dim light the gold fades into the green leather. I grab it, and another volume to place over it, and turn, my heart racing.

Before I can take two steps down the hallway, a man steps out of a shadowy doorway and into my path.

"Are you lost?" It's the man with the cold eyes.

"I'm meeting someone," I say, to indicate that I'm not alone.

"In my day, young ladies wouldn't have dreamed of reading such books." He is looking at the oversized volume that hides the one I'm clutching to my chest.

A figure is embossed on the cover. I stare at it and realize that there are actually two figures. My cheeks burn. The old man's chuckle turns to a wet cough.

"I've seen you before," he says. "We've seen you." His eyes flicker back to his friends. "Your hair is such a lovely violet."

Bony fingers caress my hair. I struggle to breathe.

"I have to meet a friend," I repeat, and step away, careful to keep the green book hidden.

"You should have brought your friend with you."

He's looking at my legs now, exposed to show that I'm not sick. I turn quickly. "Thank you for your help," I say over my shoulder, prepared to run if he gets any closer. The other men stand, dropping their cards, pushing back chairs.

My feet feel too heavy, like I can barely lift them from the floor.

"If you ever need help finding your way, you need only ask." Something in his voice makes the others stop.

"I will," I say. "I will." And now I'm hurrying down the hall.

"We're always happy to help," he calls after me.

At the bottom of the stairs I sink to the floor, leaning against the tapestry. I'm shaking so hard that I'm not sure that I'll be able to stand back up. I might have to sit here on this disgusting dirty rug forever. Elliott should have been waiting for me. And Will . . . I want Will.

But there is no one here, and I can't stay. Someone could come into this room at any moment, and both books are just lying beside me. I pick up Elliott's precious book and the other one, and stand. The birds in the tapestry watch me with beady eyes.

CHAPTER
NINE

I THROW OPEN THE DOOR TO ELLIOTT'S PRIVATE rooms, step inside, slam it behind me, and then stand, leaning against it, and panting slightly.

"Too many stairs?" he asks lightly, giving me a moment to compose myself. As my breathing evens, I realize where I am. As far as I know, even April has never gone into one of these private rooms. We joked that this was where the debauchery actually happened.

What would my mother say if she knew I was in Elliott's bedroom?

But the room we're in is a study rather than a bedchamber. In the center is a wide table, thick and angular, functional rather than decorative. An open doorway leads to his bedroom.

He puts out his hand. I give him the book.

"Good girl."

I sit and take a deep breath. The air here is just like the rest of the club, scented with sweat and a hint of subversion.

"You told me it was dangerous," I say. "But there was a man who said that he'd seen me before." I want him to understand how scared I was.

"One of them spoke to you?" He looks up from the book.

"Yes. He touched me." I put my hand to my hair. It feels oily.

"They would notice you," Elliott says.

Across the room I see our reflection in a gilded mirror.

"Do they . . . watch us?"

"Oh, yes. My uncle is an astute businessman. If bored young women will pay exorbitant dues to play at being debased, there are those who will pay for a glimpse of that."

I feel ill.

"I thought you said that they had no money."

"There are different kinds of currency. Surely you know that." He shakes his head and smiles to himself, amused at my naïveté. But I saw the way he glanced into his bedroom when he spoke of currency. I wonder if he has companions here. The rooms are quite elegant. I can see heavy silk curtains in the bedroom, and the color, a deep blue, is mirrored in the walls of the study. I have the impression of pillows and rumpled bedding. I look away.

Bookshelves line one wall of the study, but the books look unread. Formal leather classics. Perhaps those are the sorts of books he likes. A sideboard carved with lions is pushed against the wall perpendicular to the bookshelves.

"Interesting choice." Elliott indicates the larger book that I used to hide the first one, and now I'm blushing again.

He pauses, waiting for me to speak, and when I don't say anything he focuses his attention on the green book. In the stillness, the sound of ripping paper is unexpected and loud. Elliott folds the pages and puts them in an inside pocket of his vest.

"What is so important about that book?" I ask.

"It documents the building of the city. A man who memorizes this book will know ways to get around without being seen, will know its secrets. Only four were printed, and my father had one, but it was lost. I've searched the city for the others. One of the maids told me that there was a shelf of dusty books on the top floor, but she couldn't retrieve any of them. The men upstairs have ways of questioning people. They would have discovered that I wanted the book and guessed why. They won't be able to get to you the same way."

The gas lamp flickers, casting shadows up into his face.

"It's reassuring that they may hesitate before torturing me," I say. "That's what you mean, isn't it?"

He ignores the question and starts flipping through the book.

"I love this city and all of its mysteries and depths. I want to save it." Strange; I've never heard anyone speak of the city with such passion. His expression is earnest, and I want to believe him. "And I'd love to see my uncle dead." He says it so softly that I almost don't hear him.

He's found the map he wants, and he dips his quill into a bottle of ink and draws a large red X over the cathedral that we passed on the way here. And another, and then another.

"Why do you suppose they are burning churches?" I ask after a moment's silence.

He smudges the ink with the side of his hand and curses.

"There's a new leader trying to organize some sort of revolt. He calls himself Reverend Malcontent."

He's said that name before. Malcontent. An unpleasant word, and even more unpleasant as a name. I think of the blasted and burned churches, their beautiful interiors exposed now to the elements.

"Malcontent can't be his real name," I say.

"Obviously not. Did you think that my uncle's name is really Prince Prospero?"

I won't admit that I never thought about it.

"But why would a minister burn churches?" My mouth is dry. I wish he would offer me something from his ornate sideboard. Even if it's only water.

"If people get indignant about churches being burned, then they are thinking about the churches. Maybe even regretting not using the churches."

"They might pray. They might ask God for help, or they might ask Reverend Malcontent." I tear my eyes away from the decanter.

"Yes, exactly. He's setting himself up as a prophet. If he's convincing enough, he could seriously challenge the prince." Elliott speaks slowly, like he thinks I'm stupid.

I try to curb my irritation, staring at Elliott's elegant writing quill. Red ink drips from it like blood. "You're going to need acting lessons if you are going to convince my parents that you're in love with me," I say finally.

"You could be less annoying."

"Possibly." I flip my hair the way April would if some guy were insulting her. Elliott studies his book, ignoring my irritation. "So Reverent Malcontent is the force you've been worried about, the one who will rebel before you have the opportunity?" I ask.

"We'd be no better off with a mad fanatic than we are with Prospero."

"If Prince Prospero's not his name, why do *you* call him that?"

Elliott grabs me, pulls me close, and slides my hand under the back of his shirt. His skin is warm, and even as I'm frantically pulling my hand away, my fingers find raised skin. Scars.

"I'm glad you asked," he says in his most bored and

aristocratic voice. "I slipped once and called him by his former name. He had me whipped. His court considered it fine entertainment." His voice remains conversational. My fingers feel unnaturally warm where they touched his skin.

"It must have hurt dreadfully," I say, my voice small.

"Yes. But don't worry; I'm not going to tell you his real name. I wouldn't want you to slip, like I did. See, I love you so much, I need to protect you." There's pain under his sarcasm, but I can't ignore the ugliness of his tone.

"Like you protected your sister?"

"Ah," he says. "Accusations. April should have protected herself."

I know he's looking at me, daring me to argue, but I won't. He's visiting me with flowers, pretending he's in love with me, and though he says the prince has April, he hasn't given me any proof. The prince would love some reason to accuse my father of treason. With what I've done for Elliott, I could bring the prince's wrath down on my family. I might never see April again. And this place, the club, my refuge, has become tainted now, with fear.

"Have you copied the plans? Can you return them soon?"

"Soon. And yes, I've copied them very carefully. I have a friend who is an inventor. He's already working on a prototype."

"Good," I say. "Very good. I want the first mask. It should be the smallest size."

"Of course, my love."

I stand. I need to get some air, something to drink. Elliott is a poor host for not offering me anything. "I'll be back in a few moments."

He doesn't try to stop me. When I'm out of the room, he'll be free to pore over the pages that truly interest him. The ones that he's been careful not to show me.

The hallway outside Elliott's private apartment is empty and dark. I hurry back to areas of the club that are more familiar to me, keeping an eye out, just in case, for the guy April was kissing on the night she disappeared.

As I reach the bar, I'm surprised to see Will. It's unusual for him to circulate. He usually stays near the entrance, endlessly testing patrons.

"Araby," he says.

I stop. "I wasn't sure that you remembered my name," I say.

"Yes," he says. "I do. Of course I do."

I gesture for the bartender to bring me a drink, because if I don't have something in my hands, I'll just stand here uselessly, staring at Will. But the bartender is busy with a girl at the other end of the bar.

"I need some fresh air," I say.

"Then by all means go outside. If it doesn't clear your head, it will probably kill you." Will might be teasing. I can't tell.

The bartender finally sees me. He pours something into a tall glass and slides it to me, as Will takes my elbow to pull me away.

"You seem different tonight."

I'm not sure what he means by different. I grab the glass and take a long drink. I'm afraid of his expectations.

"Araby? I'll take you for some fresh air. I wasn't serious about it killing you."

I drain the glass and follow him. He leads me down two flights of carpeted stairs, to a door that I've never noticed. I thought I knew the layout of the Debauchery Club, but tonight it feels unfamiliar, as though I only know it from a dream.

"I want to show you something," he says in a whisper.

We put on our masks and go out into a tiny courtyard. Buildings loom above us, four and five stories high.

The moonlight is directly overhead. I know it's cold—I can see our breath—but I don't feel it. We take six steps across the flagstones.

"This is what I wanted to show you."

I tear my eyes from his face. In the center of the courtyard is an ancient flowerpot, an urn, partially crumbled on one side. A vine climbs out of it.

One white flower blooms on the vine.

"It only opens in the moonlight, and only for a few hours, when the full moon is directly overhead. Maybe someone planted it here before the plague, when the world was hopeful. At the end of the day, after sweeping the floors and cleaning up vomit, I come here. It reminds me that there are still beautiful things."

"It's lovely," I say—but instead of the flower, I look at him, feeling light-headed and odd. Happy. I think this feeling is happiness. I turn to study the flower petals, tremulous with dew. He is still holding my hand, and he is leaning toward me. He's so close.

More than anything, I want him to kiss me.

But I wiggle my fingers, trying to disentangle my hand politely. He ignores my attempt to keep my distance and pulls me toward him, gently. But I am serious about the vow I made at Finn's grave. If it doesn't involve sacrifice, then what is the point? I pull away, hard. It catches him off balance, and I stumble forward. My foot hits the flowerpot.

It teeters for a moment and Will lunges forward, but he isn't fast enough and it hits the flagstones and crumbles. The vine is broken. Will stares at it.

"I . . . can't hold hands with anyone," I tell him in a rushed whisper.

I'm too embarrassed to look at him, even though I can tell that he's turned toward me. Tears build up behind my eyes.

"I should take you back to your friend," he says, his voice barely a whisper.

As he leads the way back into the building, I remember the way our arms touched, casually, when he was walking me home, and I long for that quiet sense of companionship.

On our way in from the courtyard, we have a nearly unobstructed view of the bar. A chillingly familiar man stands exactly where I stood when Will approached me, holding a glass that might have been mine. Will makes a disgusted sound and pushes me up the stairwell, out of sight.

"They never come downstairs," he says. "If you see any of those gentlemen, avoid them. Drawing their attention is . . . unhealthy."

Voices, laughter, drift up from the bar. I won't tell him that I have drawn their attention. That I'm already involved.

"I have to get back to work," Will says. I nod again. Choked by regret. He takes two steps away, and then waits, as if to see what I will do. I give him a wry smile and head back to the third floor, to Elliott's private apartment.

"There you are." Elliott has placed his silver syringe in the center of the table, offering it as some sort of incentive for me to do as he commands. Reminding me how little he thinks of me.

"Have a look at these while I light more lamps." He pushes some papers toward me, flyers that look like they might be posted on buildings and folded pamphlets. Even with the additional lamps, the light isn't good enough for reading. The words blur, and all I see are symbols. Red scythes, black.

I put my finger on a black scythe. "I saw these in the lower city."

His eyebrows go up, wondering, perhaps, what I was doing there. But he doesn't ask, and I won't offer him the information.

"The good reverend is using that symbol for *his* rebellion. Have you seen these flyers?"

"No." I flip through the pages, reading headlines. The Prince Is a Villain. Science Will Save Us. The Disease Is in the Water, Not the Air. Lies and half-truths designed to frighten the reader. I crumple a pamphlet that says the plague is a curse, before I realize what I'm doing and attempt to smooth it out.

"Do the pamphlets follow the mood of the people, or do the pamphlets encourage certain opinions among the masses?" I ask.

"That's a good question, and not one that I can answer. There was a lull in the anti-science activity for a few years, thanks to your father. His invention gave people hope, and now that hope has been stripped away. My uncle doesn't realize how bleak . . . There should have been a sort of renaissance when the masks were created. Not this desperate fight over too few."

I flip over a pamphlet sketch of the prince and realize how much I despise him. My father wanted to save lives, but the prince has made an industry out of death and disease.

"Violence is about to escalate, Araby," Elliott says.

My stomach lurches. Violence is mindless. It doesn't listen to reason. Elliott seems to have men who are trained to fight, but how many? More than the prince?

"But maybe, just maybe, we can use this unrest for the betterment of the city." His eyes catch mine and hold them.

A clock strikes from the bedroom behind us. It's the middle of the night, and we're here, in this private place that belongs solely to him.

Elliott stands, stretches, and walks to the sideboard. He pours drinks into heavy cut-crystal glasses and hands me one.

"To the betterment of the city."

A light knock interrupts our toast. It's Will.

"I located your sister's steam carriage," he says. "Thieves were tearing the gold leaf from the sides, and one of the doormen moved it to the stables."

"Stables?" Elliott interrupts.

"Where the horses were housed—"

"I'm familiar with the term. I'll want to examine the carriage in the morning."

"It will be morning soon." Will is looking at me, not Elliott.

I push my chair back from the table. "I need to go home."

"Driving through the city could be dangerous. We should spend the night here." Elliott gestures to the bedchamber. "It would be safer."

"No," I say. Because Will is listening. Because I touched Elliott when he was struggling with his mask, and then again when I felt his scars. Because of the way he was looking at me when he was pouring the drink.

I hate the mock intimacy in Elliott's voice, and that Will is hearing it and might think it's real.

"The streets are no longer safe," Elliott says.

"My mother worries," I say. "I can't stay here."

I heard the way he spoke to my mother, like she was someone who needed to be protected. So I'm not surprised when he says, "In that case . . ." He turns to Will, who is making no effort to hide that he is listening to our conversation.

"Have there been any disturbances tonight?"

"It's been quiet throughout the district," Will says. He's looking at the syringe. I had forgotten about it lying there on the table.

Elliott follows his gaze and pockets the syringe. "We don't want to upset Mrs. Worth. Or the venerable Dr. Worth." His tone is slightly obnoxious, but he is doing what I want, so I don't say anything.

We follow Will down the corridor and two flights of stairs. A few people linger in the club, in corners, in the rooms and alcoves.

"Your sister's steam carriage will be here when you are ready to examine it," he tells Elliott. "Be safe."

"She's always safe with me." I look back and forth between the two of them. Exhausted, mute. Elliott, never at a loss for words, says, "Come along, my love." I flush.

Will is paler than usual; his tattoos stand out on his skin. He belongs here so totally that I almost can't believe that he belongs in other places just as completely. He mouths something, but I've never learned how to read lips.

Elliott takes my arm, and we walk outside and into the darkness.

"There used to be gas streetlights in some parts of town." He lights two lanterns and hangs them on hooks at the front of his steam carriage so that our visibility is slightly better than nothing. The full moon doesn't illuminate as much as you might expect. The buildings lining the street absorb the moonlight.

As we leave the Debauchery District, the darkness is briefly illuminated by torches. Robed figures slither in and out of my line of vision. Elliott's eyes follow them through the gloom. I breathe in, hard, and point, though they are moving quickly and have disappeared.

"Malcontent's men." He drives slowly, uneasily.

The full moon casts oblong shadows. And then, for a moment, everything goes dark. Something blocks the moon. I'm reminded of Henry's toy airship, but when I look up, the sky holds only clouds.

Elliott pulls a lever, and the steam carriage jumps forward. "If you ever need a place to hide, there are entrances to the catacombs throughout the city. They look like sewer covers, but they are marked with the open eye."

"The catacombs are mapped out in your book," I say.

He nods quickly. "Many of the passages have deteriorated along with the city, but at least now I know where they were."

"You are looking for places to hide your soldiers," I guess. "Or ways to move them through the city."

"I need a way to organize. My father knew that the architects and masons who constructed the city built secret rooms and tunnels just for the challenge of it."

"The soldier in the Towers had a pin on his lapel, with an eye. Like on the note you sent me. And on the book."

"It was the symbol of my father's secret society. I've adopted it. Prospero murdered all the members, so their secret places are mostly still unknown, and now I have what might be the only complete set of maps, thanks to you."

I scan the buildings that line both sides of the street, wondering how many men are loyal to him, wishing that we could hide in the catacombs now. If someone attacks us, it will be my fault for demanding he take me home.

"Next time I will insist we wait until morning to leave. You can sleep at my apartment."

He takes my silence as discomfort and continues. "Don't worry. I can sleep in the dressing room."

"I wasn't worried," I say, straining my eyes to see through the thick night air. "You don't even really like me."

"You underestimate yourself." His voice reminds me of the first time I met him, when he asked what a girl like me needed to forget.

"No. I don't. My parents don't even like me. They wish that I had died and my brother had lived. Everyone liked my brother."

He laughs.

"So I'm risking my life to take you home in the middle of the night, and your parents don't even care?"

I don't laugh with him, and of course he notices. He always notices. When he speaks again, his voice is gentle. "My father wished that April had been the son. She was ruthless, and I was a dreamer."

The moon shines dully from behind a cloud. We live in a haze of humidity. Even at night when it's cool, the air is heavy with moisture.

The buildings here lean over the street, which is little more than a muddy track. April's carriage would never have made it through the back alleys that Elliott seems to prefer. A clothesline is stretched over the street, with garments swaying with the movement of the wind. This was a working-class neighborhood, back when there were jobs to be had. The air here is scented with the greasy smell of fried meat, and a pleasant aroma, like some sort of spice. Elliott's hands on the steering wheel are less tense, and I take a deep, calming breath.

Something shimmers across the street in front of us. "Elliott!"

Wires have been stretched across the road, and I brace myself as the steam carriage lurches to the left and we hit a pile of rubble.

I search the darkness for cloaked figures, anything moving.

"He set a trap for us," Elliott says quietly.

I grip his arm just above the elbow, so hard that it has to hurt. We are vulnerable, with our lanterns shining brightly in the darkness.

I see a pendant with the black scythe hanging from a nearby window.

"Elliott?" My voice is shaking. I want him to back up, to get us out of here, but instead he's fumbling for something behind his seat. The street is silent except for the purr of our engine. Elliott attaches a vial of liquid to a small candle. He hands me a match. "Light the fuse."

I light it with unsteady fingers and hand it back to him. He looks at it for a moment, then tosses it into the street ahead of us.

It bursts, and there's a flash of light before an explosion rocks the narrow street.

Elliott smiles and turns the carriage in a tight circle. "Which one of us do you think the reverend wants?"

I glance at the crucifix in the back of the steam carriage.

Elliott grabs the crocodile skull, tossing it out into the street, where it shatters into a million white pieces. He does not discard the gold crucifix. And now we've turned. The fire is behind us. With no one to put it out. Wooden beams start to blaze, and then shingles on a roof high above.

"When I'm in charge of the city, I'll re-form the fire brigade," he says.

My hand throbs where the crocodile tooth scraped it.

The air is so dense in this part of the city that I can put out my arm and feel the condensation settling on my skin. In the light of the blaze I can see row upon row of arched windows. The glass is completely gone, and bats screech from within and beat their wings in the darkness.

The journey home is interminable. Elliott veers back onto the main street and stays there. The husks of churches sadden me as we pass them. They tie the neighborhoods together, tall and proud, solid stone buildings with their steeples and bell towers.

Finally the Akkadian Towers loom over us. "Almost there," Elliott says.

I want to be home. At least in April's carriage we had guards.

"When you have a chance, take another look around your father's laboratory. See if you can find any correspondence from my uncle. Both my uncle and the rebels will want to use your father. We need to know what they might be planning so we can decide how to help him."

I saw the way Elliott looked at my father, and I'm not

convinced that he wants to help him. Elliott is willing to sacrifice anything for the sake of this plan, I am beginning to realize. And he thinks I am, too.

"I'll look," I say, but I'm really just breaking the silence.

My parents have always warned me about the dangers in the city. It occurs to me that though I've seen countless explosions from my own window, the only person I've actually seen blow things up is Elliott.

CHAPTER
TEN

MOTHER AND FATHER SIT ACROSS FROM EACH other, eating breakfast.

In the placid light of morning, it doesn't seem possible that Elliott and I risked our lives so that I could be here with my parents, who have barely acknowledged me.

The roses in the centerpiece are wilting. Mother nibbles at some bread. She eats sparingly, mourning either vegetables that are no longer grown here or fruit that used to be imported. She says I don't understand because I never had the delicate sauces or the tiny mushrooms that she dreams about. When Father stayed in his laboratory for days on end, Finn and I had to forage. Finn made a game out of mixing the most outrageous foods and daring me to eat them. I was ill several times as a result of his creativity.

Mother complains that there is no butter for the

bread. I take a large bite, not caring that it's dry. I eat to keep myself alive, because if I die here in this apartment, she will be the one who finds my body. No matter how much we disappoint each other, I won't do that to her.

I sigh, and both parents turn to look at me, but neither asks what is wrong. Perhaps they are afraid of my answer. Perhaps they don't care.

"I'm thinking of doing some charity work," Mother says.

"Don't forget that the poor have burned their own factory. No one can save the world. Not when it doesn't want to be saved." Disillusionment is making Father old.

It's unusual for them to talk like this. Once they shared an interest in their children, but that was when there were two of us.

"I'm going to go downstairs and ask about conditions in the city," Father says. "If it is safe, Araby, perhaps you will walk with me."

I nod. I can't stop thinking of what I've done. Even the smallest gestures could put my family in danger. It's easy to deflect the worry in the heat of the moment, when Elliott sounds so sure. But now, away from him, breaking the prince's hold on the city seems impossible.

Mother disappears into one of her fancy sitting rooms. The vases of flowers are wilting in there, too. When Father returns from downstairs, I'm happy to spend some time with him, despite my guilt. We walk, followed by his guards, through the lobby and out to the street.

"Your mother wants flowers," he says. "She has taken a dislike to the roses your friend brought."

What he means is that she dislikes Elliott, but getting flowers provides us with an excuse to leave the penthouse. To leave the building. The staff watches us. Perhaps they find it odd, how often we come and go. Most people stay inside, especially those who are rich enough to live on these tree-lined avenues.

It is a short walk to the market.

Father adjusts the collar of my coat. "You should have a scarf." He looks down, embarrassed by the fatherly comment. "If there are flowers, we will take them home to your mother. If not, we'll go to the pier."

Beggars hover around the periphery of the market, more numerous than shoppers, and not a single vendor has flowers. Too frivolous for an overcast day like today, I suppose. I wonder where Elliott finds such beautiful roses in a city where beauty is no longer important.

Instead of flowers, Father buys two bushels of apples, and we lug them to the fence that has been erected to keep the beggars out. He polishes an apple with the edge of his shirt and hands it to a little girl. Other children line up, their eyes full of hope. Starving children are a dirty secret of the upper city. If they ever left, they'd not be allowed back in past the checkpoints. People don't expect to find the poor here.

Many of the children have cloth masks tied around

their faces. These makeshift masks may make them feel safer, but the idea of breathing through burlap makes me gag.

A bigger boy than most pushes to the front of the line. Father leans forward and speaks to him. The boy tries to grab an apple from the basket. One of Father's guards comes to attention, putting his hand on his musket, but Father just smiles, shakes his head, and points to the end of the line. The boy considers the dwindling fruit and lines up behind a child who can't possibly be more than five years old.

"Araby," Father calls, "buy more apples."

I buy all the apples I can find and drag them, bushel by bushel, over to Father. By the time the boy who pushed gets back to the front, many more children have lined up behind him. Father hands him a coin as well as an apple, and he walks away beaming.

I look away from Father's charity, distracted by a little girl. She eats two bites of her apple and then puts it carefully into her pocket. It isn't hard to imagine that she is saving it for someone, though it is hard to imagine a person who might be hungrier than the tiny girl. I want to give her a second apple so that she can finish the one she started and have another to take home. I look for her, but there are so many children. I've lost sight of her.

When they see that Father has given out the last of the fruit, the guards gather around us and hurry us away from all the outstretched hands. Father glances at the apple in my hand and raises an eyebrow but doesn't say anything. We walk, side by side, down to the harbor.

There are countless red scythes on the doors of the houses we pass. And then one black scythe. Clever to make the symbol of the rebellion so close to the symbol for the disease. Unless you are looking for it, you might not register the difference.

The water in the harbor smells of salt and fish and death. But the new steamship, the *Discovery*, is shiny and clean among the shipyard decay. I consider the ship, the copper accessories, the great wheel that will drive it forward, as I turn the cool apple over and over, passing it from hand to hand.

Father stares out over the waves.

"Something unexpected has happened," I say.

I struggle with the words. It's hard keeping everything to myself. April is gone. Mother is out of the question. Elliott would laugh. And of course I can't speak to Will. That leaves Father.

"Your mother says that you have fallen in love."

Surprise leaves me speechless.

Falling in love would be too much of a betrayal of my vow and of Finn.

"Tell me." It is a command, but his voice is gentle. It's something he used to say when we were children. After a fight with Finn, I would shut myself in my room and brood. Mother thought it was best just to ignore me, but Father would come in and sit with me, sometimes for an hour or more. Finally, when I was ready to break down and cry, he would say, "Tell me." And invariably I would. And he would listen, and at least pretend like he understood.

"I'm not in love," I say softly, "but there is someone who could make me happy." It is frightening to speak of this intangible thing that keeps going through my mind. What Elliott is doing is important, and I want to help him. But at every turn I keep coming back to Will. I could feel something if I let myself. It's a terrifying possibility.

I can't tell if Father has any desire to hear this. I remind myself that Finn will never meet someone who could make him happy. Guilt chokes me, even as I try to find the courage to speak.

"He's raising his two younger siblings," I say. "One of them needs a mask. The little boy. He saved enough money for the girl, but . . . I was trying to get a mask for Henry. Then the factory was destroyed."

"One child without a mask. That's dangerous." His voice is soft. I got the mask. Finn died. Neither of us ever forgets.

I want, right now, to ask Father if he blames me. If he thinks that I was right to make a vow that keeps me from happiness, and from Will. But what would I do if he said yes? How could I live with the guilt? And if he said no, how could I ever trust him again?

"I'm glad you don't think you're in love with the prince's nephew," he says, and then there is silence except for the guards shuffling their feet and the waves hitting the dock. I'm glad I'm not in love with Elliott, too. That would be . . . disastrous.

Some part of me believes that Father is preparing to say something meaningful and deep, but when he finally breaks the silence, all he says is, "I always wanted a house overlooking the water. The sea intrigues me."

He's changing the subject. I can taste my disappointment as surely as I taste the salt in the mist from the sea.

"Do you think there will ever be peace in the city?" My voice sounds normal. Conversational.

"I used to think that we were capable of learning from our mistakes. But now I'm not so sure. The only thing that might hold us together is if we find other people."

He gestures toward the shiny new ship.

"Do you think . . ." My voice shakes a little. "Do you think there are other people out there? Towns and cities that survived the plague?" He is the scientist who saved all of humanity.

"It seems impossible that the germs reached every place. In fact, we may take germs to new destinations."

"We could give people masks. The factory has been destroyed, but we know how to make them."

"We didn't even give them freely to our own people. Why would our benevolent prince give them to others?"

The guards are too far away to hear Father's treasonous words.

Out of the corner of my eye, I see a child sitting at the edge of the pier with his legs dangling, looking out at the steamship. He is the same color as the rotting pier, all browns and nondescript shadows. I take two steps forward and hold out the apple.

The boy stares at me for a moment. Unlike the children in the market, he does not associate us, and our entourage of guards, with free food. He does not put out his hand, but after a long moment of staring at the apple in my hand, he snatches it and then sits there, clasping it like a great prize.

The thud of running feet startles all of us, and we turn to see a man in a brown robe running across the pier. When he sees that he has our attention, he screams. "Science will destroy us!" His robe falls back to reveal bright purple bruises and seeping wounds. He raises his hand. A black scythe has been tattooed onto the palm.

I grab Father's arm just as a guard dives in front of us. The other guards move in carefully. They don't want to touch the man.

I stare at him, amazed. His robes are not enough to hide the extent of the illness. He should be dead.

His unmasked face is twisted with hatred. The guards shove musket barrels in his face. They won't risk direct contact. I adjust my mask to be sure I'm not breathing the same air as this walking dead man, and I see one of the guards doing the same thing. They prod him, forcing him away from us. He glares at Father, and I expect him to lunge at us, but all he does is murmur, "Science has failed," in a voice so sad and soft that we can barely hear it. And then the guards take him away.

"Don't hurt him," Father calls.

"Of course not, Dr. Worth."

Father and I pretend we don't hear a gunshot from behind the building.

"It's going to rain," the guard who stayed with us says.

The choppy ocean reflects the darkening sky.

We trudge back toward the Akkadian Towers.

"He had the disease," I say in a low voice.

"Yes," Father says. "Some of them last longer than others."

I shudder.

The guard was right. It is beginning to rain. I think of Father's furtive meeting in the bookshop. I could ask him if he is doing anything to endanger us. But then he might ask me the same thing. The only sound, as we walk back to the Akkadian Towers, is the raindrops falling on the sidewalk.

CHAPTER

ELEVEN

THE DOORMAN IS BOWING AND USHERING US
into the ornate foyer of the Akkadian Towers when a
movement from a doorway across the street catches
my attention. Instinctively I move closer to Father. But
there's something familiar about these movements. It's
Will. My heart misses a few beats.

I'm not sure how to separate myself from Father and
the guards. But it's almost dusk, so I know Will has to
get to the Debauchery Club and I don't have time to go
upstairs and slip back down.

Before I can think of a plan, I've been swept into the
building. The guards are settling into their upholstered
chairs. One of them shuffles a deck of cards.

I touch Father's arm. "I'm going to stay in the lobby
for a few moments," I say.

Father is too dispirited to argue.

The hateful attack, followed by the gunshot that we pretended not to hear . . . these things take their toll.

No one seems to be watching me, so I step back outside, opening the door myself so the doorman won't have a chance to ask questions. I hesitate in front of the building as two steam carriages pass. It's unusual to see more than one an hour, but at this time of the evening people are looking for entertainment.

Will meets me halfway across the street. He reaches for me, but then his hands fall to his sides and he gestures me back to the alcove where he was seeking shelter from the rain. It's the entrance to a store that closed years ago. The door is boarded up, and the display window holds nothing but dust and the disintegrating husks of insects.

A bit of fabric lies in the back corner of the alcove. I touch it with my foot. It is a small cloth cap. Whoever owned it probably slept here, out of the wind and rain. And I walked in and out of the ornate doorway across the street, never realizing that a child was living in the empty entrance of this abandoned building.

"What are you doing?" I ask him.

"Waiting. For you."

I feel a burst of total happiness. And then the doubt creeps in.

"Waiting?"

"Last night, after you left, I couldn't stop thinking about you. I was worried—"

The rain has evolved into a fine mist. Moisture beads dot his bare arms, and his dark hair is plastered against his face and neck.

Across the street, our doorman is taking a quick look around, pacing back and forth. He turns, speaking to someone . . . a guard?

"Let's walk," I suggest.

"Good idea," he says. Even though he walked a very long way to get here. Even though it's dangerous and he'll be trudging back across town to work soon. "You're fine?" he asks finally. "Nothing happened last night?"

I think of the terrifying ride home, ropes stretched across our path. The shattered crocodile skull.

"I'm fine."

"The club isn't safe for you. Not anymore," he says. He clears his throat. "The men on the top floor rarely come downstairs. But last night they were looking for you. The girl with the violet hair. Elliott's private rooms were ransacked."

Elliott had the book in his hand when we left the club, but who knows what else they might have found?

"Those men were murderers before death became a daily occurrence," he says.

I remember the old man's eyes. Will doesn't have to convince me that he is dangerous.

He gives me a quick look that I cannot interpret. "It seems they expected to find you in Elliott's bedchamber."

"How well do you know him?" I ask. "Elliott."

We've reached the end of this city block and turn to walk down the alley that runs directly behind the Akkadian Towers.

"Not well. And I don't want to know him any better than I do."

I start to question him, but I'm distracted by something partially hidden behind a stack of wooden crates. A shoe, and when I look closely, I can see a thin ankle.

A child's foot in a well-made boot.

It's starting to drizzle again. No one would lie in the mud with the rain. . . . The boy is dead. He died in an alley so narrow that the corpse collectors cannot come for him. We are in the shadow of Akkadian Towers Building Two, the unfinished building that people say is cursed.

Will makes a sound that is somehow both horrified and unsurprised. The dead boy is wearing a mask. Perhaps he is a runaway. Or maybe he stole it. Will stares at the boy's mask. It is pristine white, unusually clean for a child's mask.

"I have trouble believing—," he begins, and I know what he's going to say.

"I know better than anyone. You can't share." I grab his other hand and stand facing him, though I can't look him in the eyes. "My brother . . . was supposed to get the very first mask. He was frail, and Father had been especially worried about him. We'd lived underground for almost two years, trying to shield him from the air above."

I've never told anyone this story. It's difficult to find the words.

"I grabbed the mask from my father and put it over my own face. I was laughing. We laughed at odd things because we had so little to entertain us. I breathed through Finn's mask. I didn't know."

I let go of Will's hands.

"The mask became acclimated to me, the way that they do, and wouldn't work for Finn."

"What happened?"

"He died. When Father tried to change what he considered a malfunction in the masks, the prince told him no. He was pleased that the poor couldn't steal them from the faces of the rich."

Will looks at the dead boy. "It isn't your fault," he says. "You can't possibly think it is." When I don't say anything, he takes my arm. "I didn't walk all the way down here for you to stand in the rain and catch cold."

He thinks I'm going to fall apart. But I won't.

"Araby?" he begins again.

"Did you take the children downstairs early?" I ask, desperate to change the subject.

"I never went home."

"You never went home?"

"I walked up here this morning. And waited for you. I hoped that eventually you would come outside. I didn't realize how rarely people come and go in this part of the city."

"You waited all day?"

"I had to. You didn't come outside, and then when you finally did, you had guards. Listen to me. If you go back to the club, I'm afraid that you will disappear and there will be nothing I can do to help you. Elliott shouldn't go back either. But I'm not worried about him."

"Is that what happened to April?"

"No. I don't think so. I saw her leaving. She must have disappeared from her carriage, outside the club."

I won't let myself look into his eyes.

"Who is watching the children?"

"A friend. Thank you for sending food, by the way."

I have so many things to say to him, but it is almost dark. I know he has to go. So I don't say anything. He's the one who breaks the silence. "And thank you for telling me about your brother."

When he pulls me close, there is no flirtation, no suggestion of anything except comfort. My heart beats faster anyway.

"I'm sorry that you lost him. And that you've chosen to punish yourself because of it."

It was my fault. But there is no point in arguing. We are almost to the end of the alley, and I know he must leave me in just a few steps.

"Be very careful," he says. "If you aren't, I won't get a chance to convince you that you are wrong."

We are back to the front of the Akkadian Towers, and once again I'm lifting my hand without meaning to, reaching out to him, and once again he doesn't see. He's walking away, with his shoulders hunched against the wind and rain.

Everything is changing. April gone, the club off-limits. I don't want to go inside, but then two of Father's guards push through the door. The doorman looks nervous.

I smile at them all and sweep into the building. My bravado carries me up the first four flights of stairs, but with the elevator still broken it's a long climb in near-darkness. When I stop to catch my breath, I imagine that I hear footsteps behind me.

Our hallway is empty. The courier has gone home for the night, but Mother is waiting for me, with Father standing slightly behind her.

"A message was delivered for you," she says as soon as I step inside. She hands me an envelope sealed with red wax in the shape of an eye.

I hold the letter for several moments, not wanting to open it in front of Mother, but she is standing, waiting.

I break the seal with my fingernail and read quickly.

Had a wonderful time with you last night. We have been invited to visit Prince Prospero's castle. I will pick you up tomorrow before noon.

E.

My first thought is that he must have found out something about April, but as I stare at the note I realize that the word *invited* looks odd. Holding it to the light, I can see that he started to write something else. Summoned? It isn't really an invitation. I fold and refold the paper.

Mother rearranges roses in a jewel-encrusted vase, pretending that she isn't watching me.

"What should I wear for a meeting with the prince?" I ask.

The vase shatters on the tile floor.

"Don't go," Father says. "It's dangerous, Araby."

"So is breathing."

"Not in the same way. Araby—"

He's said my name twice, within two breaths. I could almost acquiesce when he says my name like that, as if he cares.

Our front door bursts open. Two soldiers in the prince's livery step over the threshold.

"We wanted to make sure that Dr. Worth was safe," one of them tells us. "The prince said we should check inside the apartment periodically." They are both carrying weapons. Inside our home. I search their uniforms for the emblem of the open eye that would indicate that they really work for Elliott. Nothing.

Mother collapses onto the couch and Father goes to her. "I'd appreciate it if you knocked next time," he says. "My wife has a nervous disposition." The soldiers shift from foot to foot. They are embarrassed, but not as polite as Father's regular guards.

I've brought them here. Through my interactions with Elliott, or through some other mistake. Somehow this, too, is my fault.

CHAPTER
TWELVE

WE TALK LESS THAN USUAL AS EVENING TURNS
to night, aware of the guards listening just outside
the door. Father comes to my bedroom and mixes my
sleeping draft himself.

"Araby—"

I hold Elliott's missive between my fingers. "It isn't
an invitation."

"No. But I've gotten around his commands before.
There are ways . . ."

This is the time to ask him what is going on.

"Who were those men in the bookshop?" I ask.

His surprise is genuine.

"Young scientists the prince is not aware of," he says.
"They need guidance."

I think of the drawing in his desk, with the enigmatic
caption. *Tell the boy this will never fly.* He hates the prince's

control of science. Is that all it is, his connection to those men?

He finishes mixing my medicine and leans forward to give me an awkward hug. I'm too surprised by the gesture to ask him anything else.

In the morning, our courier is two minutes late. I notice because Mother comments on it. "Your father has gone downstairs to consult with his guards about the new soldiers. He's very concerned." She waits, but I don't say anything. "Your father," she says tentatively, "says that maybe I should walk with the two of you. . . ."

I gag on my dry bread.

She rarely leaves the apartment and never leaves the building.

"I would go if you were with us, Araby."

I sigh and don't answer her. I hate the way she ignores things that upset her. I have to go to the prince's castle. Even if I could hide behind Father somehow, there's still a chance that April needs me. Mother goes to the piano and begins to play scales.

Father is out of the apartment, and this is my last chance to go through his lab before we leave. Elliott wants me to look for evidence that Malcontent might be communicating with Father.

I slide the laboratory door back, paying close attention to the positioning of it. Not quite closed, not fully open.

The lab looks the same way it looked before. Counters cluttered with colorful liquids, empty desk.

Last time I stopped at the drawer with the blueprints. This time I reach for the bottom drawer.

It's empty. But when I push the drawer shut, it sticks. I pull the handle hard, removing the drawer completely from the desk, and put my hand into the cavity. My fingers touch a small book bound in leather. A thin volume that feels insubstantial in my hands.

The journal falls open to a page that says *Everything is my fault.*

I catch my breath and hold the journal to my heart. I know exactly how he feels. In this moment, I am closer to my father than I have ever been.

But I can't stop now. Placing the journal on the floor, I open the second drawer, the one filled with receipts and papers. If there are messages, this is where I will find them. I'm on my knees, riffling through a stack of letters, when Father returns. He enters the lab soundlessly, laying a paper on the table before he looks up and sees me. I watch the emotions as they cross his face. Shock. Anger. Betrayal. And something I can't read. Guilt?

"Araby?" His voice is nearly normal. But he knows I wasn't in here looking for him. He doesn't say anything else for a long time. Maybe he can't.

"Your friend will be here soon. I saw him in the lobby."

My friend? I realize that it's nearly noon, and Elliott is coming to take me to the prince's palace.

"Father . . ." He won't meet my eyes.

Time stops for a few seconds as Father picks up

objects without seeing them, sets them down.

Elliott's knock is either arrogant or angry, possibly both. Father turns his back to me and I finally stand, pushing in the drawer as I do. The journal lies on the floor. I could give it back to Father now. But instead I pick it up and hide the dark leather against my equally dark skirts.

Elliott has come to the apartment without flowers. When I walk out of Father's lab to the foyer, he's toying with the silver handle of his walking stick.

"I have to change," I say before escaping to my room.

Mother follows me. She waits for me to speak, and when I don't she shuffles through my closet, eyeing my ripped dresses with distaste.

I choose a red corset.

"That won't do," Mother says. "The prince hates red. Let me loan you something." She hurries to her room and returns with a dark purple dress. "This will be beautiful."

I don't want to take it, but I'm sure nothing in my closet is suitable.

"The prince hates the immodesty of the new fashions," she says. She fumbles with my hair, pulling it back from my face with her clever, nervous fingers. When it's fastened with a pearl clip, the violet streaks are almost hidden.

"You can make it up to your father," she says softly. "When you return. Araby," she continues. "I've always wanted to tell you . . ." She puts her hands on my shoulders and turns me toward her. The look on her face is direct, intense. There is no confession that I want from her, not now. Not today.

I pull away. She is so nervous that this gesture halts her confession. I pack a bag quickly and slip Father's stolen journal inside.

Elliott and Father are standing together, silent and uncomfortable. Heavy footsteps, pacing back and forth, remind everyone that there are guards in our foyer. Elliott taps his walking stick against the tiled floor, seeming to enjoy the sound it makes.

Mother comes through the doorway behind me, the sound of her long dress against the floor reminding me of the times before the plague, a world of swishing skirts. A world without masks.

"Be careful," Father says. Elliott meets Father's eyes, and some understanding passes between them. It hurts that Father will look at Elliott but not at me.

My poetry book is lying abandoned on a side table. When I pick it up, Elliott's note, the one about meeting him in the garden, flutters to the floor.

Mother moves to retrieve it, but Elliott steps forward. His foot slides over the note as he moves in front of Mother, removing a small square box from his pocket.

He opens it to show her. "Do you think she'll like it?" he asks.

"No."

She realizes how terrible that sounds and covers her mouth with her hand. "It's just that Araby doesn't care about things like diamonds," Mother says. "Another girl would like it."

Elliott laughs a little. His inappropriate laughter is my favorite thing about him. He kneels and retrieves the slip of paper.

"We may be asked to spend the night," Elliott tells Mother. "Don't worry. She'll be safe."

My parents' eyes move over my face, as if memorizing me. I wonder how often they wish that they had done the same thing with Finn. For a second I'm not sure if I can leave them. I want to run to Father and beg for his forgiveness, to wipe the frightened look from Mother's face.

But if I do that, I'll be trapped here, with no way to help April, no way to help anyone.

We move toward the doorway, where the unfriendly guards are standing. I don't think they are blocking our way on purpose. One of them is looking at me, and I move to adjust my skirt before I realize that I'm wearing Mother's sedate purple dress. When we reach the hall, I still feel the weight of their eyes.

Three chairs clutter the hallway where there used to be just one. Is it acceptable for the prince's soldiers to sit while they spy on us?

"Those were members of the prince's private guard," Elliott says.

"What does that mean?"

"It means that the prince is very concerned for your father's safety."

Elliott hands me the folded slip of paper.

"You want to be more careful."

"I'll try," I say. "It's hard to be as sneaky as you."

"You flatter me," he says, smiling. He looks directly at me for the first time today. "You are very elegant," he says, picking invisible lint from his sleeve.

"Thank you." I never know how to take his compliments, or whether they are sincere.

We walk down the stairs together, sometimes in step, sometimes with him a few steps ahead. Finally we reach the lobby.

"I've never been to the prince's palace," I say, eyeing our usual guards, who are lounging in the lobby. They see that Father isn't with me, nod to Elliott, and go back to rolling dice on a low table.

"You should be thankful," Elliott says darkly. "It's a testament to how much your father loves you."

And yet here he is lifting me into his steam carriage, taking me there. Father loves me. Elliott does not. And I've betrayed Father at Elliott's request. I close my eyes as the city rushes by.

Once we're out of the city, I open my eyes and pay attention. It's been years since I've left the city proper. The air feels different here, but as much as I want to take off my mask, it still isn't safe. Forest creatures carry the contagion, too.

When Finn was alive, Father used to borrow a horse and wagon and take us outside the city for picnics. It amazes me, how we thought life would stay the same. The drive takes more than three hours, but I stare at the scenery and the time passes quickly.

Slender evergreen trees line the road, and I long to walk through them and touch the deep green needles.

As if he can read my mind, Elliott stops the steam carriage. He's wearing some sort of protective goggles, and I don't like the way they work together with his mask to hide his entire face.

We are on a ridge overlooking his uncle's stronghold. Below us is a huge castle, complete with turrets and a drawbridge.

Maybe it's the driving goggles, but his eyes are faraway and sad.

"Elliott?" Comforting him might allow me to forget my own misery.

"I hate this place. When I visit, I always stop here." He gestures to the overlook. "To remind myself that we aren't that far from the city. Even on foot, it isn't much more than half a day's journey, and there are ways to escape the castle. See those caves?" He points to some dark areas on the side of the cliff, which, if I stare long enough, could indeed be the mouths of caverns.

"Passages in the castle lead to those caverns," he says.

"Is there any structure in this city that doesn't have a tunnel underneath?" I suppress a laugh, because it's so silly, all of these passages that I have never seen and don't really believe in. But Elliott doesn't even smile.

"According to the book you so cleverly retrieved, all the passages in the city connect. If I'd known, I could've escaped to the city instead of staying here for years as Prospero's prisoner."

I stare out over the imposing landscape. "It's obvious that you hated living here. That's reassuring to know before we go back in."

"I didn't mean for you to be reassured. You should be afraid, Araby. Do you care enough for April to go inside?"

Even from here, in the dreary light of afternoon, I can see that there are bars on every single window of the castle. We could turn around, could be back at the Akkadian Towers before the sun sets.

But April is in there, and she would go inside for me. I'm sure of it. Regardless, we have been ordered to come.

Elliott must know what I am thinking.

"Who would come for me if I were inside?" he asks.

I can't answer, because I don't know.

Elliott reaches into his pocket and brings out the tiny box he showed my mother.

"Will you wear this?" he asks. He tosses the box to me. When I open it, the sun glints off the facets of an enormous diamond.

"I don't—"

"It wouldn't mean anything," he says quickly. "Except to my uncle." His hair falls over his goggles, and he looks particularly young and wistful. I take the ring.

"Sometimes I have a hard time not trusting you," I admit.

"Don't trust me." The ring twists and turns on my finger. The diamond is sharp and very cold.

We drive down a narrow incline and pass a stone guard tower. Elliott slows, and the guard bows and waves him through. Next is an iron gate. A tall fence goes on as far as I can see. The gate closes behind us with a clang.

"Well, we're in. Now I just hope we can get out." He puts his hand on my arm. "Don't trust me," he says again. "It would make me feel even worse if you got killed."

The fear sinks into me now. I don't want to die here.

We take a sharp turn, and the castle looms above us. I wasn't prepared for the immensity of it. Like a giant hulking toad crouching out on the peninsula, coldly menacing and exquisitely drab.

"My uncle had the road engineered to turn in that exact spot, just to give people that response."

"What response?"

"The one you are having. Awe? Fear?"

From this angle I can see that it isn't just a medieval castle, it is a cathedral and an abbey all meshed together into something magnificently ominous.

"Hideous, isn't it?" Elliott pulls his steam carriage through a final stone archway and stops. "Be cautious. Do not tell my uncle anything about either of your parents, and don't give him any indication that we aren't madly in love."

"We aren't madly in love?"

"You scorn me. But I am infatuated with you."

"You're a better liar than I thought," I say lightly.

"I'm a fabulous liar." He swings down from the carriage and walks around to lift me down. He pulls me close and says quietly, "And you need to be too."

It is sunny, if humid, in the courtyard. But once we get inside, it is cold and dark. The quick change in temperature is a shock. The entranceway and the adjoining chambers are completely empty, and I feel as if every movement I make is likely to echo throughout the castle.

Servants in blue-and-purple livery scurry out from the shadows and follow us. Elliott ignores them, stopping only when we reach a large open doorway. A herald hurries around Elliott and into the room. "Your nephew!" he announces in a loud, official voice. "Your nephew and . . . his female friend."

The room is huge but also crowded.

We step into the throne room. Elliott bows.

"Hello, Uncle. I've brought my fiancée, Miss Araby Worth, to meet you. As you suggested."

His fiancée. I feel my face turning pink. The diamond ring cuts into my finger.

The prince turns, and the weight of his attention makes me want to hide behind Elliott.

He looks as if he might be posing for a portrait, standing beside his throne with his hand resting on a carved dragon's head. He is taller than I expected, balding, with sharp dark eyes.

"It is good of you to visit," he says, as though we had some choice in the matter.

He isn't large, or physically imposing, but as soon as he speaks, I feel cold.

"I know how busy you are," Elliott says.

"Never too busy for family, surely?"

A muscle flexes in Elliott's jaw. This is the man who killed Elliott's father. His uncle looks past him at me.

"Your father once did a great service for me," he says.

I won't let him see my anger. My father did a great service for mankind, not for power or money, and certainly not for the prince himself.

"We are very proud of his accomplishments," I say.

The prince rubs his chin thoughtfully.

"You should be. And since you are here, I have a request for you. I had hoped that your father would come and live here, in my palace."

The prince's voice sounds reasonable, though I feel the danger beneath every word. A wave of nausea hits me as his eyes meet mine. "Your father insists that you and your mother are happier in the city. But since you've struck up a friendship with my nephew . . ."

I wait for him to say that April is here too, that he's used her as bait. But he doesn't, and though I feel increasingly ill, I know I have to respond. This is treacherous ground. I stare past him, struggling to come up with the response that won't anger him. A black spot, a shadow, is burned into the stone wall at the back of the throne room.

The prince follows my gaze and looks pained.

"Not all of my scientists are as fortunate as your father," the prince says. "Dr. Roth caused an unfortunate explosion when he was working on the steam carriage. I had him put to death, but I find his steam carriages quite useful. Do you have one?"

I shake my head. He already knows this. No one can purchase a carriage without his approval.

The soot running up the wall looks so fresh that it would probably smudge onto my fingers if I reached out to touch it.

"He was Elliott's mentor, of sorts. Has he told you? Elliott spent hours with him, learning all about the steam engine."

This room reeks of fear. Expensively dressed people gather around the throne, listening. The prince raises one eyebrow, reminding me for an instant of Elliott.

"It's a good thing I never accidentally blew anything up, or you might have executed me."

Elliott is trying to sound nonchalant, but he's failing. He seems inexplicably innocent, which isn't a word I would normally use to describe him. Maybe vulnerable is a better term?

Since I'm staring at Elliott, I hope I look like a girl who is in love.

All around us, people are pressed tightly together. This is the most crowded room I've ever been in, at least since the plague happened, but there is one area they avoid. A line of tables beneath a stained-glass window against the left wall. Green light seeps through the tinted glass. I recognize some of the items spread over the tables. A microscope. An intricate clockwork device. Part of a steam carriage. But my eyes linger on unfamiliar tools.

"We have ways to help the geniuses among us find inspiration," the prince says. He has stepped off the dais now and is standing so close I can smell something sharp, like cinnamon. I force myself not to move away. "Do you like parties, dear child?"

Torture implements. He wants to bring my father here and torture him. And now he's asking me about parties?

"Of course I do," I stammer.

The prince smiles a frighteningly kind smile. His teeth are stained. "Perhaps we can celebrate your—" He stops. "Your friendship, at my next ball."

He purposefully did not use the word engagement. Because he knows we're faking? Because he won't let his nephew marry me?

"That sounds wonderful." I don't recognize my tiny, high-pitched voice.

"It will be," the prince says. "There's nothing like a masked ball to change your perceptions. Elliott may walk right past you, and you would never know." Is his threat directed at Elliott, or at me? "A masked ball is so exciting," he continues.

"Except that we're always wearing masks," Elliott says in a flat voice.

"Ah, but these masks—anonymity can be intoxicating, don't you agree?"

Despite myself, despite the danger, the prospect of a masked ball is enticing. It seems like something April would love. I wonder why she never suggested attending one of her uncle's balls.

And I realize that if April was afraid to attend a party, it must be frightful indeed.

"Have you set a date for your next event, Uncle?"

"Yes. And of course we'll celebrate when your sister returns. If she returns."

CHAPTER

THIRTEEN

A SERIES OF DISCORDANT CHIMES SUMMONS US to dinner. Elliott leads me to a sumptuous dining room. As in the throne room, sculpted dragons are everywhere. The chandelier is a cacophony of hatchlings.

"It's one of the reasons I've always hated the Debauchery Club," Elliott says. "My uncle's peculiar taste in decorating."

"Will he tell us—" I start to ask, but Elliott squeezes my knee, telling me to be silent.

Dinner is served by servants who won't meet our eyes. Elliott keeps his hand on my leg while we eat. I want to brush it away, but since I'm wearing a long skirt it feels prudish to do so, especially when he's probably placed it there to communicate with me.

A man across the table spears his meat with a knife and announces, "I tell myself every day how fortunate we are that the plague didn't kill the cows like it did the horses. Every horse in our stable fell down dead within a week."

"April loved horses." Elliott's quiet voice is meant only for me. "She spent her childhood in the stables. I was taught to ride, of course, and I rode every day for the exercise and fresh air, but April loved it. She was sadder the day her horse died from the plague than the day our father was—" He realizes what he is about to say and stops himself. People are listening.

I meet his gaze, and maybe because he almost made a mistake, or because of the sadness I heard when he spoke of April's loss, I actually like him.

During the last course, servants roll a piano into the room.

"Do you play?" the prince asks. Several moments pass before I realize that he is speaking to me.

"No," I say.

"A pity," he says, and gestures for a young woman to go to the piano. I'm homesick, suddenly; Mother plays that song over and over, especially on gloomy days.

When the concert is finished, the dinner guests trickle out and Elliott stands and takes my hand. I follow him without question as we leave the main part of the castle. He pushes a tapestry aside, and we enter a dark corridor.

"My uncle wants to see me. While I'm gone, I need you to do something for me."

"Fetch a book?" My teasing tone falls flat in the semidarkness.

Elliott takes off his mask and leans close to me. If anyone came around the corner, they would think we are about to embrace. As he moves closer, I'm tempted to pull away, but he's speaking so softly that I wouldn't be able to hear him. It's more feeling the words he's saying than hearing them, as his lips move against my hair.

"There's a girl," he says. "She has information. Meet her in the dungeon." He gives directions quickly, but the movement of his lips is distracting.

"I hope April isn't in the dungeon, but if anyone knows where she is, Nora will." He checks his pocket watch. "I have to go. My uncle hates to be kept waiting."

I step away, but he grabs me.

"One last thing. Whatever you do, don't go into any of the cells."

And then he's walking away.

I stand alone for several minutes, watching the shadows move across the stones. The mortar that holds them in place is coarse and thick, as if the stones didn't exactly fit together and had to be glued into place. The prince had the entire castle moved from across the sea. A prop for his megalomania. I shiver.

Hurrying down a dank stone stairway, I take a candle from a candelabra in the hall and hold it carefully as I descend into the dungeon. The castle smells dark and wet and wrong. I hear mice scurrying, a great many small feet scrambling against stone, and almost lose my nerve. Three more steps. Then five. Then ten. The floor is uneven, so I step gingerly. The ceiling is so low that if Elliott were with me, he would barely be able to walk upright, and Will would have to crouch. Thoughts of Will come unbidden, and I want more than anything to be out of this foul place and in his apartment. I'd settle for the Debauchery Club. Anywhere but here.

But I move down a wide passage, lined with iron doors that presumably lead to cells.

I hear a slight sound that could be a footstep, or might be the castle settling above me.

Turning toward the sound, I almost scream. A girl is close enough that I could touch her if I stretched out my arm. She waits, pressed against a stone wall, and I don't know how she stands being so close to it. The wall is covered with fungus that glows green in the feeble light. Water has seeped out from between the stones, pooling in fetid puddles on the floor. The stones glisten. Water drips.

The oozing of the wall reminds me of the Weeping Sickness.

I force my eyes back to the girl. She is holding a lantern, but there's a cover over it. She pulls it off, smiling a little, amused by my discomfort. She is very beautiful.

"Elliott sent me," I tell her in a low voice.

She adjusts her apron and looks me over.

"Tell Mr. Elliott that his sister isn't in the palace,"

she says. It takes a moment for the words to sink in. I'm distracted by the way the corners of her mouth turn up when she says his name.

"She has to be here," I say. Where else could she be?

"She isn't. She hasn't set foot in the palace, not since last year when they visited together. Tell him that he should leave as soon as he can."

A sound from inside one of the cells startles both of us. She puts the cover on her lantern, takes two steps back, and disappears, leaving me alone in the near-impenetrable darkness. My eyes search the shadows beyond the light of my candle. This place, with the seeping wall, appears to be the convergence of multiple corridors. I count five passages, all leading away.

I've turned in a complete circle twice and am horribly disoriented, unsure which corridor leads back to Elliott and safety. I pick one and start to walk, careful not to get close enough to the doors of the cells for anything to reach out and grab me. I hear a grating sound, a door opening, and I scurry down the corridor, straining to hear. . . . Are there footsteps behind me?

At last I find the stairs. My toe connects painfully with the uneven stone, but I keep moving, ascending so quickly that the faint light in the hallway above seems blinding. I hear something above me and look up. It's a bat. A big black bat, beating its wings. I lunge to the side, ready to scream, but before I can draw breath, someone grabs me.

And pushes me against the rough stone wall, pulls his mask aside, and kisses my neck.

"Are you scared?" Elliott asks.

Footsteps clatter behind us, and he grips my shoulders harder, as if that will make it more convincing that we are embracing here against these mildewed wall hangings.

A servant passes, and when she's out of sight, Elliott lets me go so abruptly that I almost fall.

"Sorry." He uses the edge of the tapestry to help me remove the dungeon muck from my shoe. "We don't want anyone to know——"

"She isn't here." My voice sounds strange, filled with disappointment.

"No?"

"You don't sound surprised."

"I never sound surprised. That doesn't mean . . ." A second set of footsteps is approaching. I brace myself as he reaches for my shoulders, but his hands are gentle this time. He leans in, looking into my eyes, and for a moment I'm so certain he's really going to kiss me that I grab my mask, holding it so he can't pull it away from my face. No matter what risks he is willing to take, I'm not comfortable breathing the air in this place. And I don't want to kiss him.

I don't know him well enough to be sure of the emotions that cross his face. Guilt, distrust, maybe desire. I feel myself going rigid, even as I try to relax into his embrace.

"You're way too stiff. No one is going to believe you are enjoying this," he says.

"I'm not enjoying it," I mutter.

Two servants walk by. I look, but neither turns out to be Elliott's pretty serving girl.

"I don't think anyone would believe that you had brought me to this dank passage to . . . embrace me," I say finally.

"You'd be surprised at the places people will embrace."

"People . . . lovers . . . come down here for those purposes?"

"They have been known to." Something in his voice lets me know that his lips are quirking behind his mask.

I can't help myself. "Have you?" I ask.

"When I was younger."

"With that girl? Is that why she looked at me like—"

"I don't remember," he says. "Different girls, different places."

"That's despicable."

"Probably. My uncle kept me prisoner here for years. He didn't keep me in a cell, but I was still a prisoner. Everyone knew it. I did a lot of silly things to try to annoy him. Including meeting girls in most parts of his precious palace. None of it meant anything."

"Not to you. Perhaps it meant something to them."

"They were fools. It wasn't safe for anyone to be friendly with me." Elliott's voice is low and angry. "It probably still isn't."

"I hate it here," I say.

"As do I."

"We'll leave tomorrow?" I ask.

"We'll leave when the prince allows us to leave." We walk out into a hallway and up another flight of stairs, and then down a long corridor lined with fluttering wall hangings that would be easy to hide behind. Elliott stops outside a door. "This is your room. I'm across the hall. If you need anything"—he smirks—"just knock on my door. In fact, *I* need something. We should practice. Every time I put my hands on you, you freeze. People are certain to notice." He pulls me close. "Some girls enjoy . . ."

I push him, and he takes half a step back. "I'm sure they do, but you just called those girls fools, and I don't care for unexpected intimacy."

He's still too near, but I won't back away from him.

"As long as we're playing this game, expect intimacy from me. Then it won't ever be unexpected."

"No." I put my hands on his chest and push him harder than before. "That was never part of our agreement."

"Forget agreements. Just try not to look so upset when I touch you. My uncle notices everything. We are in danger."

I open my door.

"Araby?" He's dropped some of his arrogance and just looks sad. "Come to my room for a drink before bed?"

"Not tonight," I say, and I back into my room. I close the door carefully, bolting the lock.

The room is opulent but uncomfortable, decorated to impress guests. I settle into bed, but as the hours pass it becomes obvious that I won't be able to sleep without my sleeping draft. I keep seeing Father's face.

I tell myself that when I return home we'll walk down to the pier together. Time will temper the hurt, and maybe Father will listen to my reasons. But I'm terrified that all the familiar things in my life are about to change. And maybe I'll never walk with Father again.

The clock watches me from across the room, a gold dragon with red eyes, under a crystal dome that ticks incessantly, just a little slower than the beating of my heart.

Thinking of Elliott and his near-embrace, I realize I've come too close to breaking my vows, and that makes me think of Will. Why must sleep be so difficult?

Footsteps approach from down the hall. I wait for them to pass, but instead they stop. Someone is going into Elliott's room.

As I listen for footsteps to come out, my mind drifts to Elliott's intensity in the humidity of the hidden garden, when he told me how his uncle had slit his father's throat. He didn't say anything about the blood, but I'd guess it stained the Oriental carpet, and I'd go even further to bet that the stain never came out.

I wake up screaming, covered in sweat, disoriented by a dream that feels more real than this dark unfamiliar room. A hand moves the blanket and pushes my hair back from my face.

My heart is faster than the dragon clock now, much faster.

"It's okay. You're safe." The mattress shifts as Elliott sits on the bed beside me. "Is something wrong? Did you have a nightmare?"

My dream was about blood, gushing red blood.

I start to ask how he got into my room—maybe I didn't bolt the door after all—but my throat hurts. I've screamed it raw. Again. And now I'm sobbing.

"I thought someone was attacking you. I wouldn't have come in otherwise." He swings both legs up onto the bed and sits against the headboard.

"No," I say. I am shaking and scared, but I won't let him use this as an excuse. I won't let my guard down.

"We aren't enemies, you know."

"I know," I whisper. We aren't friends either.

"I'll stay here. I'll keep you safe."

"Not in the bed."

He gets up and pulls an armchair close enough that he can touch my hair.

"I didn't realize you disliked me so much," he says.

I open my eyes and look up at him. His voice is nearly as raw as mine. I've hurt him.

"I don't dislike you." And it's true. I don't. I like when he's vulnerable, but even his arrogance can be magnetic.

"Is there someone else?"

Will's profile hovers at the edge of my consciousness, but there's disgust on his face. I remember the way he looked at me after I crushed the white flower in the courtyard. Will is fascinated and disgusted by girls like me.

"No," I say. "No one."

"You're April's closest friend. I wasn't expecting you to fall into bed with me, but the two of you haven't exactly been living chaste lifestyles."

"I was." My voice is small.

"What?"

"Chaste. I made a promise." This is the first time I've tried to explain.

Whenever I consider abandoning my vows, when I think maybe it would be okay for me to be happy, I remember standing over the grave where Finn was never buried because the corpse collectors took his body away.

"So there you are, drinking and taking drugs to the point of incapacitation, and you've been missing out on the best part of debauchery?" He isn't interested in my story. I almost revealed everything, and he doesn't care.

"I wouldn't know."

"If you want to know, tell me." His voice is flirtatious, but when he speaks again, the suggestiveness is gone. "I used to sit with April when she had nightmares," he says softly.

It's the middle of the night and we are both tired. Maybe if I ask questions, he'll tell me the truth.

"Elliott, why are we here? Do you really think you can make things better?

"Yes," he says. "If we aren't working toward change, what's the point?"

The problem is that right now, I can't see the point, and I'm not sure if I ever did. "Tell me something we can actually accomplish."

"Move people out of the lower city, away from the swamps and the mosquitoes. Renovate the buildings along the river and let families move in, give them masks. Open stores and businesses. Remind people that there are reasons to live."

"And how will you do that?" I ask.

"Start with the masks, hire workers. Work through an entire neighborhood, repairing one building at a time and then moving on."

I remember stores. Particularly a candy store where Finn once stole a lollipop and I got blamed. It would be nice for people to have places to go. Things to buy. Masks so they aren't afraid to breathe.

"I'd like to think that you could do all that."

"My uncle doesn't care about the city, but I do. And I'm not the only one." He yawns, still stroking my hair. It feels good, and with him beside me I sleep deeply for the first time in years.

I wake to comforting morning light. It's the same poor quality here in this dismal castle as it is in our penthouse apartment. Elliott is sitting in the armchair, fast asleep. I slip out of bed so that I can wash and dress quickly, before he wakes. While I'm brushing my hair, I meet his eyes in the mirror. They are bluer than ever in the light streaming in through the window. Deceptively innocent under those pale eyebrows.

"Good morning, my dearest Araby." He has to catch his balance on the side of the bed. "I'm not going to recommend sleeping in a chair, not if you want to move properly the next morning."

"I'm sorry."

He smiles. "I'm not. Consider it my good deed for the day, and the day has just begun. That means I can be very bad today." He hesitates as if waiting for me to say something in return, something flirtatious. I play nervously with the engagement ring.

"Do you trust her?" I ask.

"Who?"

"The girl who said that April wasn't here."

"Unfortunately, yes." He stands and goes to the washstand. He splashes water into a basin. "I choose my informants well. She knows everything that happens in the palace."

Elliott's shoes are at the foot of my bed. His right shoe is stained with dungeon muck.

"Elliott?"

He comes back toward me, smoothing his shirt, and follows my gaze.

"I met last night with some of my people. That's how I heard you screaming. I was in the corridor, returning to my room."

"Was your meeting productive?" He is not telling me the whole truth, not mentioning the visitor I heard at his door, but I let him have this secret.

"Yes, but nothing conclusive about April." He checks his reflection in the mirror. "I want to go to the tower before we leave."

"Do you think she'll be there? Maybe?"

"No."

His answer is simple and harsh. I don't want to ask more, but I feel I must.

"Will we be allowed to leave?"

"I'm not certain. But I find the best strategy is to act like he'll let us walk out of here when we want."

His answers are not reassuring. I'm sure he doesn't mean them to be.

Elliott leads me down the hallway, up two flights of steps to another hallway that's filled with antique cannons. "My uncle collects oddities," he says.

We come to the end of the corridor and climb a stairway that spirals into the tower.

"This is where the prince keeps important prisoners. A room in the tower is kept in preparation for April." We climb another set of stairs. He clears his throat. "And for me and for our mother. At least this is where he would keep April if he wanted people to know she was here. Otherwise she would be in the dungeon."

The room is empty, save for a bed and a desk.

"You were so sure that he'd taken her." I can't keep the accusation out of my voice.

He slumps against the wall and puts his head in his hands.

I can't help thinking that Finn and I would do better. I would never lose him.

Except that I did lose him. To death and disease. And murder.

Elliott paces back and forth in front of the barred window, clenching his fists. He touches various items, a child's jewelry box. A doll.

"It's dusty. He hasn't been preparing these rooms. He's left them the way they were." He looks relieved, and then sighs.

Across the room is a door that's been painted the same color as the wall. "What's through that door?" I ask.

"Nothing."

I see him reaching for me, but I'm already pushing the door open. This room is much like the other, except that the walls are covered with a thick textured wallpaper. The sort my mother would have had installed throughout our apartment if Father hadn't objected. I see a bed, a desk, a wardrobe. Under the single window is a piano.

"Araby?" Elliott puts his hands on my shoulders. "You were right. We should go."

It's a beautiful piano. I step forward to feel the finish, touching one ivory key with my finger. Sheet music is still open on the bedside table.

There's a gentle tap at the open door. Elliott pivots. I can't help noticing how graceful he is. A guard stands in the doorway. He gives Elliott a quick salute.

"Sir, Miss Worth is not allowed in the tower." The guard seems profoundly uncomfortable.

I cross to the wardrobe and pull it open. Dress after dress hang waiting, all modest. Not a single one is red.

"My mother was here," I say softly.

"You must have suspected. . . ."

"No." I never suspected, but it all makes sense. The way Father worked, day and night. Mother's nervousness.

The window is barred. The door is heavy, fitted with multiple iron locks. Mother was a hostage. I trace the outline of a butterfly in the wallpaper. He caged her up here and surrounded her with butterflies. And I've treated her horribly.

A second guard steps into the doorway, and the three men consider one another. This guard does not salute Elliott, and his expression is angry.

"I am to remove the young lady," he says. "The prince has ordered it."

Elliott takes a step forward. When I put my hand on his arm to restrain him, the diamond on my ring flashes. I move my hands to his shoulders, and I can feel his tension easing.

Elliott glances meaningfully toward the bed. "We'd like a few minutes alone."

I choke, but I let him touch me. His hand is at the nape of my neck.

"Sir." The first guard is nervous.

"It's okay, Elliott, we have our own room." I pull him toward the door. The guard behind us laughs, and the nervous one looks away. He's one of Elliott's men, I'm sure of it.

Elliott's thumb slides from my hairline to my shoulder in one movement, and I feel myself blushing.

"Yes, we both have rooms." He leans forward and kisses the side of my face along the edge of my mask, a gentle kiss, but suggestive. "But the view from this window is lovely."

He guides me to the barred window, and I stare out at carefully manicured green lawns, and then there are trees and the edges of the marsh curling around the castle. Elliott turns me slightly toward the hillside. I cannot see the caverns that he told me were there, but I understand that he is reminding me of them.

"You must leave." The second guard seems ready to call for reinforcements.

Elliott pulls me out of Mother's specially designed prison, through the outer room, sliding his mask back into place. He twines his fingers through mine. We walk slowly, though my instincts tell me to run, past the cannons, down the circular stairs of the turret. When we're back in the main part of the keep, he drops my hand.

"Excellent. They won't be talking about the prince's nephew skulking around where he isn't supposed to be. They'll be whispering about how Mr. Elliott and his beautiful fiancée can't keep their hands off each other."

It's silly, but I think of the serving girl, Elliott's spy. I wonder how she will feel when she hears the whispers. If she's risking her life to spy for him, she is probably in love with him.

"Come on, it's time to wish my uncle a good morning," he says.

I feel like someone has wrapped his hands around my throat. How can I be in the same room with his uncle? I never want to see Prince Prospero again.

"I am sorry," he says, turning back when he realizes I've stopped beside a rusting suit of armor. "I was sure that you knew."

"No," I admit.

"Until last night, I thought it was the reason . . ." He falters, and I wait for him to continue. "I thought it was the reason you never wanted me to touch you, because of my uncle and your mother."

I shake my head. "I avoid touching everyone. Not just you."

His uncle and my mother. The truth is starting to sink in. She didn't abandon me.

"Elliott, I can't look at him."

"You have to. Smile. Act normal. Don't let him see that you are angry."

My need for oblivion now is stronger than ever, stronger than the night I met Elliott. I don't have to ask him for it. He eases the syringe out of his pocket.

"Will this help?"

I shouldn't accept it. I know that, but I need to stop thinking for a little while. So I hold out my arm.

It's just like before, only now I know Elliott, and almost trust him.

Afterward, I can walk and make a facial expression that I'm pretty sure passes for a smile. I've perfected the art of the fake smile. It's not so difficult when you are completely numb.

I glance into a mirror, wondering if my eyes are dilated.

"You look fine," Elliott says. "You always do. It's pretty amazing. The first time I saw you, you were passed out on the rug in the green room on the first floor of the Debauchery Club. I thought you were dead. I guess that's the first thing I suspect when someone is lying on the floor. You were beautiful, and I was glad when your eyelashes fluttered and I could see that you were alive."

He reaches out and fingers the collar of my dress, as if adjusting it, though I'm quite sure that it doesn't need adjusting.

"And I'm not easily impressed by beauty," he adds.

CHAPTER
FOURTEEN

ELLIOTT STOPS TO COMPOSE HIMSELF, BREATHING deeply several times before we reach the throne room. I should feel dread, or disgust or fear, but I feel nothing.

People are flowing through one of the doors, and servants follow them, carrying bottles of wine and hampers of food.

"We're going for an outing," Prince Prospero says. "Did you enjoy your time together?"

"The paddleboat?" Elliott asks, ignoring the innuendo in his uncle's question.

The courtiers study me. I play with the diamond on my finger, wondering, in a world where disease slithers through the air and down our throats, what value does a diamond really have? The hateful ring refracts the lights from the gaslit chandelier into a thousand colors, lovely and useless.

"It's beautiful," a female courtier says. The look on her face is unadulterated envy. "Elliott doesn't visit the palace often enough."

"Very true." Elliott throws his arm casually around my shoulders.

"But you could live here," the girl says.

"Yes." His tone is neutral. "I can't imagine anything more horrifying, can you?" he murmurs for my ears only.

"We live in fear of displeasing your uncle." She shudders. "Of being sent back to the city. And yet you choose to live there. You must be very brave."

Elliott removes his arm from my shoulder. "I'm sure you would never displease the prince," he tells the girl kindly.

"I hope not. My cousin tells terrifying stories about the things that happen in the city."

The girl puts a handkerchief up to her mask, as if to block out some horrible smell. I had never seen this gesture, but the ladies of the court seem to do it over and over again. Even with masks, they are afraid of the air and petrified by the idea of the city.

The servants take us to the water's edge in a wagon that is pulled by a large steam engine. The boat is also propelled by steam and has two large decks with colorful pennants and small pavilions spread about them. The people who have not been invited stand on the banks and wave as we make our way downriver.

"There are crocodiles in the water today," I hear someone say.

He's right. The channel is churning with reptiles, and I take a step back from the rail. Elliott laughs. I don't like his laugh so much right now.

"They eat people, you know," he says. "The corpse collectors figured out a few years ago that it's easier to dump the bodies in the river and let the crocodiles do the rest."

I picture the baby, a tiny body wrapped in blankets. Do the crocodiles eat the blankets? Or leave them to float in the water? The slithering of the reptiles makes me feel faint. Even the water, slapping gently against the sides of the boat, horrifies me.

"I always liked boats," Elliott says. And I'm reminded for a moment of the steamship that Henry was driving back and forth across the table when I ate breakfast with Will. And then of my father's fascination with the harbor.

"There's a steamship being outfitted in the harbor," I say.

"Yes. It was my idea. He has offered to put me in charge of the voyage."

"Do you believe there are other people out there?" My father has a book with sketches of famous places around the world. Places that are whole and healthy and beautiful. I want Elliott to tell me that there are other people out there. That we could visit those places someday.

"If we survived the plague, then others must have.

There may be other methods of preventing the disease. And we've heard that there are people who are not susceptible. Perhaps you and I don't even need these masks."

"It's strange that no one has come to the city. If other people survived, what's stopping them?"

"What has stopped us? Internal strife, fear, desperation? I'd love to find others. But the voyage isn't about that. Not for me."

A string quartet plays soothing music as Prospero's boat turns the bend, and for a moment we have a view of the city. Beautiful, virulent, smoldering.

A musket fires, making me jump. After a moment of stunned silence, the passengers laugh and applaud.

"Don't look." As Elliott grabs my shoulders to turn me away, I see three figures standing among the rocks on the shore.

"Are they diseased?" I ask.

"Yes."

"And they left the city for the marsh? To die?"

"They don't always die." He looks at me for a long time. "I knew a boy who lived with the contagion."

"What happened to him?" I'm not sure that I want to know.

"He bruised easily, his skin oozed. Everyone waited for him to die, but he didn't even seem sick, certainly wasn't bedridden. Instead people who came in contact with him died. At first it was deemed coincidence. When his own mother came down with the contagion, he hung himself."

I gasp.

It isn't unheard-of for people with the contagion to kill themselves. But it still horrifies me.

"They are dangerous, these people with the disease. Especially to the people who love them. Most of them leave the city voluntarily for the marshes. Others are run out of the city. Or killed."

I've never been in the swamps, but it seems like an inhospitable place, full of reptiles and biting insects. I see a few chimneys, maybe a village with four or five houses. I wonder if Father knows that there is a village here. He must.

Among the heaps of stones that line the shore, I see a statue. It has been shaped like a girl rising from the rubble with her arms outstretched. I point to it.

"Talent doesn't disappear when you get sick," Elliott observes.

"Not until you die. Then it's gone forever," I say quietly. "Does the prince know that people can survive for so long?"

"Yes. Of course. Why do you think it's legal to kill anyone who has the disease?"

We hear laughter from the bow of the boat, and the well-dressed passengers surge toward whatever diversion is being offered.

I can't look away from the three figures on the shore.

One falls to the ground. Another runs, hiding behind the heaped stones. The last figure sits staring out at us. We're too far away to see his face, but I imagine that his expression must be defiant. Either he's daring the guards to shoot him or he doesn't care.

A volley of musket fire startles me again, even though I should be expecting it. Sparks fly as the musket balls hit the limestone. I breathe deeply, relieved that they've missed.

But with a last burst of fire, the man slumps forward.

The body falls with the hand palm up, close to the water, and as we watch, a massive crocodile lurches out of the swamp.

Tears course down my cheeks. My oblivion should have lasted longer. Reality is proving stronger than Elliott's drugs. Blinded, I hurry away from the merriment.

"See?" Elliott is following me. "See what I mean about savages?"

I hate the look on his face, as if he's happy about what is happening because it proves his point. I close my eyes.

"Just because you don't want to see something doesn't mean that it will go away. Do you think inhumanity doesn't exist if you pretend not to see it? Or maybe get too drunk to understand? We've forgotten the things that make life worthwhile."

I put my hands over my ears to block the sound of his voice.

Mother believes that music makes life worthwhile.

Music, art, literature . . . maybe the survivors in the swamp believe that too.

Elliott pulls my hands down. I understand that the gesture irritates him. But I don't want him to touch me. Anger clouds my vision. I can't even look at him I'm so frustrated. Disgusted. He's brought me to this terrible place and won't tell me anything. Twice he's asked me to risk myself. Twice I've sneaked into Father's laboratory. And I don't even really know why.

"You're playing at revolution." I say it in a low voice so the other passengers won't hear me, but I put all of my scorn and frustration into it. "You say you want to change things, but you can't do anything."

I turn away from him, and then, with no warning, he wraps his arms around me and lifts me. He twists my body up, above the low railing on the side of the boat, dangling me out over the water. I go limp with shock.

"Don't look down," he hisses. "The water is swarming with crocodiles. Do you know that they pull people under the water, lodge them beneath a rock or a fallen tree to snack on later? They don't just eat the dead, Araby. There's a place, just around the bend, where there was a cage. People put human sacrifices out for the beasts. They've taken to worshipping them. I witnessed it myself. Human beings chained a girl there and left her to die. That is what my uncle has done to us, to our city."

Elliott's gone mad. My back is pressed against his

chest, and I can feel his heart racing. He's gasping for breath. If I struggle, he might drop me. I look for something to grab on to, but there is nothing close enough. Nothing but him.

The other passengers are mostly in the bow, fawning over the prince. As far as I can tell, we are alone. The water reflects the midmorning sunlight, blinding me.

I suck in my breath, wanting to scream, but I can't make a sound.

"I didn't get there in time. It was terrible. We tore down the platform and threw the chains into the water. Two days later they had put up another platform and killed another girl."

Elliott's arms are very strong. He pulls me back, but my legs are still dangling.

"So why are you doing the same thing to me?"

I feel him flinch.

"I told you not to trust me." His voice is harsh. I'm sure, for a moment, that he really is going to drop me. "But you started to, didn't you? Last night. This morning. I could see it in your eyes." He drops his forehead against my hair. For a torturous moment, as one of my shoes begins to slip, he doesn't move.

"And I'm falling in love with you," he whispers. "But I would throw you in the water and watch crocodiles tear you to bits, if I thought that doing so would accomplish my goals. Do. Not. Trust. Anyone. Especially me."

He pulls me in. When I move, one of my toes touches

the wood railing. The deck is below me, but I'm still too afraid to struggle. His thumb caresses my cheek.

"What's wrong with you?" I gasp.

"I don't know." His sincerity is almost more frightening than anything else.

He is actually panting as he pulls away my mask and searches my face. His is already gone, though I have no idea when he took it off.

He kisses me.

I'm trembling all over from the intensity of the last few moments. I allow him to kiss me. And then I tear myself away.

I put all of my rage behind my fist, connecting, hard, right below his eye.

It's been years since I've fought, but I had a brother. I know how. Both of us collapse onto the polished wooden deck. I scramble to get my mask back on.

He has his hand up to his eye, touching where I've hit him. Now we're both gasping for breath. His mask is on the deck beside him. I hold it out to him.

There is a barrage of shooting from the front of the boat, but the prince isn't watching the murders. He's leaning over the railing of the top deck of the ship, watching us.

Suddenly Elliott scoops me up and carries me below into a storage room.

"I'm sorry," he says in a low voice. He's still trembling, hiding behind his mask, trying to pretend that the depth of emotion he just revealed wasn't real. He's trying for nonchalance. But I know better.

I see with satisfaction that his eye is already turning purple. He takes the silver syringe from a pocket. He's offering me a few more moments of oblivion. He looks so devastated, so earnest. But he just held me over a crocodile-filled river.

I consider the syringe and feel an odd burst of strength. "I don't need it."

"Really?"

"Put it away."

Later a servant tells the two of us that we are to ride back to the palace in the prince's enclosed carriage.

Prospero has barely settled himself into his seat when Elliott asks, "Where is my sister?"

"Is that the only reason you came? Because you thought April was also . . . visiting? You wound me, nephew."

"You asked me two weeks ago to stop her from making such a spectacle of herself. And before I could do anything, she was gone."

"And you think I had something to do with that?" the prince asks. He gives Elliott a slight smile.

Elliott doesn't answer.

I struggle to remain completely still, to keep my face impassive. The prince cannot see how much I despise him. That would be disastrous. The silence stretches out. Unbearable.

"I do not have your sister. If you discover her whereabouts, send a courier to tell me, immediately. Whatever you think, everything I've done, I've done to make you and your sister stronger."

I don't move or make a noise, but the prince's attention shifts away from Elliott. His eyes crawl over me, and I wonder if I remind him of my mother. "I will send men into the city to make inquiries about April. Will that please the two of you?" His gaze returns Elliott's. "Three days from now, you will captain my steamship. Your project. Your voyage of discovery. The scientist's daughter can go with you. While you're gone, we'll move her parents to the palace so that they won't be so lonely without their only living child."

He pauses on the word living. It was his fault, and I'm just now comprehending the depth of it. His fault that Mother missed the last year of Finn's life. So many moments when we could have been together. He's hurt so many people.

"Dr. Worth has always claimed that being in a medieval palace stifles his creativity," Elliott says. "Don't do this."

"Why? Are you trying to get her to trust you? Tell her how I used to make you dip your chubby little toes into the water with the crocodiles when you were a boy. Maybe she'll feel sorry for you."

The prince chuckles. If I had any sort of weapon, I could kill him right now.

"You look pale, my dear," the prince says, "Here, I have something that will rejuvenate you." He pours white wine from a glass bottle into a tarnished silver cup.

The wine burns my throat, but with his eyes on me, I have to empty the cup.

"We're going back to the city to search for April," Elliott says. I can't tell if he is saying this for my benefit or for the prince's.

"And I wish you luck in finding her," the prince says. "Though I am pleased that she hasn't been making a spectacle of herself of late."

"It's difficult to embarrass your family when no one has seen you in days," Elliott mutters.

"Indeed. Now here's your steam carriage, waiting by the gate, all packed with your bags."

I'm relieved and surprised that the prince is letting us go. He recognizes my relief and smiles to himself. Mocking me.

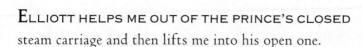

CHAPTER

FIFTEEN

Elliott helps me out of the prince's closed steam carriage and then lifts me into his open one.

"That was too easy," he says. "Maybe he does have April after all."

"Will he take my parents prisoner?"

"He wants to. He has always wanted to."

And now I've meddled, captured his attention. If he takes them now, it will be my fault.

Elliott drives too fast, careening around the twists and curves that we traversed just yesterday. We are both relieved when the palace is out of sight.

"I don't feel well," I say, maybe an hour into our journey. My face is hot, but my arms are covered in gooseflesh and I am shivering. My first thought is the Weeping Sickness. Is this how it begins? My mask was never off, except when Elliott was kissing me. And it was askew the morning I woke at Will's. I suppress a shudder.

"You'll feel better the farther we put that place behind us," Elliott says. But I don't feel better. I lean back and watch the passing trees, trying to ignore the pounding in my head.

Finally I reach for the silk scarf Mother loaned me, but I lose my balance and fall against Elliott.

"You're feverish," he says. As he touches my face, I note that his fingernails are impeccably clean, but that one of them is slightly blackened.

"Araby?"

"I think I'm sick," I whisper.

"Tell me exactly how you feel." He's concerned now, stopping the carriage.

I'm glad he's concerned, but I can't answer his question because I'm doubling up over the side, gagging. He pulls my hair gently back from my face. "Get it out of your system," he says. "That bastard may have poisoned you."

"Poison?" I ask weakly. I wipe my mouth with the back of my hand and collapse back into the steam carriage.

"Your eyes are dilated. Hell and damnation, I should have realized . . ." His hand is still on my hair.

"How are you going to tell my parents?" My voice breaks, and I realize that I am crying, but there's no moisture left in me, so it's only dry, heaving sobs.

Elliott fumbles with some vials and bottles that he's

grabbed from under his seat. "I don't have the right ingredients for a general antidote. I have to get you to a friend in the city."

He hands me a bottle of water.

"We're going to drive fast, but if you need to throw up again, you should. The more you can get out of your body, the better."

"Am I going to die?"

Either he doesn't hear me or he chooses not to answer.

I curl up on the seat of the steam carriage, trying to ignore the pain. I'm not stupid. Even if he finds his precious antidote, there will be negative effects. I think of Will. I want desperately to live.

Elliott hands me a handkerchief. "I'm sorry. This has nothing to do with you. This was an attack on me. He's showing me that he can take away anything that I care about."

I close my eyes. Right now I don't care about his uncle or his rebellion. I'm going to die in the middle of this unending forest, and I'll never have the chance to apologize to my parents.

"It's only another hour back to the city." Elliott takes my hand, and I bite my lip and pretend that my crying is from the pain, for tree roots and debris jolt the carriage mercilessly.

"I'm not going to let you die," he says. "I won't let you die." He repeats it over and over until it blends with the sound of the wheels and the grinding of the engine.

Eventually his voice is all I'm aware of, and then I close my eyes.

When I open them, we are in the city. The hot-air balloon of the Debauchery District floats above us in a haze of low clouds. Elliott pulls his steam carriage into an alley and through an opening in the back of a building.

When it stops, I stumble out of the carriage, awkwardly catching myself as my feet hit the stone. They don't stay on the ground long, because Elliott sweeps me off my feet.

"Where are we?" I ask.

"The workshop we are using to manufacture masks."

"Really?" At some point, even before his madness today, I had stopped believing in him. It was easier to hate myself, to think that I'd betrayed Father for nothing than to believe Elliott might keep his promises.

"Look at me," he says. I do. The only reason I haven't panicked is because he's been so calm, but now he's starting to look worried. I want my parents. When we met, Elliott accused me of not being afraid to die, but I am terribly afraid right now.

"I'm glad you had such faith in me," he says.

He carries me down a set of narrow cellar stairs. He only stumbles once.

In a subterranean boiler room, illuminated by gas lights, a young man is bent over a table, fiddling with pieces of porcelain. Above his mask he is wearing a pair of thick spectacles, and there is a magnifying lens on the left side. He doesn't look up as Elliott bursts through the door.

"I was expecting you yesterday with the money. I can't finish these without—"

"Help," Elliott says simply.

The young man jumps to his feet. "Is that the daughter—"

"Kent, I think she's dying."

I gulp when he says the word dying. And then my stomach burns and I twist back and forth in his arms. He lays me on a metal table. I'm sweaty, and my hair is soaked.

"It's an ugly poison," Elliott says.

"Your uncle?"

I try to complain because the tabletop is metal and I am shivering with cold, but Elliott and his friend Kent ignore me. They are fumbling with jars and bottles.

"Let me do this," Kent says. "It's too personal for you."

Could Elliott have meant it when he said he was in love with me? No, I can't trust that.

"Araby, can you hear me?" Kent asks. "Did you taste anything out of the ordinary? Any particular flavors?" I make eye contact with Kent and realize, with a start, that I recognize him.

"I've seen you before," I croak. "At the bookshop."

"Yes," he says. "I suppose we almost met, once."

He gives me a beaker full of thick, cold liquid.

"Drink this."

I choke it down.

"I didn't notice any . . . flavor," I say. "Maybe it was overly sweet?"

He pours something from a test tube into a cup. It foams and fizzes.

"I'm going to make an injection," Elliott says. I focus on the magnifying lens that Kent is wearing.

"You're a scientist," I hear myself say. A rogue scientist in hiding from the prince. Helping Elliott with the revolution.

"I'm actually an inventor. My father was a scientist."

And then Elliott puts a needle in my arm, and I lose consciousness.

When I wake up, Elliott is holding my hand and we're back in his steam carriage.

"I couldn't protect April, but I swear I will protect you," he is whispering. "We're home." I lift my head to see that we are in front of the Akkadian Towers. Hours must have passed, because it's late afternoon. Elliott helps me out of the carriage and smooths my hair.

"I'm not sure how you manage to look pretty—"

"Sir?" The doorman is standing behind him. "The elevator is still not safe," the operator says. "I am so sorry, sir. Is Miss Worth ill?"

"My driving nauseated her," Elliott says quickly. He doesn't want the doorman to think that I'm contagious.

The last thing anyone wants in this city is to be suspected of harboring the plague, but he should realize how many times I've stumbled past these same workers, coming home from the club.

The sunlight hurts my eyes, and my head pounds.

I should ask Elliott if the poison has done any lasting damage, but I'm not sure I want to know.

The lobby of the Akkadian Towers is as elegant as ever. Three guards sit in a semicircle, but today they are not throwing dice. They are staring across the room, at an armchair upholstered with gold-and-white striped silk. The girl in the armchair turns and smiles. April.

Elliott's arm, wrapped around my shoulder, goes rigid.

"Can you stand on your own?" he asks under his breath.

"Yes." My voice is shaky.

He lets me go, waiting until I've grabbed the back of another armchair for support, and then he takes three quick steps across the floor and pulls his sister out of her chair and into an embrace. She squirms away.

My relief at seeing April alive is followed by frustration. Why couldn't she have returned two days ago? Where has she been?

"I've been waiting all morning," she says to me, ignoring Elliott. "I didn't think you were ever coming home." I sway on my feet, and Elliott is instantly back at my side.

"If I help you, do you think you can make it up the stairs?" he asks me.

"I'll help. I've had enough practice supporting her," April says.

She puts one arm around me and leads me into the stairwell. The left side of her face is bruised and swollen.

"One of your concoctions?" she asks Elliott.

"The prince poisoned her."

"Did you find a way to fix her? An antidote?"

"Of course."

"You both need to be careful. There are terrible things happening in the city." She says this earnestly. She's worried about him, about us, but he doesn't see it.

"April, you have to tell me everything—" Elliott begins.

"Yes. So you can use it. You'll want to know who took me, and what they did to me. Your enemies."

Elliott flinches.

April is staring up into his face. He looks away first, as if he can't stand seeing the bruises.

"Yes. I want to know all of that. But first I should take you to Mother. She's worried sick. And Araby wants to spend some time with her parents, I'm sure. Shall we reconvene this evening, to make plans?"

"Not in the secret garden," April says. "In our living room."

"Of course," he says. And we begin to climb again.

It's warm inside the stairwell, and I'm sweating. I push

my hair back from my face.

"Nice ring," April says.

"Thank you," Elliott and I say at the same time.

We pause at the top of the first flight of stairs, and Elliott puts his hand to his mask.

"Sometimes I just can't breathe through this thing."

"You have to force yourself. It isn't safe—" I stumble, and Elliott grabs me. We teeter on the edge of the stairs. He pulls me back, and we fall against the wall. He laughs, and for some reason I laugh too.

"That's funny?" April asks. "Almost falling down the stairs?"

"It's funny because she was lecturing me about staying safe, and then she almost . . ." Elliott's smile fades. He frowns at his sister. "I found it slightly comical. Absurd."

She puts her hands on her hips and glares back.

"I bet you like the big words he uses," April says.

I could say a lot of things to her. "I don't actually like him at all," I say.

We climb the rest of the stairs in silence. I want desperately to get away from April and Elliott for a few hours. To be safe in my home with my parents. I practice my apology in my mind, and then we're on the top floor and home is right in front of me. I lift my feet, stumble forward. As we turn the corner, our courier opens the door. I dive through, away from conflict and conspiracies, and shut and lock the door behind me.

"Mother? Father?"

I am alone.

I walk through each room, calling for them, surprised by the way my voice echoes through the empty spaces. Sinking to the floor of the living room, I put my head in my hands. Mother isn't here to bring me crackers. Father isn't here to look at me as if I'm a stranger. For all I know, the poison is still running through my veins, and without my parents, I cannot make amends before I die. I've put them in so much danger. I want them to comfort me, to tell me everything is going to be okay. Even Mother. Especially Mother.

I hurry through Mother's room, to the closet, and stare at her dresses. Are any of them gone? Maybe a leather trunk has been removed from her closet?

How did Father negotiate his freedom, in this apartment that once belonged to the prince? Removing Father's journal from my bag, I open to his words. *Everything is my fault.* I need to know what he meant. But the words blur, and I find that my head is pounding.

The clock chimes. An hour passes, and my parents are still not here. I am beginning to suspect that they are never returning.

The scent of the prince's cologne clings to my dress.

The light in my bedroom has changed. In the back corner, a small window looks into the garden. I've never paid much attention to it, as it's always been covered with vegetation. But the tree branches have been pulled back and away. For the first time since I've lived here, I can see through the window. And anyone who is in the garden can see into my room.

I turn to get a blanket, and that's when I see the box, placed on my bed like a gift. Sometimes Father buys books for me and places them among my pillows, but this is larger than a book. It is a heavy box, and the wood is glossy and varnished. Inside there is a small mask.

I catch my breath. My fingers find and trace the name that has been etched into the surface. It is engraved. FINN. Father must have commissioned this mask after Finn died.

A mask for a dead boy.

It will probably be a little big for Henry. That's one reason that the poor don't always buy masks for their children. They grow into and out of them.

I need to get this mask to Will. This can't wait. I watched Finn as he came down with the infection. I know how fast it can strike. I put the mask carefully back in the box, pull a leather satchel from my closet, and place the box inside.

I take off my dress quickly, kicking it across the floor, and pull on a favorite, velvety black, appropriately tattered, with a skirt beneath that nearly reaches my knees and a corset top that is easily laced. The dress is comfortingly familiar but not warm. I pull on a coat that is long and sheer so that my legs are visible, and I put Father's journal in the pocket.

Hurrying though the interior rooms, I almost expect to see Elliott watching me from the garden.

Our courier was sitting in his chair outside the apartment when I arrived. He undoubtedly lives in the lower city. We can walk together at least part of the way to Will's apartment. It'll be light for another hour, so Will and the children will be there. The children never go outside, after all. The courier smiles tentatively when I open the door.

"Did my parents leave any messages for me?"

"I wasn't here this morning. They sent me to search the carts again, to look for the young lady's body."

I shudder.

"Did you have to touch the . . . bodies?" I can't help asking, thinking of the horrible black carts, the arms and legs.

"I had to turn them over, if the faces weren't visible. There were several nicely dressed young ladies." His voice is conversational. Is this what passes for small talk now?

"During the hours when you were here, you didn't see anything suspicious, people who would wish my father harm?"

Something flickers behind his eyes before he shakes his head. Whatever he is withholding, it makes me feel less guilty about lying.

"They left instructions that you were to escort me. I have an errand to run in the lower city."

"The lower city?" He sounds as if he's never heard of the place.

"Isn't that where you live?"

"Yes, but . . ."

"You may walk with me, and then go home early. I don't expect we will need your services tonight."

He stands. "You're sure that your parents gave permission for me to leave early?" He doesn't want to call me a liar, but he's certainly thinking it.

"Yes. You are delivering me rather than delivering groceries." I try to smile, but it's difficult.

"The lower city is dangerous. If we are attacked, I will not be able to protect you."

"We won't be attacked." I say this with more authority than I could possibly have, but he seems to trust me.

I hold the leather satchel close to my body and hurry down the stairs, through the lobby, and out a side door, with the courier following close behind. The streets are deserted. The only people we see are workers cleaning the front of the old opera house.

As we pass by, I reach out and touch a gilded molding, turning the tip of my finger gold. On the side of the building, someone has painted a black scythe. It's smeared right over the fresh gold paint that hasn't had a chance to dry.

"They say the prince may put on an opera and force people to attend."

It sounds like something the prince would do. Or a

lie that Malcontent might spread. I've seen the seats in the opera house. The thought of so many people in one place is enough to make anyone panic.

We continue on. With each step we take down the broken sidewalk, the buildings become more dilapidated. We pass easily through the checkpoint. The soldiers don't stop people who are leaving the upper city.

Every dirty window seems capable of hiding an unfriendly face.

Maybe Elliott is right. There is something inhumanly sinister about masked faces. A man makes obscene gestures toward me from a doorway.

We walk faster.

Since the horses are dead and steam carriages are rare, the side streets have returned to muddy paths. The sidewalks that line the taller buildings are better than the street, but still deep with debris that would make it difficult to run.

I watch for cloaked figures, but instead I keep seeing a group of teenage boys, trailing us by half a block.

"Do you live nearby?" I ask.

"I live a few streets to the west," he says.

My eyes catch a flash of red. A young man in a red shirt. I tell myself that just because the streets are mostly abandoned doesn't mean that every person on the street is suspicious. As we turn a corner I see a row of brick buildings, long and squat. I repeat the number of Will's building over and over in my head. It can't be far.

We round one more corner, and I get a better glimpse of the group following us. They are young. Wiry youths carrying makeshift weapons.

"Why are they following us?"

"You're dressed too elegantly for this area of town."

I almost laugh. My skirt is so worn that I doubt anyone could really tell that it was once expensive. Perhaps they covet the corset itself. Has whalebone become a sought-after commodity?

It's likely that they are following because I'm a female, which is more frightening. I glance back again, re-evaluating their ages. They may be older than I first thought. They wouldn't be the first boys to have their growth stunted by malnutrition.

I watch for a tree at the edge of the sidewalk near the door of Will's building. I remember it from when I walked with Will. A pendant flutters from a window we pass. Another black scythe. I've stopped seeing the red ones that mark the doors of the dead, but the black ones scare me.

"What is your daughter's name?"

"Leah."

One of the boys is carrying a heavy wooden cudgel. I can't help imagining it coming down, breaking my mask, here in the street where the air must be vile. Crushing the precious mask that I'm carrying.

"We're near my friend's building. See where that tree stands, near the front door? In a few steps, we will separate. You keep walking forward. I will go in through the front door and straight to my friend's apartment. Once I'm gone, they won't follow you."

"Miss!"

"Think of your daughter. We'll part in four steps, and you will be safe."

I count the steps precisely in my head, my mind racing. One.

Now that we're farther down the street, I can see the apartments stretching into the valley. And I see that there is a single tree in front of this building and the next. Both trees stand alone, and both are slightly bedraggled.

Two.

I read the brass number on the side of the building. Three.

I'm walking away from the courier, and it's too late to tell him that this is not the right building after all.

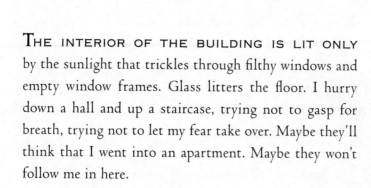

CHAPTER
SIXTEEN

THE INTERIOR OF THE BUILDING IS LIT ONLY by the sunlight that trickles through filthy windows and empty window frames. Glass litters the floor. I hurry down a hall and up a staircase, trying not to gasp for breath, trying not to let my fear take over. Maybe they'll think that I went into an apartment. Maybe they won't follow me in here.

As I'm entering a stairwell, desperate for a place to hide, I hear the door opening. I pause, afraid the stairs will creak and give me away. There are heavy footsteps in the entranceway. Some of them go in one direction, and some in another. I have to risk the noise of the stairs. If I don't, they will find me for sure.

When I reach what must be the top floor, the hallway has no windows, so it is completely dark. I shuffle forward, touching the wall with my left hand and holding tight to my bag with the other. I barely wince and don't stop as a sliver of wood from the wall lodges itself under my fingernail.

The wall ends abruptly, and I feel my way into an alcove. At the end there is a door. I turn the handle, but it is locked. My entire body is shaking. Collapsing to the floor, I pull my legs to my chest to make myself as small as possible, praying that no one will come into this alcove, that they don't have torches.

I graze the carpeting with my fingertips, searching for something to cling to. The texture of the carpet is surprisingly spongy, and I imagine that my fingers are green with mold from some unidentifiable fungus that probably carries noxious germs. I ease the box with the mask from the satchel and slide it to the back of the alcove. The box is dark wood. Perhaps, even if they find me, they will overlook it.

I grab my skirts, trying to stop shaking.

I can hear heavy footsteps echoing from the floor below.

What will they do when they find me?

Voices carry from the stairwell, and I hold my breath, afraid that the tiniest noise will give me away.

"The top floor is abandoned."

"She could be hiding up there. Did you get a good look at her? Was she carrying a purse?" a crackling adolescent voice asks.

I shiver. They have no idea of the value of the thing I carry.

I hope they have let the courier go. I try to focus, try to think. It feels like Elliott's drugs are still in my system, or the poison. Or the antidote. A wave of nausea washes over me. I focus on soundless breathing. Throwing up now would be a very bad thing.

I wish I had stayed on my feet, but I can't think how to stand without making too much noise.

It has to be nearly evening. Soon it will be dark, and even if I get away from these attackers I will not be safe in the lower city. I have to get to Will's before he leaves for the Debauchery Club.

A voice startles me. "Maybe she went out onto the roof."

He's so close that I can hear him breathing. I hold my own breath, so scared and sick that tears are running unheeded down my face.

There is a sliver of light as they open and pass through a door to the roof.

I lurch to my feet. The bag flaps against my knees. Empty. If I go now, I might make it down the stairs and outside. The door has been closed for less than a second. I stumble out of the alcove, leaving the box behind.

I run as hard as I can down the stairs. I hear someone behind me. Something crashes into my shoulder, and the cudgel clatters under my feet, tripping me. With all the drugs in me, what I feel is not exactly pain. The guy grabs my arm, but I'm falling, and he doesn't have a good grip. I land at the bottom of the stairs, cursing my impractical heeled shoes, and start running again.

The boy behind me calls to his friends, but they are on the roof.

I've had plenty of time to guess the distance to Will's building. If the numbers on this one are correct, then it is two blocks away.

I see two more boys come out of the building. They look down an alley, and then pull back quickly. I don't want to know what has frightened them in that alley.

Pulling the shreds of my sheer coat around me, I feel the weight of my father's journal and clutch it to my body while I run. Soon I can see the door to Will's building. I focus on the door. It represents safety.

And then my ankle twists beneath me, and I fall to the cold sidewalk.

CHAPTER
SEVENTEEN

PAIN SHOOTS FROM MY ANKLE TO MY KNEE. SO much for the dulling effect of whatever is still in my body.

The sidewalk is very cold. I am not wearing enough clothing, and I know without looking that something is emerging from the shadows between the buildings. Figures in black cloaks.

I scramble to my feet and up three stairs into Will's building, slamming the door behind me.

The interior of Will's building is not that different from the one where I was hiding, except that the windows are unbroken and mostly clean. His apartment is on the top floor, so I limp up a flight of creaking stairs. I stand outside the door for a moment, unused to one without a courier or at least a doorman, before I hit it several times with my fist and then abandon courtesy and try the knob. It's locked, of course.

After a long pause, my heart begins to beat in my throat again. What if they aren't here?

As I am abandoning all hope, a wooden slat on the door opens and a pair of blue eyes peers out.

"Araby!" I hear clicking and fumbling as locks are unlocked, and then the door swings open.

I push in, past the children, and lock the door.

"It's dangerous out there," I say.

"You sound like Will." Elise is wearing her mask, and I hate the way it hides her face and emphasizes her small brother's vulnerability. "He's in the kitchen."

Will is sitting in one chair with his feet propped on another, holding a mug with both hands.

In this moment, he is everything that I ever imagined.

He is the guy who works at the nightclub, thin, well dressed, and dangerous with his tattoos and shaggy hair. Tired from working late, but still mysterious.

But the kitchen around him, the children, one holding my hand, the other gripping what's left of my skirt—they tell the story of the Will I have been given the privilege of glimpsing. The secret Will.

My eyes shift to a mirror in the hallway. My face is dirty. He looks up and sees me.

"Hi," I say.

His first response is a tired smile, and then he takes in my appearance and jumps to his feet.

"You're bleeding," he says.

"I don't think so. . . ."

"Come here." He puts his mug on the table and walks me to the sink, then pours water from a pitcher onto a rag and dabs at my face.

I take off my mask and raise my face. He isn't wearing his mask.

The water is cold. His voice is warm.

"You are very trusting."

"No," I say. Not after being held over a river filled with crocodiles and then poisoned. I'm starting to shake again. "Some boys chased me. I had to hide, and there were people in dark cloaks—"

"You're safe now. They won't come into a building, but they will prey on anyone who looks vulnerable."

I don't tell him that they did follow me into a building, because he's so close, touching my face. He pulls me into a gentle embrace and then eases me into a chair, handing me the mug that he was holding when I arrived.

"Probably isn't hot now, but drink it anyway. Your hand is bleeding, and your knee." He wipes the blood from my knee before placing my hand on the table. With a clean rag he dabs at the blood on my hand, and then slides the diamond ring off my finger.

It looks odd against the tablecloth. Glittering, abandoned.

"The ring wasn't in the way," I say.

"No."

Will calls for Elise to bring a needle.

A clock hangs above the sink, and I watch it as he works to extract the splinter. Ten excruciating minutes.

His hands are gentle, but every time he touches me, my nerves flare. As he concentrates on my hand, his dark hair brushes against my upper arm.

I stare into the mug, willing myself to breathe normally.

"There." He holds up an ugly sliver of wood. "All better." He leans forward as if to kiss my hand, but Elise scampers into the room.

She twirls, pointing to her mask. "Just like yours, Araby!" she says.

My failure today comes crashing down on me.

I grab Will and hide my face against his shoulder. "I had a mask," I whisper, "for Henry. I was bringing it to you." I wince, thinking of how differently this scene played out in my head, how I imagined handing the box over to Will. "Father bought it for Finn."

Will reaches for my hand, but I pull away, more aware than I've ever been of how little I deserve even the smallest happiness.

"I told Father about Henry needing a mask, and he gave me something that must have been precious to him. And now I've lost it."

I've cried too many times today. Will hands me a handkerchief and I dab at my eyes. I'm not pretty when I cry.

"You're punishing yourself for Finn's death," he

guesses. "This is why you won't hold my hand?" His voice is painfully gentle. But I'm not sure how he's figured this out. Sometimes it isn't logical, even to me.

"I made a vow."

I won't cry. When the guilt is this heavy, you can't. It just settles and stays with you, and it's cold. Grief is warm, but guilt is very very cold.

"I promised myself that I wouldn't ever experience the things . . . that Finn won't."

"You were bringing a mask for Henry?" There is hesitation in his voice, as if he won't let himself believe, but he is smiling slightly.

"Yes, but I hid the box before I was attacked. Why are you smiling?"

"Because that means it's okay for me to notice you. To like you. I wondered what was wrong with me when I kept watching for you at the club, anticipating speaking to you. I started to despise myself for being so interested. I wondered what you would say when I was testing you, what you and your friend were giggling about."

This must be breaking my vow, somehow. I am too happy for it not to be.

"I never giggle," I say, trying to mask my feelings.

He grins.

"You wondered what was wrong with you because you liked me?" I ask finally.

"You already know that I'm partial to girls with

bright hair and glossy lipstick, but usually the attraction evaporates. Except with you."

He looks away. His cheeks are flushed.

"William," Elise says. The urgency in her voice startles me. "It's getting dark outside. You shouldn't be walking to work after dark."

So Will isn't immune to the danger on the streets. I don't want him to go.

"She's right. I should've left already, but I was distracted." He smiles a slow, flirtatious smile, and then checks himself. "Sorry." He looks down for a moment, as if weighing some decision. "Stay here. Sleep. I'll tell my neighbor that Elise and Henry are staying home tonight. Tell me where you left the box, and I'll do my best to retrieve it. I don't want your bravery and generosity to be wasted."

I feel a sense of wonder. Bravery and generosity? I'm not brave or generous, but it's nice that he thinks I am. I tell him the house number and describe the dark third-floor entranceway.

He hands me one of his shirts, a red one. It is soft when I touch it to my face. "You can't possibly sleep in that dress. Wear this, think of me." The flirty tone is back. He frowns. "I want you to do one thing for me. Think of a story that you can tell me about your brother. Not about you and your guilt, but a story that celebrates Finn."

I go with him to the door. He stops for a moment and

then squeezes my hand before walking out. I turn each lock carefully and slip into the other room to change out of my dress.

I slide Will's shirt over my head, and then I collapse into his bed. It feels odd to be here again. His last smile stays with me until a tiny hand touches my shoulder.

"Do you know any stories?" Elise asks. Her face is anxious, as if my telling her a story is very important. I close my eyes. My mother used to tell us stories. It was the thing I missed most during our years in the cellar. Finn would get restless, but I loved her stories.

"I know lots of stories," I say. "My favorite is about a princess who has to battle a dragon."

As I begin to speak, I can't help remembering how it felt to be where she is now, nestled with my brother, listening to a story.

Three stories later, both children are asleep, and I blow out the candle.

I wake once, what must be hours later, in almost complete darkness. I've been dreaming, not of crocodiles, but of being held over the water. Of struggling uselessly. Someone is holding me.

When I check that my mask is in place, I brush against Henry. His unmasked face is soft and sweet. Elise, on my other side, is wearing hers. I don't know whether she always wears it, or if she is trying to emulate me.

I pull the blankets over both of them and settle back,

listening to their rhythmic breathing. I wonder where my parents are. I can't stop thinking of the way they looked at me as I was leaving. As if they might never see me again. I wonder if they still grieve for Finn, or if they feel guilty because they've forgotten to feel the grief every day. Like I sometimes do.

It's morning when the door creaks open and I sit up, frightened. Will is in the doorway, taking off his coat.

"Hello, sleepyheads. I have a present for you," he says. I see that the bakery box is balanced on a heavy teakwood box.

"You found it," I breathe, amazed.

"Your directions took me right to it." Henry and Elise are rubbing their eyes.

"They rarely get to wake up at home," Will says. "Look, Henry, Miss Araby brought you a very precious gift. Now you can be like Elise. You'll be able to go to school."

Henry holds the porcelain mask carefully. His hands are chubby and dimpled. Will shows him where it will rest on his face.

"Before you put it on, let's eat breakfast. There's a technique for eating in your mask, and no reason to get it all dirty on the first day you own it. Your favorite brother brought home cinnamon buns."

I follow him to the kitchen. I'm still wearing his shirt. The way his shirt clings to me feels more revealing than anything I own.

Will smiles, and it's obvious that he's going to continue to flirt with me. It isn't pushy, not like Elliott, and I don't feel like he expects anything from me, but there's warmth when he looks at me. An appreciation that I don't deserve.

"Today is an auspicious day," he tells me. "We're going to take the children outside."

CHAPTER
EIGHTEEN

I WAS ALONE WHEN I LEFT THE CELLAR FOR THE first time. All I really remember is that the weak sun dazzled my eyes. I had imagined that when it happened, Finn would be beside me. But he wasn't.

As I take off Will's shirt, I tell myself that nothing bad will happen. Both children have masks now.

By the time I manage to get the remnants of my dress together, the children are devouring cinnamon rolls. After my first bite, icing gets in my hair, and Henry stands in his chair to carefully wipe it out.

Will takes a long look at the disaster that is my wardrobe and gives me his coat. I leave what's left of my own coat hanging in his room. He puts scarves on the children, and we set out. Both children grasp my hands.

The wind is pleasantly cool against my face, reminding me of childhood. Winter seems cleaner, especially when a light dusting of snow covers the city for a few hours. Henry laughs and points to a bird.

"We've only seen birds from the window," Elise explains.

Will looks pained. Guilty. He shouldn't be. He kept them alive.

"We won't go far," he says. "But there is an open space, a little park, a block from here."

Will is carrying a ball, a rather large one that is easy to catch, and when we get to the park, he throws it on the ground, hard. The children watch it, mesmerized by the satisfying bounce, the sound it makes as it hits the earth. Henry follows the pattern, moving his head up and down, and then he drops my hand and tears after the ball.

We stand watching them play. It isn't until Will shifts his weight from one foot to the other that I realize my hand is in his.

Elise touches the grass with tentative fingers. I pull gently away from Will and sit on the ground with my bare knees touching the brittle brown grass.

The surrounding buildings throw shadows across the tiny park, and my happiness is tinged with the fear of unseen things creeping from the dark corners and shadows.

"Look how tall the buildings are!" Elise doesn't see them as menacing. I pluck a frost-burned clover from the grassy area and twirl it between my fingers.

"If you find one with four leaves, it's good luck," I say. "You can make a wish."

"I'll find you one." Henry looks up at me with big eyes.

"What would you wish for?" Elise asks me.

"Maybe I would give it to you, so you could make a wish." I feel uncharacteristically content, sifting through the plants, touching the earth with the tips of my fingers.

"Oh, no. I'd give it to you," Elise says seriously.

I pause with my fingers still trailing through the grass, but I am no longer looking at it. I'm unsure whether I should feel sad this child thinks I need the wish so desperately, or flattered that she would give it to me without considering the things she might desire.

Will smiles and shrugs, amused by my reaction to Elise's words. After I've met his eyes, the clover can't command my attention.

He is sprawled on a bench, a bemused expression on his face. He yawns.

"You haven't had any sleep," I say softly, wondering how I can ask him to take me home tonight. He looks exhausted.

"Later," he says. "I can sleep like a normal person tonight. The club is closed because of the upcoming expedition."

Like a normal person. I wonder how he and the rest of the staff feel about the patrons of the club and our late-night hours. In the year I've been frequenting the Debauchery Club, it has never been closed.

"The prince has decreed that no businesses will be open until the launch of his new steamship."

"You spoke to him, the prince?"

"Briefly. He was in the club for a few moments last night. Said he had to retrieve a friend who had been living in the city."

My mother? My stomach drops. Oh, God, my mother. I have to get back to the Akkadian Towers and Elliott.

"You're killing the grass," Elise tells Henry.

Henry pulls his hand away guiltily. I start to tell them that they probably couldn't do much to harm the dried husks of grass, but they're already playing a new game, rolling the ball back and forth.

They didn't have to speak to make this change. Finn and I could communicate wordlessly, too. I'm envious, but surprisingly, watching them doesn't hurt. And Elise won't lose Henry. I made sure of that.

Will yawns again.

"Time to go home. This neighborhood seems quiet, but I won't be much good at protecting the three of you if I fall asleep."

A wet snow starts to fall, clinging to our hair and masks before it melts. Despite the snow, I feel warm and . . . happy. I hate that we have to leave this.

The apartment house, with the one tiny tree in front, feels . . . not exactly like home, but safe. It feels safe. As

Will locks the door behind us, I take it upon myself to help the children remove their coats and hats and hang them in the closet, pairing the gloves together. Will lays out a paint set, two brushes, and a large sheet of paper.

"I borrowed this from the club," he tells me. "From your boyfriend's office."

Elise frowns, either at Will's words or at the tone of his voice.

"Elliott isn't—"

Will makes a dismissive sound. I can't tell if he doesn't want to discuss Elliott, or if he doesn't believe me.

"I took the paper and paint a long time ago, when Elliott only visited the club to get the money for his uncle. Back when he didn't wear a mask because he thought he was invincible."

I hate feeling compelled to defend Elliott.

"He didn't discard his mask because he thought he was invincible."

The children paint happily. Elise has drawn a bright yellow sun at the top of her paper. Will stops to take a quick look. "She doesn't usually draw things from outside." He looks pleased.

I follow Will into the bedroom. I know he doesn't want to listen to me talk about Elliott, but I can't help trying to explain.

"It wasn't strength or invincibility that made Elliott put aside his mask." Will takes the blankets down from over the windows.

"Now that we all have masks, we can have a little more light, maybe a bit of fresh air will seep in." He smiles, but it's obvious that he's ignoring what I'm saying.

"He believes that the masks are making us inhuman because we don't see people's faces. And part of me agrees with him."

"Or maybe he just wants you to take off your mask so he can look at your face without the obstruction." Will touches my cheek. His fingertips graze my cheekbone, ever so lightly. It's warm in here, but I'm shivering. "And it's impossible to kiss someone with a mask on. In case you haven't noticed."

I feel my face flushing.

"I don't think that's it. He doesn't try to get me to take off my mask. Elliott doesn't really like me very much. We're working together—"

"He likes you. I've seen the two of you together, remember? He isn't pleased that he likes you." Will frowns. "It won't keep him from using you."

"I need Elliott's help. I have to go home." I feel terrible for asking this when Will can barely keep his eyes open.

"I wish I could take you, but there is no one to watch the children. I'll rest now, so I'll be able to escort you back to the upper city this evening." He unfastens the top button on his shirt, but undressing seems to be too much effort and he collapses into bed. "I've been waiting for your story. Will you share it with me?"

I hesitate. He closes his eyes, and the lashes are dark

against his cheeks. It is amazing that I am here with him. The memory comes unbidden, of Elliott sitting beside my bed all night, protecting me from nightmares.

"Araby?" Will pats the side of the bed. Like he would for Henry or Elise. My hesitation is silly.

I slide into his bed, facing him, but not touching. It's comforting, and . . . that's all. Comforting. I can tell that he is exhausted. His voice is soft. "Tell me about Finn."

Whenever I think of Finn, I remember that he always believed in Mother, and that makes me feel worse than ever. I don't have a specific story. Instead I focus on what I felt, watching the children today at the park.

"It was hard, learning to say I, after he died. As children, it was always we. We want cookies, we are afraid of the dark. Terrified is probably a better word; Finn and I were always afraid at night. One of Father's first inventions was a small light for our bedroom. The fear bothered Finn."

There are so many stories about Finn, stories of heroism and unfailing sweetness. But the one that comes to me isn't one of those.

"The cellar was frightening. There were dark corners and places where the bricks had settled into the earth below, places where creatures could crawl in, lizards or spiders, and there was never enough light.

"At twelve, he liked to deny that he was afraid of anything, and he didn't want me to be afraid either. My fear spilled over and affected him. And I spent the nights in the cellar tossing and turning, afraid that something was going to creep out of the corners and touch me with tentacles or hairy spider legs. I barely slept.

"One evening, I was reading beside one of the lanterns, and Finn dropped an enormous white spider onto my lap. I don't suppose it was that big, the size of a coin, maybe." I shudder at the memory. "I don't know what he thought I would do—kill it maybe? Perhaps he thought I'd see that my horror was illogical, that a spider was easily killed. Instead, I fell out of my chair and hit my head against the wall.

"My head started bleeding, and then he was holding a rag against it to staunch the blood, and I knew that he was sorry. For two months after that, he would sit beside me until I fell asleep. Sometimes, when the clocks told us that it was morning, he was still sitting there."

I take a deep breath, prepared to continue, and realize that there is nothing more to say. Instead of a sweet story about my gentle brother, I've made him seem awful. But Will laughs.

"It's the sort of thing a brother does to a sister. My bond with Henry and Elise may be different from yours with Finn, but if I die, I would hate to think that either of them chose to live half a life because of me."

He eases the mask off my face.

"And your brother would not care that I am going to kiss you before I go to sleep."

He kisses me. Very gently, on the cheek. How tragic

it is that my mask is off, and he's just kissing my cheek.

He hands me back my mask. By the time I get it in place, he's asleep.

I sit beside Will for a long time, until a commotion from the other room distracts me. When I investigate, the children are all smiles, holding up their paintings for me to admire.

We share the last cinnamon buns. Their cabinets are stocked with food. I smile. I've helped.

Elise invites me to put a wooden puzzle together. I'm not particularly good at puzzles, but I like the look of happiness on Henry's face each time he places a piece in the right spot.

"I have a game called chess," I tell Elise. "You would be good at it. Next time I visit, I'll bring it to you." Our chessboard has been put away since Finn died.

"That means you'll be leaving," she says. I nod. "But if you bring me the game, that means you're coming back!" She hugs me so hard that it throws me off-balance.

As I'm helping Elise with the evening meal, the unthinkable happens and Henry starts to sneeze and cough. Will is out of bed immediately, touching Henry's forehead, asking him how he feels. I back away. Not because I'm afraid that Henry will make me sick, just horrified by the idea of sickness.

"He has a fever," Will says, tucking Henry into bed. "Children get these things, it happens." But his face is pale.

I position a chair beside the bed. There's nothing I can do for a sick child, except to entertain him, so I spend the evening telling Henry stories that my mother used to tell me. He squeezes my hand during the exciting parts and eventually drifts off to sleep.

I realize, surprised, that it is fully dark. Elise touches Henry's face, around the periphery of his mask, and then pulls a trundle bed out from beneath the big bed and gets in. Will stands in the doorway.

"I'm not going to make it home tonight, am I?" I ask.

He shakes his head. "I can't take him downstairs, not if he's sick."

"He's going to get better," I murmur, but it's just something you say. Father told me over and over that Finn would get better. I've questioned everything he's said since, but at the time I believed him.

"We should get some sleep," he says, handing me another of his shirts and gesturing to pillows that he's placed on either side of Henry. I carefully disentangle my fingers from Henry's and go to change.

Exhausted, I fall asleep nearly as soon as I climb into bed.

I wake in the middle of the night, shaking. I push my hair back. Even though it is cold in this room, I am dripping sweat. The only thing I can think about is Elliott's silver syringe. Oblivion. My mouth is dry, but Will has no alcohol in his apartment. I wasn't looking; I just noticed when I glanced at the food in the pantry.

Will and the children are asleep. I try to ignore the tears that are sliding down my face and soaking Will's spare pillow.

I turn the pillow over, and lie awake, watching Henry. It isn't until the morning light is streaming through the uncovered window that I realize he is no longer burning with fever.

"I told you that children catch things," Will says when he wakes up. "Illnesses aren't always fatal."

Henry opens his eyes and blinks, probably wondering why we're all staring at him. Will turns to get something from the wardrobe for Elise. His shirt is untucked and halfway unbuttoned, and the light gleams off his tattoos.

Plenty of guys at the Debauchery Club have tattoos, but I've never seen anything quite like his. I want to touch them.

"I've wanted to ask you about those," I say.

Henry stretches, climbs out of bed, and goes to the kitchen to join his sister. Will gives me a shy look, so different than the way he looks at me in the semidarkness of the Debauchery Club.

"I told you I hang around in the Debauchery District because I like girls with tattered dresses and unnaturally colored hair."

I feel a twinge of jealousy when he talks about girls in the plural.

"Tattoos attract that sort of girl like nothing else."

"Well, I'm glad you have a reason," I say, hating that

my voice sounds like I'm judging him. I know I have no right to judge anyone.

"Actually, that's the story I give . . . other people. My mother was an artist. The design is from something she made for me before she died." He stares out the window for a second. "The print in the other room is her work."

"I want to go to the park," Henry says from the doorway.

Will closes his eyes. I sense his struggle. He doesn't want to expose Henry to dangerous germs, but in a world where a child could die at any time, can you deny such a simple pleasure?

"If the streets are clear, then we can go to the park for a few minutes," he says finally. "I wish there was something better, but I don't feel comfortable walking far, not with all of you." His eyes move to my bare legs and negligible dress, and then away. "Not in this neighborhood."

On the way to the park the children walk between us, fighting over who gets to carry their precious ball. They bounce the ball back and forth, laughing when it hits Henry's mask and bounces harmlessly sideways.

"I don't know what I would have done if he had caught the contagion," Will says. He hesitates. "Do you ever hate people, when the people they love get better?"

The question hurts, because he's right. I have hated people who still had their brothers. But not him. I was terrified at the prospect of Henry being sick.

"I brought you the mask," I say.

"I wasn't suggesting that you didn't want him to get better. I saw how you were with him last night."

"I don't want people to go through what I did," I say.

"If Henry died, I would feel guilty for not protecting him. But you were a child. It wasn't your fault."

I shrug, not because I don't care, but because I can't put the depth of my guilt into words. He knows more than I've told anyone else, but not everything.

"Finn wouldn't want you to deny yourself."

I don't like him speaking casually, like he knew Finn. Sharing the pain was good for me, but it's my pain and I've hoarded it for a long time. I've done regrettable things to forget my guilt. How many times have I lost consciousness, only to wake up with the pattern of the floor tiles imprinted on my face?

"I've been doing everything wrong, haven't I?" I whisper.

He puts his hand under my chin and searches my face with his dark eyes. "Do you think you could take off your mask for just a few moments? We could try not to breathe."

I'm reaching up to my face before he's finished asking the question.

His mask is already off.

He looks at me like he does in the darkness of the club. His eyes are half closed, and there's something almost languid in his movements. He raises my chin and gazes into my eyes for a long time. He slides his hands under the coat until they rest on my bare shoulders.

I close my eyes.

"Araby!"

It's April. Will fumbles with his mask, as shocked as I am. Such a lack of awareness could be deadly. I feel breathless and guilty, as if we were doing something wrong.

The most lavish steam carriage in the city is parked at the curb. April's servants wait in the carriage, dressed in spotless uniforms, but there are also men wearing the uniform of Prince Prospero's private guard.

April is smiling. Maybe because she's managed to find me, or maybe because I was about to kiss Will. She's always said that my vow was stupid, though she never delved into the depths of it.

In this light, the bruising on her cheek and neck is even more prominent. Elliott steps up beside her and crosses his arms. He is wearing his bored expression, but I know that his jaw is clenched.

"Thank God we've found you," April says sweetly. "We've been looking everywhere. Elliott was concerned."

Elliott uncrosses his arms and toys with his walking stick.

"She might have been kidnapped," he says. "Her family disappeared. We didn't know where she was. It was concerning."

I know his anger is deep, but in front of Will he'll

be cool, arrogant. He won't show anything that might suggest jealousy.

"I can't believe you abandoned me, Araby. I wanted to take you to the club last night, to celebrate my return." This isn't April's usual brand of gaiety. It's forced and a bit mean. "It was frightening when we couldn't find you." That is genuine. April is frightened, and she covers it up by acting flippant. Every word she utters has a grim undertone. She has painted her eyelids purple, as if that will camouflage her bruises.

Will feels me removing myself from his embrace and lets me go. Without the warmth of his arms, the temperature drops.

"What happened to your dress?" Elliott asks. His eyes are on my legs, which are exposed because Will pushed the coat back. He sees where my knee was skinned when I fell. "Are you hurt?" With the question, he's lost a bit of his nonchalance. I wonder if Will was right. If Elliott could actually care for me.

"There is a new illness. People are dying, lots of people," April says, her voice serious.

"A new illness?" Will asks. He sounds incredulous, but there's an undercurrent of fear. A plague robbed all of us of our childhoods. All of us fear unchecked disease.

"Not another plague?" The words feel alien on my tongue. Impossible.

April puts a gloved hand to her mask. If she's wearing gloves, she must really be afraid. "It kills instantly. You fall down dead, bleeding from your eyes. They are calling it the Red Death." She is both terrified and relishing the terror, like a child telling a ghost story.

I'm already telling myself that I don't believe it. I can't.

"She isn't exaggerating. I need to speak with your father," Elliott says.

And that fills me with a cold, foreboding horror. I stare at his very serious face, unmoving.

But the children don't understand what's happening. Elise inches close to April. "Can I touch your dress?" she asks.

April smiles down at her. "You are very pretty," she says. "Like your brother." She means Will, not little Henry.

Will squeezes my hand, but then Elliott moves quickly between us, breaking us apart.

"My uncle has your mother. He says he is keeping her safe." He gives me a second for this to sink in, not looking into my eyes.

"And Father?"

"He evaded the guards."

Father is on the run and Mother is alone. Elliott wants to speak to Father. So he needs me as bait.

"I know this is difficult, and I've been trying to find the best solution. You will go with me on the expedition, as planned. The ship sets sail tonight, and when we return . . . things will change."

His voice holds a sense of authority that wasn't there

two days ago. What has happened while I was here with Will?

Elliott turns to Will. "My sources tell me that things will get ugly tonight. The upper city is already in chaos. Stay inside with the family."

"Did someone hit you and black your eye?" Henry asks in a high-pitched, excited voice.

"Yes," Elliott says without inflection. "A very bad person hit me."

The soldiers pace restlessly. We have to go.

Elise buries her head in my skirt and whispers, "I wanted you to stay with us."

I lean over to tell her that I will see her again soon, but April pulls me back.

"Thank you for keeping her safe," Elliott tells Will. His voice sounds sincere, but I don't trust sincerity from him.

"I will always keep her safe," Will says, raising his eyebrows.

They stare at each other, over my head. I look back and forth between them, trying to think of something, anything, to say. April rolls her eyes.

The buildings surrounding the little park seem more sinister than they did just a few minutes before. The empty windows, the door hanging from its hinges. The lack of sunlight . . .

"How will you protect your little siblings, if you are trying to protect Araby?" Elliott says. "Be careful that you don't spread yourself too thin. The more people you care for, the harder it is to protect them. Come—"

We are turning away when two men in dark cloaks run toward us. One of them is carrying a torch; the other has a cudgel. The man with the torch throws it through the only unbroken window on the building that stands to the west of the park. He runs directly for us.

I stand frozen until the sound of breaking glass convinces me that this is real, and by then the man with the cudgel is only a few steps away. He leans down and almost casually scoops Henry off his feet.

Elise screams.

CHAPTER
NINETEEN

BEFORE I CAN DRAW THE BREATH TO SCREAM myself, Elliott springs into action, pulling a long sword from his walking stick. But the blade is thin, and the club the man is carrying is large and heavy.

Will tears at the park bench, ripping up a piece of rotted wood. It won't be much of a weapon.

"Do something!" I scream at the soldiers. The one who is closer aims his musket, but I don't watch. I run toward Henry. April grabs my arm, and we almost fall.

The man holding Henry raises his club over Elliott's head. For a moment I imagine it crashing down, but before the man can move, Elliott stabs him through the heart.

The man falls backward, clutching his chest.

I dive, but April wraps her arms around me, and I can see, even as I plunge forward, that I'm not going to get there fast enough.

Henry hits the ground, hard.

His mask connects with the bricks of the sidewalk with a sickening crack. The soldier finally fires his musket into the air, and Elliott is already chasing the second attacker.

"Follow him!" Elliott yells to the soldiers.

Elise stares at the dead man. Her shock is a testament to Will's care. Even in the upper city, we see death every single day. In the silence, we hear the crackle of flames as they start to spread through the first floor of the building. I hope no one is inside.

"They broke my shiny mask that Miss Araby brought," Henry says, and puts up his arms. He is speaking plainly, so he isn't badly hurt. When I pick him up, I'm amazed how light he is.

"Elliott shouldn't have followed them. They may not be alone," April says.

"Elliott has a sword," I say, to reassure her.

"It's a flimsy blade," she retorts. "Maybe Elliott would think more clearly if he wasn't distracted, wondering about you and William." She gives me a pointed look.

Henry wiggles, and I nearly drop him. His trust in me to keep him safe is painfully misplaced, yet he wraps his arms tighter around my neck.

"Take them home and keep them there," April tells Will. "Today is a violent day."

"Who hit you, April?" I reach out to her with the arm that isn't cradling Henry.

"A madman," she says. "Who has reason to hate my brother. And my uncle." She sighs. "Elliott is the one we need to be fighting for, he's our best hope, but he makes it so hard sometimes."

"You'll tell me all about it later?" I ask. She nods. Will steps forward. I hand Henry back to him and immediately miss Henry's warmth. It's too cold to stand alone, and I've pushed everyone away.

Elliott returns, racing back to us with his guards close behind.

"He went underground. If a rebel group starts using the catacombs effectively, my uncle will lose control of the city." His hands are fists. I think he's afraid that Reverend Malcontent is working faster than he is. He stretches out his fingers, calming himself, before he puts his hand on my shoulder. "We have to go." His voice is soft, and for a moment I think he understands how difficult leaving will be.

"We can't just leave," I say.

"Why, do you have another mask to give the boy?" Elliott asks. "No? Then there is nothing further we can do. William should take the children to safety."

"We could drive them home," April says.

"We'll be safer by ourselves," Will mutters, and he reaches for my hand. My heart nearly stops. I deserve a few more hours with him. Deserve to know what it's like to kiss him, before our world goes up in flames. Again.

"I'm sorry, Will." I slide my mask to the side and stand on tiptoe to kiss his cheek.

He pulls me close, but instead of embracing me, he whispers, "I've worked in the Debauchery Club for a long time. I know things, people. Maybe I could help you. It would be better than getting involved further with them."

I shake my head. I can't let him risk himself. He's the only one looking out for Henry and Elise. I hug both children.

"Be good," I say. "Listen to your brother."

They nod.

"You'll be safer." I say it more to convince myself than anything else. Will picks up Henry and takes Elise by the hand.

"And I thought he was irresistible before," April says in a dreamy voice. We watch their retreating backs, and I realize that I'm holding my breath.

They've left Henry's ball. I place it carefully on the floor of the steam carriage, which is littered with pamphlets. I pick one up.

"It says the water in the lower city is poisoned."

"Another attempt to frighten people," Elliott says. "Malcontent."

Smoke from the burning building stings my eyes. I steady Henry's rubber ball with my foot. The world seemed safer yesterday. Maybe not for me or my family, but for everyone else.

The guards climb into the carriage, beaming at Elliott like he's the greatest hero on earth. We ride in silence for several miles.

I start to ask about the Red Death, just as April speaks.

"I can't believe that you went home with Will," she says, laughing. "Every female member of the club has been trying for him. And it was wasted on you, wasn't it? Or did you break your vow?"

"I didn't . . ." I begin, and then trail off. She's looking from me to Elliott expectantly, and I realize that she's trying to reassure him. She thinks he cares what I did or didn't do with Will.

"Of course you didn't—"

"Shut up, April," Elliott says. Maybe he does care.

Now he's annoyed her, so she teases him. "Did you see the way they were . . . "

Elliott makes an angry gesture.

"It was nothing," I say.

"Nothing? You were with him for two nights."

"Henry was sick."

I picture the faces of the children, innocent with sleep, but then I push the image away. Mother is a prisoner and Father is in hiding. Elliott's right. It's dangerous to care about too many people.

"Araby is good at getting men to sleep beside her without anything . . . happening," Elliott says grimly, surveying the city.

His voice is strained, and there is a crease in his forehead that I never noticed before.

"You weren't hurt in the fight?" I ask.

"Of course not."

We pass building after building. Homes with quilts and blankets covering the windows. I'm in pain too.

We're both looking out over the city, trying not to feel anything.

"I didn't know you could fight with a sword like that," I say, to break the silence. In the distance I can see another building blazing.

He makes a dismissive gesture. "They were untrained, clumsy."

"When we lived in the palace he used to challenge the guards to fight him," April says. "Until the prince made him stop because he had killed too many."

"That's not the way I remember it," Elliott says softly.

One of the guards frowns. Elliott shakes his head, and the guard looks away, flushing.

It is starting to drizzle. I pull Will's coat closer around me, hoping he won't be cold without it. I am ridiculously pleased to have something of his.

We've pulled up to a crossroad, and I realize that it's the same one where I first saw dark-cloaked men slipping in and out of the shadows. No cart blocks our path this time. There is no young mother, giving up her infant. Instead April ignores the cold wind and Elliott does his best to shelter me from it.

The canvas roof of the young woman's building has been torn back, exposing the grim living quarters inside.

I realize then that we are not going home. We're going to the Debauchery Club. The thought of going into our empty apartment horrifies me, but Will warned me not to go to the club. I should tell them. But for some reason I don't.

When we get within a block of the club, Elliott leans over and says to April, "This is where we separate. You take the guards, as we discussed earlier."

April wants to say no. I can see it in the tilt of her head. But Elliott's voice is plaintive. For Elliott, this is close to begging.

We climb out of the carriage, and April gives us one long look before hurrying to the back entrance of the club. Elliott's steam carriage is parked at the end of the alley.

"You'll have to go with my sister," he tells the guard. "She needs your protection. We will rejoin you in a few hours."

The guards who were with us in the carriage nod and turn away, but two others come out of the Debauchery Club. I recognize one of them; he was watching my father.

"Loyal to the prince," Elliott mutters.

"Sir, you can't—," the guard begins.

But Elliott has turned away. He hands me into his carriage, cursing because the engine is cold, and when he tries to start it, the motor makes a strange grating sound.

Three guards have gathered on the sidewalk now.

"Sir, you should come with us," one of them begins. More are approaching. Two of them have unslung their muskets.

"Elliott, they're going to shoot us!"

"No, they aren't." Above his mask, his blue eyes are sparkling. He's enjoying himself.

He hits the side of the steam carriage with his fist, and the engine comes to life with a loud roar.

Elliott's soldiers appear to be arguing with the prince's men. Elliott smiles. One of the guards who was with us in April's steam carriage hits the man who was trying to stop us. And then we turn a corner, and they are all out of sight.

"What will your uncle do to my mother?" I ask.

"It depends on your father. No matter what happens, I don't think my uncle will kill her."

"You don't think he will kill her," I say flatly. "She has to live, Elliott. I owe her a lifetime of apologies."

"Sometimes I think that's all we owe our parents." Elliott adjusts his driving goggles. "I didn't crawl out from behind the curtain when my father was murdered. If I'd done so, maybe I could have bought him some time; he could have fought back.

"If he had lived, my mother wouldn't be a paranoid wreck, and maybe April wouldn't be so self-destructive.

But I can't even tell my mother that I'm sorry for being a coward. If I say one word about it, that would be treason.

"My mother is so scared of the prince that there is a chance she would turn me in. Wouldn't that be amusing, if my own mother betrayed me? For trying to apologize?"

"But you've thought of apologizing."

"Of course. Haven't you?"

I hadn't, not before two days ago.

Maybe Elliott is a better person than me.

"My uncle doesn't understand people who can make things. All he knows how to do is destroy. Your mother makes silence into music. He is fascinated by that."

I don't know how to respond to this observation, so I stare out at the city.

Something is burning on the sidewalk. Usually I'd assume that such a fire was an attempt to generate warmth. But today it might just be a random act of destruction.

"We've always wondered why Uncle Prospero let your mother go. You had a brother, right?"

How can he not know this thing that defines me?

"We were twins."

Elliott can't comprehend what this means, but he has the decency to say, "I'm sorry."

I fight back tears. Losing Finn never stops hurting.

"You are sure he's dead?" Elliott asks.

"Yes."

"You're sure he's not a captive?" When I shake my

head, he continues, "Your father has held the prince at bay for years. But all of a sudden, the prince has decided that he doesn't care. Either he no longer fears your father, or there is something he fears more."

Elliott picks up a handful of flyers, but instead of handing them to me, he lets them fall through his fingers. Still, I see the words DOWN WITH SCIENCE repeated over and over. "I don't want to live through another plague. This Red Death. I never want to see . . ." He gestures out at the city. Whatever sunlight there was is gone, and the buildings are dreary and dark. "I don't want to watch this city burn to the ground."

His voice wavers. Not enough that most people could hear, but I notice.

He makes an abrupt turn.

"After my uncle released us from the palace, my mother begged me to live with her and April in our old apartment in the Akkadian Towers. But it held too many memories of my father, so I lived in an apartment on campus. I was writing real poetry then. Agonizing over words. I was happy until I realized that I was the only one who could do something about the deterioration of the city. I could make something, the way my uncle never could. It is what I was meant to do."

I wonder how he can be so arrogant. And why I believe him.

He falls silent as we approach the university. This place has strong memories for me, too. Father in his white lab coat. Finn standing on a chair to peer into a microscope, looking at germs, while I pretended not to be bored. I haven't been here in years.

We drive past a domed building and a row of white columns. The lawn of the university campus is lush and green and the white buildings are clean of graffiti. The buildings gleam in the late afternoon light, and the shrubs have been cut into neat squares.

"The people who live here choose to spend a large part of their time on upkeep," Elliott explains. "There are even unofficial classes held in some of the buildings. Though I guess they've canceled them now." He points to a message that's been painted above an arched window. THE CONTAGION WAS CREATED HERE. "Ugliness has seeped into every part of the city."

"Or maybe the ugliness is in us. Father says that's just the way we are. Underneath the pretense of civilization."

"That's an odd thing for him to say. He saved humanity, after all. Do you think he regrets it?"

"Sometimes, maybe," I say, mostly to myself, because it isn't the sort of thing Father would ever admit. "Especially after Finn died."

Elliott parks his steam carriage behind a tall building and leads me up a set of narrow wooden stairs to his apartment. Every surface inside is covered with books except a table under the window, which is littered with vials and beakers. I feel a stab of desire looking at all of the residue in the beakers. With what Elliott could concoct, I could forget all of this for a little while. I'm not sure what is deeper, my disgust with myself for wanting oblivion, or the wanting itself.

Through the window I see groups of maskless young people sitting together in the courtyard. I put my hand to my own mask. It's cool to the touch, like it always is in late fall and winter. How wonderful it would be to discard it, even for one day. But I never will.

Elliott is gathering papers from his desk and from a table near the desk. He crumples them into a large metal bowl. The basin is blackened already; these aren't the first papers he's burned. I wonder if he ever made copies of the blueprints I gave him. I don't suppose it matters now.

Smoke stings my eyes. I like this apartment much better than the one he keeps at the Debauchery Club, but the smell of smoke reminds me of earlier today, and I feel slightly ill.

"I'm going to walk over to the science building," I say. "You can watch me from the window, if you want to check on me."

He's pacing back and forth, muttering to himself.

"Be careful," he says, looking up at me for a moment. "You know this campus pretty well, though, don't you?"

I'm fairly certain that I never discussed the university with Elliott. I don't answer before I walk out the door.

The wind outside is cool.

The science building was Father's favorite place,

before. Finn and I played beside the stream that runs behind the building while Father did research in the university laboratory. I find that stream now, and sit beside it, wondering how to question Elliott. How to ask him for details about his rebellion. He must have more in mind than what he has revealed to me.

I am startled when someone puts a hand on my shoulder.

"I have some questions for you," I say, surprised at how completely I welcome Elliott's presence.

Except it isn't Elliott.

CHAPTER
TWENTY

"I HAVE SOME QUESTIONS FOR YOU AS WELL,"
Father says. "And warnings. The prince has your mother."

"Will she be safe?" I choke out the words.

He sits down and puts his hand over mine. He is wearing a heavy coat and has cut his hair and shaved. Somehow he looks both younger and more worn.

"How could you not have told me?" I whisper.

"That she was a prisoner?"

I hate knowing that Finn died believing that Mother had abandoned us.

"It was her secret, Araby."

I pull my hand away.

"She thought it was worth your anger to protect you both. There is no right answer. Did you feel you were doing the right thing when you stole plans from my laboratory?" When he puts his hand back over mine, it's as if I never pulled away. "Nothing is easy, I know." His voice is impossibly sad.

"I'm sorry." It seems inadequate, and also, somehow, unnecessary. I'm worried about him. "How will you hide from the prince?"

"It's better that you don't know, but I won't let Prince Prospero take me into custody without a fight."

A fight? My father is the most peaceful man I know.

"Elliott wants me to go with him on the voyage." The wind scatters the dead heads of a row of dandelions, the fluffy kind that children blow and wish on. Father was once excited about the possibilities of the steamship.

"I have nothing left to bargain with. The prince's nephew may be the only one who can protect you now. Stay away from the prince and the religious fanatics. Go, get out of the city."

"But—"

"Araby, I have a question for you," he interrupts. "The most important thing I've ever asked."

I stare at a blue fish darting back and forth in the stream.

"Are you ever truly happy? Could you be?" How can this be the most important thing he's ever asked?

I want to say yes. This morning, in Will's apartment, I would have said yes, but in my mind I keep seeing Henry falling to the ground, his mask cracking. I don't say anything.

Father sighs. "So your answer is no."

No is too final. I grip his hand the way I might have held on to it as a child, before . . .

"I don't know. The plague happened." My voice catches on the word plague.

"The plague happened," he agrees.

"And we lost Finn."

"And we lost Finn."

Mother said that he must believe there is good in the world, so I promised never to tell him. I couldn't wash Finn's blood from the crease between my thumb and my forefinger, no matter how much soap I used. But I kept the secret.

"You've given me the answer I need," Father says.

But I've given the wrong answer. Dread settles over me. I pull Will's coat tight and struggle to think of a way to tell him that I could be happy, I might be happy, but I have no words. And now Father is speaking again, his voice low and rushed.

"Whatever happens, remember that I love you, and your mother loves you."

I can feel him pulling away, and I want to cling to him. But we've never been that open.

"Don't take your mask off, not for any reason." He hands me a vial filled with clear liquid. "If you get into trouble, drink half of this and give the rest to the person you love most."

I start to ask what it is, what it does, to ask what he knows about the Red Death—but before I can, someone grabs me from behind.

"So you found him," Elliott says. One arm is snaked around me. In his other hand, he is holding a knife.

"I didn't find him," I gasp, trying to figure out what he thinks he's doing. "He found me."

Is Elliott suggesting that I meant to find Father, that perhaps I've betrayed Father? Again?

"My uncle wants you dead," Elliott tells Father.

I kick him and he lets me go. With both eyes trained on Father, he shifts the knife from hand to hand.

"I know." Father stands, and for the first time in years, I see the heroic father of my youth. The father who could do no wrong. He's a hero to many people, but that never mattered to me, not after Finn died.

"Who are you working with?"

Father blinks, surprised.

"I'm not working with anyone. I'm not working at all. I'm hiding." Father's eyes bore into Elliott's, and I can't tell if Elliott believes him. Or if I do.

"I need to know everything there is to know about the Red Death."

Father gives Elliott the look that he reserves for incredibly stupid people. I see Elliott's knuckles turn white around the hilt of the knife.

"Please—," I begin, trying to find a way to stop this.

"It's a virus." Father's voice is low and unfriendly. "The masks help, but they don't guarantee immunity. I have pages of notes about the illness. You can read them, if you think the information would be helpful.

They are in a journal I kept as I studied various diseases. It's hidden behind the third drawer in my desk."

The journal isn't in his desk. It's in the pocket of my coat, and my coat is in Will's wardrobe.

"I want those notes," Elliott says. He takes a step backward, as if to make himself less threatening. "Are they enough?"

"Nothing is going to be enough. But I recorded everything I know."

"And did you include the information that has prompted my uncle to command his guards to kill you on sight?"

Father laughs. "At this point, blame is useless, wouldn't you agree?"

Elliott stares at Father for a long moment. "Not for Araby," he says. "Did you even consider—"

A bullet zings past my face and hits the wall of the science building, dusting us with bits of red brick. I stifle a scream. Elliott scowls and turns, and Father starts to run. Without thinking, I grab the sleeve of his coat.

"Father, I—"

"Soldiers are coming," Elliott says. "They've been following us."

"They will kill me," Father says simply, looking at me. Before I can open my hand to let him go, he's ripped the coat away, knocking me off-balance and into Elliott. Soldiers surround us, their muskets aimed at Father.

"No." Elliott holds up his hand. The soldiers point the loaded muskets skyward.

"Nearly all the soldiers within the city are loyal to me now," he says. "But there are a few who still look to my uncle for rewards." Elliott turns to the man who shot his musket at us.

"Deal with him," Elliott says to another soldier, who I recognize now. It's the man who I spoke to in the dark hallway at Akkadian Towers, what seems like years ago.

He gives me a tiny nod of recognition and then asks, "Did you get what you want from him?"

Elliott shrugs. "Enough for now. I need you to disappear for a few more days."

"Of course."

Elliott pulls me away. "And you thought I was playing at revolution?" His blond eyebrows nearly touch the fair hair that is hanging over his forehead. "We really should go. There was too much damning evidence in my apartment, so I set a small fire. Except it got out of hand." He smiles. "Oh, and I have something for you."

Two presents, one from Father, one from Elliott.

He hands me his knife, the one with an ivory handle. The one he was toying with while he spoke to Father. "Hide it, in your boot or under your skirts." His eyes travel up and down my body. "Not that you have much left in the way of skirts."

I take the knife, holding it nervously.

"We really should leave now, before something explodes."

The air is thick and heavy, as though the city is closing

in on us. Elliott lifts me up into his steam carriage. We have to get out.

"Why do you hate my father?"

"I don't hate him." I can't tell if he's lying, and before I can ask more questions, we round a corner and Elliott has to swerve to avoid hitting a black cart that's sitting in the middle of the road. An emaciated arm dangles over the side, white and limp.

"Where are the—" Then I see one of the corpse collectors, dead in the middle of the road. Blood streaks his face.

"The other one is probably dead, too." Elliott's words are calmer than his hands, working the controls. "People are dying. Like before. This voyage might keep the two of us alive, and the return I have planned will surprise my uncle."

But who will keep Will and the children alive?

I expect to see the body of the other corpse collector as we pass the cart, but instead, in an abandoned doorway, I see a girl.

"Don't look," Elliott says. His face has gone a sickly shade of green.

She's lying half in and half out of a doorway, and her skirts, ripped and tattered as mine, are pushed up around her waist.

I swallow hard and look away.

Elliott picks up speed until we reach the Debauchery District and then swerves to a stop in front of the club.

My face smacks against the side of his carriage, and I put my hand up to my mask to make sure that it is intact.

"There are two swords in the back of the carriage," he says. "Take one. I'm going to teach you to hold it. You will never end up like that poor girl. Not if I have anything to do with it."

He opens the double door at the front of the club and leads me into an enormous room with high gold ceilings and murals of dragons feasting upon the entrails of fallen knights. The carpets are red, the exact same shade as the bloody intestines featured in the paintings.

"I never knew this room was here."

"It's a ballroom," he says.

It's a direct violation of my vow. Finn will never learn to fight with a sword. And I know he wanted to. When we were little he was always hitting things with a wooden sword that Mother gave him. The handle was painted gold, and he used it so much the paint flaked off.

Finn will never do this. But I can.

Elliott grins. "I won't be teaching you to fight so much as teaching you how to look like you know how to fight. Stand here." He grabs my shoulders and pulls them back. "Hold the sword like this."

The corners of the room are dark and far away. An ornate balcony extends the length of the room.

"Hold your sword stable," he says. "And keep it upright, even if I hit it hard."

I grip the hilt and grit my teeth, bracing for his blow.

"You can take off your mask in here, you know."

"I'm going to keep it on," I say. "Wearing it doesn't make me uncomfortable, so it will be to my advantage."

"You'll need every advantage you can get."

Elliott circles me. He is amazingly light on his feet, and he keeps his mask on too. It's a tiny victory.

"If you take off your mask, I guess I'll know you're ready for a kiss. Like in the park today. With Will."

"I wasn't—"

Finally he attacks. It doesn't hurt me so much as jar me. I hold the blade steady, challenging him with my eyes.

"Sorry we interrupted your moment. What did you do with the diamond ring I gave you?"

I left it on Will's kitchen table.

The sudden awareness that my ring finger is bare makes my sword wobble. His blade makes contact with mine, ever so gently. He's insulting me with meekness.

We fight in silence, except for the echo of his blade hitting mine. It reverberates throughout the room, but our voices don't carry. And our footsteps, as we move from the ornate gold-and-white tiles to the red carpet and back, are silent. My arm throbs. Elliott hits and I block.

Soldiers gather on the shadowy balcony, watching.

"Elliott." My voice is plaintive, and I hate myself for it. "I don't know more right now than I knew that first night in the garden."

His blade slides toward me and I fall back, tripping over my feet.

"Stay focused! Hold your wrist like this." He twists my wrist around a little. "If you want to keep this up, you'll have to strengthen your arm."

"I can strengthen whatever I need to strengthen."

He hits again, hard, and I would wince, but I can see anger in his eyes.

"That's good," he says. "Always act sure; it will throw your opponents off."

"Always act sure," I repeat. "Just like you."

My feet slide on the polished floor, and my arm has gone numb.

"On the boat, I revealed more of myself to you than I've ever revealed to another person." He swivels and turns, waves his sword at me, showing off.

"You were holding me over water that was filled with crocodiles." I hit my blade against his, hard. He smiles and gives me a slight bow.

He raises his sword, and I ready myself for his next blow. I don't think Elliott knows how exhausted I am, but the blow never comes.

"I told you that I was falling in love with you."

Someone ignites the candelabra above us, and the shadows that I've become accustomed to waver. The darkness of the room shifts, and now it's all reds and golds.

"Love requires trust. You told me not to trust you," I say finally.

"You trust Will?"

"Will has nothing to do with this."

"Remember the pamphlets I showed you? The papers rustling around in April's steam carriage? There's a printing press in the basement here that doesn't run by itself. Do you think he prints inflammatory pamphlets for extra money, or does he have his own agenda?" He waits for the accusation to sink in. "Either way, I want you to stay away from him."

"You can't tell me what to do."

He is standing over me. Too close. I could hit him with my sword if I wanted to.

"I'm looking out for your safety."

I raise my sword. Elliott pivots and knocks it from my hands. Then he leans down, grabs the hilt, and gives it back.

"Do you want to know how I became such a good fighter?"

I raise my eyebrows. He can interpret that however he wants.

"Put your sword down. I know you're exhausted. My uncle hired an instructor to teach me. I was clumsy and weak at first, so my uncle forced me to fight in his throne room. Against his soldiers. Every time I lost, he executed someone I considered a friend. The other boys in the castle, boys I had played cards with. Once it was a boy who simply laughed at one of my jokes. Then it was my tutors, people who had done me kindnesses. He killed them one by one."

He's pacing, running one hand through his hair while the other grips the sword that seems an extension of his arm. A draft turns the candelabra, and his face moves from shadow to light and back to shadow.

"I improved and sometimes won. But my uncle insisted that I fight to the death every single time." He leans forward and touches me, right above my heart, with the tip of his sword.

I stand as still as I can, appalled by his story, uncomfortable because his stance has changed. The pain in his eyes has turned to something else.

"I never made friends," he says. "For fear I would lose them. One or two stitches more and this dress is going to fall off you." He toys with the lacing on my dress with the tip of his sword, slicing my corset.

He drops his sword and steps forward until his body is touching mine. I hold the bits of my dress together, my hands creating a tiny barrier between us.

"April says that my inability to trust makes me weak. So I'm going to tell you everything. I still don't know how Malcontent thinks he can take the city from Prospero, but I've been preparing to take it for years. I have the military. The prince's guards and trained soldiers. They have families. They live in this city and know how little the prince cares. They've sworn to fight for me. Now, with the maps of the tunnels, we have a way to move unseen."

His breath is warm against my hair, his mask is

suddenly off. "We will leave on the steamship, but we will return in two days. I have men stationed throughout the city. But only my uncle and those closest to him need worry about bloodshed. We will give away masks and provide food to the poor. The followers of this reverend may be a problem, but he has no army. Eventually we'll bring his people around to our side. Show them how life in this city can be improved." He smiles. "We'll get to start rebuilding.

"I need you beside me," he continues. "At first I wanted you because you were the scientist's daughter, and he was a hero. But now . . . I just need you to believe in me."

"I will help you," I say. "I'll do anything I can." The chandelier spins, and pinpoints of light move over the floor. I realize with surprise that Elliott is handsome. And noble. And deadly.

"Thank you," he says.

He hands me Will's coat, and I put it on gratefully, as the remnants of my dress fall to the floor.

The soldiers in the balcony applaud, and Elliott swings open the double doors of the ballroom and leads me out. The interior of the club is as shadowy as ever.

"Hello, purple-haired girl," the old man wheezes. He's standing in the shadowy hallway.

"Hello," I reply. With Elliott beside me, I'm not so terrified. Elliott ignores him until the older man moves into our path.

"We want to go to the palace," he says to Elliott. "Tell your uncle. This place is no longer—" He stops and licks his lips. His tongue is like a lizard's; in fact, his entire face is reptilian. "Satisfactory."

"Do you think I have his ear?" Elliott asks.

The man smiles grimly. "If he wanted to kill you for your treason, he would have already killed you."

"I don't think we should rate the prince's affections by who he hasn't gotten around to killing," Elliott says.

The old man chortles.

"My uncle may be in town for the launch of the ship," Elliott says. "If so, I will relay your message." He nods a dismissal to the man and takes my arm.

We climb the stairs, but when I turn and look back, the old man is glaring at us.

I follow Elliott down the dark corridor that leads to his private chambers. Will said they were ransacked, but I suppose the maids have cleaned things up. He leads me to the bedroom. The bed is neatly made, and April has spread several dresses across it.

Elliott stops in the doorway.

I stop as well. "What about your uncle?" I ask. "What will he do when you are rebuilding the city? And how will you stop him?"

He sighs. "I've considered taking the castle. He has stores of gold, and food. Things we need. But I think it will be better, with this new plague, this Red Death, to begin with as little bloodshed as possible. We'll take his soldiers away, and he will have no real power. Eventually we will take back what he's stolen from the people."

I study Elliott's face. His plan makes sense to me, but I've met his uncle, and I am afraid of what he will do.

"My mother?"

"We will rescue her. I have people in the palace. I'll get her back for you."

He's still earnest, but he's no longer meeting my eyes.

"We were going to kill him," he says in a whisper. "We were going to kill him tonight. But the Red Death has changed everything. He won't come back to the city until it's safe, and it will never be safe for him." He clears his throat and resumes speaking in his regular tone. "I have to meet with some of my men. I'll see you in two hours," he says.

"Promise?" It may be childish, but I need his reassurance.

"Yes." He hesitates, and I think, for a moment, that he might kiss me. But instead he straightens a dragon statuette on a decorative side table.

"Elliott? When we're on the ship, will you keep teaching me? With the swords?"

"Yes." His voice is soft. "Make yourself beautiful." He stops in the doorway. "More beautiful," he amends, and then he's gone. But not before I hear a key clicking in the door behind him. So much for trust; he's locked me in.

CHAPTER
TWENTY-ONE

APRIL GESTURES FOR ME TO FOLLOW HER INTO a dressing alcove. She arrived shortly after Elliott left. I'm not sure how she got in.

Her dress has long sleeves. I have never seen April in a dress that covers her arms, especially not indoors.

"Isn't this dressing room fabulous? If we end up being the last living people in the city, we can stay here with all of our dresses and try them on, one after the other."

"That sounds . . . entertaining," I say.

"Elliott has books. If we are the last people on Earth, you and Elliott can read poetry to each other."

"While you try on all your dresses?"

She meets my eyes in the mirror and frowns. She knows I'm mocking her plans. Her flippant expression drops.

"I suspect I'll be dead," she says, examining her

bloodred fingernails. "Tell me we will live through the next few weeks, Araby. Please?"

I'm not sure how we went from joking to seriousness. But she's gone pale, and her eyes are huge. She's terrified.

"A man died right in front of me. He was walking, and then he collapsed. He was shaking, and he looked terrible. Mad. Blood was coming from his eyes. And then he died. Araby, he'd been walking along looking normal just moments before."

She's sobbing a little, over this man neither of us knew.

"Before he died, the man's saliva dribbled onto my shoe. I had to make one of the guards fetch me a different pair. And now our servants are dying, both at home and here at the club."

She pushes me in front of a mirror, and I study my reflection. The violet has mostly washed out of my hair. Otherwise I look strangely the same.

"In the end, it doesn't matter, does it? No one cares what we wear or how we look." April turns away from the mirror. I have never, in all the years of our friendship, seen her turn away from a mirror.

If the plague hadn't happened, it would matter. People would be talking about what April wore, who she danced with.

"Even I don't really care anymore," she continues. "I just want to stay alive. And for you and Elliott to stay alive."

"You've seen people die before."

"Not like this." She pulls my hair back from my face and uncaps some glitter. It reminds me of the night Will told me that I should wear the silver eye shadow, that it would look better on me.

She lines my eye with something liquid and dark. Her hand is steady. I pull away so that I can look into her face, but she's focusing on my cheekbones.

"They say this one will finish us off," she says.

Panic wells up from deep inside me. The vial my father gave me weighs in my pocket.

"When did it start, April? When did the first people die?"

"Two days ago."

I let out the breath that I didn't know I was holding.

"People say this is the end. That there is no point fighting it. Some of them are going to churches and praying, and . . . some of them are attacking girls on the street. My uncle doesn't care about protecting anyone." She brushes some glitter over my eyebrows.

Elliott wants to protect the people. He cares. But he couldn't plan for this new disease, and he can't protect us from it. That is why he let my father live. Why he wants his notes.

"Araby, I'm scared. I'm too young to die."

It's selfish. Thousands of people who are younger than her have died. She's lived a better life than most of them. But it is genuine. She's scared. She is my closest friend; I put my arms around her.

"I don't want to die either," I say softly.

She returns the embrace.

And we stand there. My cheek is pressed against her shoulder. I want to tell her everything—about Will and about my parents.

"When I met you, you were going to jump off the roof."

"I was thinking about it."

"I saved you," she says.

She's right.

"If I had a sister, I would want her to be just like you," she says.

I should give her half of whatever's in the vial my father gave me. She looks in the mirror and laughs softly.

"Sorry, I didn't mean to be so embarrassing."

I clear my throat, but I've waited too long; she's pulling away. I reach into my pocket for the vial.

We turn back to each other at the same time.

"April—"

"This dress will bring out the green in your eyes."

My eyes aren't green. She gestures to a deep green corset with the tatters of a skirt attached.

"Uncle Prospero will hate it, but you'll look great," she says.

Her embarrassment is spilling over to me. I don't know how to explain about the vial. So all I say is, "Thanks." Though it isn't clear what I'm thanking her for.

"I'm going on the voyage, too," she says. "The prince wants to keep me here, but I won't stay."

"We'll go together."

She embraces me. We've hugged more tonight than in all the time we've known each other.

April walks to the door and unlocks it. Two guards wait for her in the hallway. A few seconds later, I hear the latch clicking shut.

"Sorry," she calls through the door. "Elliott says you have to be locked inside for your own safety."

I grind my teeth, glad I didn't offer her half of my precious vial.

How dare they lock me in this room?

I sit forward and lean my chin against my hands, careful not to muss my hair or makeup.

I should get something to drink, water perhaps, before I put on the green dress, but as I walk to the basin, someone grabs me and puts a hand over my mouth so that I cannot scream.

CHAPTER
TWENTY-TWO

I DON'T FIGHT. HIS GRIP IS LOOSE ENOUGH THAT I could bite. But I don't.

"You won't scream?" I feel his breath on my ear.

I shake my head and he lets go.

Will's wearing the same outfit he was wearing this morning. His hair is messier than I've ever seen it, and his expression is unreadable.

I can't help wondering about the printing press. It would be ironic if he were printing the pamphlets that vilify the wealthy here in the basement of the Debauchery Club. But it isn't amusing because if he hates the rich, where does that leave our . . . friendship?

"I know you're going with him. I won't try to talk you out of it, but there's time before you sail. Come with me for a few moments."

I hesitate.

"If I could get into this room, then other people could." He glances up at the ceiling meaningfully. He's right—those men upstairs aren't happy with Elliott. "You'll be safer with me."

He grabs my hand and pulls me toward the door.

"Stop," I say, and he does, though I can tell it's difficult for him; his body is ready to spring into motion. "I'm . . . not wearing anything . . . under this coat." I can't interpret the look on his face, so I just stumble on. "Elliott cut my dress with his sword."

He frowns. Doesn't say anything.

I pick up the green dress from the bed and slip it on, while still mostly wearing the coat. When the dress is in place, I drop the coat and struggle with the stays.

"Let me help you."

I let him.

I should offer him his coat back, but I want so badly to keep something of his. I put it on. He leads me through the door, closing it behind us. We slip down a corridor and leave the Debauchery Club through the back. The alley smells odd. There's a cloak lying in our path. Someone must have dropped . . . my foot makes contact with something solid, and I gasp. The shoes I'm wearing have an open toe. I stare down at the dead body. Will lifts me over the corpse.

"People are dying." He sounds scared.

I like that he doesn't pretend not to be afraid of death. We cross the street to the former brick factory that is now a club, the Morgue. "This place isn't owned by the prince," he explains. "The upper rooms probably won't open tonight due to his decree. But the basement is always busy."

He leads me down a narrow staircase and through a wooden door that has been painted red.

Inside, the room is dark and smoky and filled with bodies. I stand slightly behind Will as he leans forward to talk to the bartender. He downs a shot of straight liquor and then pushes the glass back across the bar. The bartender refills it without looking at Will. This is the first time I've ever seen Will drink.

My pulse quickens when someone gestures to me, offering pills. I ignore the offer. I need to be fully aware, though my head has started to throb.

"So this is the Debauchery Club's competition," I say, trying to shift his attention to me rather than the bottom of the shot glass.

The bodies are crushed in here, crowded. Bare shoulders and arms, visible above plunging necklines, remind me of the corpse in the alley. I don't let myself think about the girl in the doorway. It's easy enough to tell that these people are alive. They reek of sweat and the fear of death.

The bartender slides a couple more drinks across the bar, and I take one quickly. I sip the alcohol. It burns. I can't believe Will is drinking so much of it, and so fast.

My eyes are drawn to a couple in the corner. A girl is straddling a boy, moving against him, but what I notice is that they are wearing their masks. Somehow, kissing has become more intimate than anything else.

Will scans the room. We don't have much time together, and I want to get out of this place.

A young man approaches, emerging from the smoke. His spectacles reflect the light of the cigarettes that people are smoking behind us.

"Success?" Will asks.

"Yes. But you owe me. Are you drinking?"

I recognize Kent, the fellow who had that mysterious meeting with my father, and who saved me from the prince's poison. I'm not sure that I want him to see me here, with Will.

Will throws some money down on the bar and puts his hand on my arm. My eyes travel to the couple in the corner. The girl's head is thrown back. I feel jealous of her abandon. She isn't aware of the people around her, of this terrible claustrophobic room. I brace myself for eye contact, for a connection like I felt for the girl that evening in the rain. But her eyes pass right over mine. It feels like a slap in the face.

Will slides both hands to my shoulders, less sure than usual.

"We're going up to the roof," he whispers. "Come on." His urgency mirrors mine.

The three of us climb five flights of stairs. Will has

his arm around me by the first flight, and his hand is doing something to the hair at the nape of my neck, where April pinned it up. It makes my knees weak, which in turn makes it difficult to climb.

And now we're on the roof and Will is leading me to a great wooden basket, big enough for the two of us. It's the famous Debauchery District balloon.

"My brother always wanted to go up in a balloon."

"Well, then you should do it for him," Will says softly. It's the exact opposite of the way I've tried to deal with Finn's loss. The idea of living for Finn is alien and fascinating.

Kent walks around the balloon, stopping to inspect something. "The rope that tethers it is attached to a pulley. If you want to come down, you'll have to let out some of the air. Otherwise, I'll pull you down myself. You have fifteen minutes."

There's something else on the roof. Something enormous, under a giant beige tarp that looks like a tent, except for the way it's tied down.

Kent sees me looking at it and flushes.

"What is that?" I ask.

"Just an experiment," he says. I recognize his tone. He sounds like Father when he's in the middle of something. When he isn't sure whether his idea will work, and isn't ready to talk about it.

I'm standing scandalously close to Will, and I know I should step away, but I can't, not even for appearances.

"This is Kent," Will says. "He's the resident expert on this balloon."

"Nice to meet you." There's no reason to point out that we've met.

I don't offer him my hand. We stopped doing that years ago, due to the contagion, and both of my hands are on the front of Will's shirt, clinging to him like he might evaporate if I let go.

Kent gives a little bow. "Nice to finally meet you." He plays along with me. "Will's mentioned you."

"Are you ready?" Will asks.

He waits for my answer, and then he lifts me into the basket and climbs in beside me. The balloon rises fast enough that there's a moment when I'm actually frightened. Will clears his throat.

"All day I kept thinking of the look on your face when you were leaving. Henry's mask still works, you know. But you looked so lost. So hopeless."

I don't want to talk about being lost or hopeless.

The roof of the club is already far below us. I can see the steamship, all lit up in the harbor. Crowds are gathering.

My stomach hurts, like when Finn and I used to ride the seesaw at the park. Bursts of hope make despair harder to live with.

"I thought once that I had never met anyone so suicidal. But there's more to you than that. It's why I took you home."

"Instead of leaving me to die?"

"Instead of leaving you in the doorway of the hospital. I saw how you were changing. Then, this morning, it was like a light went out."

I'm crying. I do not deserve happiness. And if I find it, I won't be allowed to keep it. The city shimmers through my tears. I wipe them away with the back of my hand.

"It's peaceful up here," I whisper.

"Yes." He pushes his dark hair back from his face. "We can take off our masks. The air is safe this high up."

I don't dare ask if he's sure, because if he hesitates, I won't have the nerve to risk it.

I take off my mask. This act feels more revealing than taking off my dress. Perhaps because of the tears on my face. He takes the mask from my hand and lays it carefully on the floor of the basket, with his stacked neatly on top.

From up here, you can't smell the decay of the city, can't see that everything is crumbling.

"This is what I wanted you to see," he says. "From up here you can see the whole city. Look at the streets, the canal. Look at the church steeples."

"It is lovely," I say. But that's not really what I'm thinking. The city is only wonderful when you are far away from it. I don't want to go back.

In the harbor the new ship glows seductively. We'll have to navigate around rotting ships as we leave.

"There is goodness in the world. We made this city. It's beautiful and marvelous."

He's not convincing me that there is beauty in the world, but I'm happy because he wants to convince me.

He presses up against me, hard, with his hands gripping tight to the basket on either side. It should be difficult for me to turn, but I do it effortlessly. He wraps his arms around me and somehow my hands are twined into his hair, and his lips are against mine. We're kissing like it's the only thing keeping us alive.

The basket swings lightly back and forth, and he shudders. I open my eyes and look at him. He's beautiful. Completely beautiful with his eyes closed, leaning forward. He pulls me toward him without opening his eyes.

"Will?"

He kisses the side of my face. "I want to stay up here forever," he whispers.

We kiss again, and I feel like I'm drowning. So this is what April always said I was missing. It isn't as messy as I thought. His hands are in my hair and on my shoulders and my back, and I feel boneless and weak. The vow that I made, and even Finn, seem very far away.

The balloon bumps and descends slightly.

Kent is already pulling us down.

"Thank you," I say.

"You have to remember that there are reasons to live, and that at least a few people are decent, and that the world is worthwhile some of the time, okay?"

I raise my face to his, wanting another kiss, but he stops me.

"You will remember?"

The balloon bumps downward again. His eyes are still closed.

"Why don't you open your eyes?"

He opens one and squints at me for a second. "I'm terrified of heights," he says.

The basket bounces again. "We should put on our masks." He puts his trembling hands on either side of my face and kisses me once more. The balloon drops rapidly.

"I need to tell you something," he says into my hair, and then there is an explosion, and I gasp.

Reds and yellows and blues burst in the air above the harbor.

"Fireworks," I breathe. They explode over the *Discovery*, and I can hear people clapping. I've only seen fireworks once in my life, at a celebration in this same harbor when I was a little girl. Even from here I can hear the reaction of the crowd.

I try to twist toward the harbor, but Will and I are intertwined. Another round of fireworks explodes above us. The smell is acrid and unpleasant, and the sound is startling—too many things have exploded and burned in this city.

He hands me my mask, and I put it on.

We untangle our bodies and step out of the basket, onto the roof.

CHAPTER
TWENTY-THREE

"SEEMS THE CELEBRATION IS STARTING EARLY," Kent says. "His Majesty must have discovered that some religious zealots were planning to ruin his party."

Our view from the top of the Morgue isn't clear like it was from the balloon, because we are quite far away, but we can see the crowd parting for a group of soldiers.

"The prince is arriving now," Will says.

"I doubt it. If there's any hint of danger, he'll stay away." Kent frowns and glances back to the tarp covering half the roof.

"I should be down there," I say.

"If you're going, you'd better hurry." I think Kent is more worried about inspecting his balloon than about us, but then he says, "Elliott is expecting you," and looks at me. I flush.

"There's no way we can make it. The harbor is too

far," Will begins, holding tightly to my hand.

"Take Elliott's steam carriage," Kent says. He's moved from the balloon to the basket, running his hands over the straps. "As long as you ask the guard to bring it back. He left it with me so that I could procure supplies for our project." He looks at me when he says this.

I pull Will along behind me. We hurry down the stairs and out into the street. The prince's illuminations can't reach this far, and it's very dark.

I grip his hand tightly. I love the feeling of my fingers intertwined with his.

"Finn wouldn't mind," I say.

"Exactly." His voice is gentle.

Elliott's steam carriage is parked where we left it, outside the Debauchery Club. A guard stands beside it, holding a musket.

"We have to get to the harbor," I burst out.

"Miss Worth?" he says, though I'm sure I've never seen the guard before. "I'll take you as far as I can, with the crowds."

Elliott's steam carriage is only built for two, but Will pulls me up into his lap and holds me close, and the soldier drives quickly. I catch him glancing over twice, frowning at Will. And at me.

Finally, the streets become too congested and the guard stops.

"Good luck," he says. Will nods.

The streets are so tightly packed that we can barely force our way through. Vendors sell phosphorescent necklaces, and one is wearing maybe a dozen of them. They make his face green. His teeth are yellowish and the whites of his eyes are a sickly yellow. I don't think it's just the phosphorous glow from the necklaces that makes him look sick. His sleeve rides up, revealing a rash. I stifle a scream and step back. Will is right behind me. He puts his hands on my shoulders to steady me.

"It's a skin abrasion," the man says, backing away from me, and then taking another step, as if he might break into a run. If I scream, if I point to him and accuse him of carrying the contagion, the crowd will tear him apart. I've seen it happen before. Finn and I saw it happen.

One of the necklaces drops into the palm of my hand. I study it for a moment, aware that the infected man is disappearing into the crowd. The festive mood I sensed from the roof of the Morgue seems to have dissipated. People watch one another warily, never standing close enough to touch. I see the flash of a knife, hidden in a loose sleeve. People wear their cloaks pulled tight around them.

Everyone is looking toward the harbor. But their expressions are not excited, not happy. They look hungry, as if they are expecting a different sort of spectacle. A hanging, perhaps. Too many of them are wearing the glowing necklaces that make their faces green and sickly.

"We need to reach the ship!" I call to Will. Somehow I've lost his hand.

I slip between two people, but a woman shifts and I accidentally touch her. She jerks away, exclaiming, and as I stumble I come in contact with the boy standing beside her. I pull my hand back, repulsed by the warmth of his flesh.

And that's when I realize that Will is no longer with me.

I turn in a complete circle, searching for him, but the path that I followed through the crowd has closed. Other paths open and close as the crowd shifts, but I cannot tell which one might lead me to Will. I look for him, starting to panic. I can't be alone here.

A trumpet sounds, and a group of well-dressed men steps out onto the deck of the ship.

A week ago I stood on this pier, just me and my father. Other than his guards, we could have been the only people in the world. Tonight there are hundreds of people around me. I don't want to imagine the shadowy places from which they have emerged. As I slide between two men, one of them reaches toward me. I throw myself away from him, and suddenly I'm through the crowd and teetering on the very edge of the pier. I catch a gleam of fair hair from the deck of the ship.

Elliott scans the crowd. He is wearing his mask, but I can still tell that he is frowning. I raise my hand, but only to eye level. I want him to see me, but I don't want to draw attention to myself. Sailors and guards stand to either side of Elliott. I search for April but don't see her.

A man in a top hat that's seen better days hands Elliott a bottle of champagne.

I'm not that far away from him, but I can no longer interpret the look on his face. He puts his hand up to touch his mask. Then screaming starts behind me.

People fall into the water, splashing and yelling. I'm shoved backward and I grab at the people around me, only remaining on the dock because the man beside me hasn't fallen. He shoves me away, but I've regained my footing and I don't fall.

And then I see her. A girl stands in the crowd, convulsing. Red tears run down her face, and her fair hair has turned a rosy pink from sweat. She holds out her hands, begging for help, but people back even farther away from her.

"The Red Death," I hear someone say.

The girl falls.

I'm not surprised that no one steps forward. But I am surprised that the sound of her head connecting with the pier's rotten wooden planks is clearly audible.

I hear Elliott's voice and turn. He is leaning over the railing of the ship, and his mouth is moving, but I can't tell what he is saying. Someone shoves me again, and I fall to my hands and knees.

I'm not sure if he was calling to me or someone else. The skin on my palms is raw and bleeding, and as I try to get to my feet, I see someone kick the dying girl. It isn't a malicious kick, more of a prodding gesture, but once one person has done it, others join in, using their feet to push her toward the water. Her long white fingers twitch and grasp for something to hold on to. A lady screams as they wrap around her ankle.

The girl is alive as they dump her into the harbor.

Someone touches my shoulder, and I spin, knocking the hand away.

"Araby?" Will has his hand still stretched toward me. I throw my arms around him, so relieved that he, at last, has found me. Over his shoulder I see April across the pier, her dress of red sequins over strips of white silk standing out in the drab crowd.

I don't know why she's in the crowd, not on the ship, but Will can help me reach her and get us both on board. He can save us, and when we return, I'll save him.

On the ship, several well-dressed men approach Elliott to shake his hand. He is speaking to them while scanning the crowd. He's looking for me.

"Come with me."

Will's voice is impossibly gentle. A man stands beside him. An older man of average height with a silk scarf tied tightly around his throat.

"Make way for the scientist's daughter," he calls in a loud voice.

I hear people murmuring. A woman reaches out and almost touches me. "God bless you," she says softly.

"Let's get her underground," the man says. When he moves, it's obvious that he has a limp. Something he's accustomed to. Something old.

Everyone is staring at me now. A few of the maskless ones are smiling, but their smiles are not reassuring. And Will is looking away. He is not helping *me*, I suddenly realize. He is helping this man. I stop moving, but Will doesn't let go of my hand.

"Araby!" I hear Elliott and turn.

A crackling sound is followed by a boom. I look up into the sky just as flames burst from the hull of the ship and the smokestack falls forward, into the screaming crowd.

CHAPTER

TWENTY-FOUR

"GET HER TO THE TUNNEL," THE MAN YELLS. Burning scraps of timber are falling from the sky, and my eyes are watering. Something bloody splatters in front of me. I'm being propelled forward, away from the screaming crowd at the harbor, into a side street.

A faded sign with a picture of an octopus advertises a tavern that closed years ago. Will helps me over a pile of debris, and then the man with the limp is lifting a piece of canvas and gesturing for me to climb down a ladder. I shake my head.

A second, louder explosion rocks the pier. Will pulls me close to him for a moment, and then pushes me forward. We don't speak. My head throbs from the noise. I put my feet on the ladder and begin to descend. Directly in front of me, behind the rusty rungs, I see a carved eye, the symbol that Elliott wanted to use for his rebellion. Elliott is probably dead.

"So this is the scientist's daughter," the man says. He isn't asking. He just announced it to all the people on the dock. He knows.

"I've brought her, Reverend," Will says. "Like I said I would."

Of course. On the pier, the man's voice had the resonance of a minister. Who else would be at the center of such chaos, ruining Elliott's plans? I had imagined that I would meet the Reverend Malcontent at some point. But not like this.

I try to back away, but Will pushes me forward. Everything is different now. I stomp down on his foot, and he curses.

Malcontent wraps his arms around my waist. I kick and lash out as he tries to turn, to take me through a door, and I twist away from him, and for a moment I'm free. Until Will grabs me.

"It'll be better if you don't fight," he says.

My elbow connects with his rib cage, but before I can run again, the reverend pushes me roughly into a cell with a wooden door.

Through the tiny barred window in the door, I watch as Will hands the man a slim black book. My father's journal.

The reverend smiles. "Wait here," he says, and walks into another tunnel.

Will stands in the center of the room, alone. In

profile he is impossibly handsome. His cheekbones are higher, his eyelashes darker. He waits silently, showing no interest in me.

I grab the bars, ready to cry out to him, ready to beg him to help me. Before I can, the reverend walks back into the room, herding Henry and Elise in front of him. The children are wearing their masks. Henry's is cracked, but blessedly still intact. Will kneels and embraces them.

"As promised," the man says.

Will leads the children to the door, then stops and turns back to me. I don't try to interpret what he's done. Part of me understands, but that doesn't make it hurt less.

"You won't hurt her?"

The man laughs.

"If she is innocent, the Lord will protect her."

"Innocent of what?"

The man laughs again. "Take those children home. The streets will be bloody tonight."

And then Elise sees me.

"Araby," she calls. "Will, Araby is here, too! She can come home with us."

Elise pulls away from her brothers and runs to the door. I can't imagine how I look; crazy, probably. The pain of Will's betrayal hits me with the unexpected force of a punch to the stomach.

"We can't take her with us. Elise, I'm sorry." Will

stays where he is. He probably doesn't want to come close enough to look me in the face.

"I need to kiss her good-bye," she insists.

"Elise, come back."

She runs toward me, reaching a small hand to the cell window. "I never got to say good-bye to Mother."

That changes his mind. He crosses the room and lifts her. She pushes her mask aside. I am careful not to look into his eyes as I accept her kiss.

"Be a good girl," I say. "Take care of your brothers."

The reverend is standing across the room, shaking his head, looking mildly amused. He stands straight with his hands behind his back.

"I'll come back if I can," Will whispers. He's really leaving me here. I turn away.

"Araby?"

I hate myself for looking back at him. He takes his hand out of his pocket and reaches through the bars.

I put out my hand, and he drops the diamond ring that Elliott gave me into my palm. We stare at each other for a long moment after he withdraws his hand. But what is there to say? I doubt the people who are holding me will be impressed with a diamond. Especially when they could just take it from my dead body.

Will's head is bowed as he leads the children away, and the reverend follows them.

I hate Will for leaving me, and hate myself for wanting him to turn around and say something, anything, that would make me think it's worth living through the rest of this night. I miss his touch, and that makes me sick.

Across the cell is a small window just above street level. When I step up on my tiptoes, I can see out to the harbor, which is burning.

The ship has collapsed in on itself. What's left of it is on fire, probably from the gas lamps that were strung all over the rigging. Elliott was standing on the deck. Is there any way he could have survived?

Did Elliott die believing that I abandoned him? Betrayed him?

Didn't I?

Smoke billows in through the tiny window. Sometimes people run by, screaming. Two people fight, kicking and hitting each other right in front of the window.

Finally I turn away, wondering about my parents, about April. I do hope Will gets the children home safely. My cheek is still gummy from Elise's kiss.

The ship is gone. Elliott is gone. I huddle beneath a threadbare blanket but can't get warm.

The knife Elliott gave me is still in my boot. I pull it out and touch the cold metal. Press the blade to my wrist. I could end everything right now. Oblivion. I'd never have to feel guilty again. Never have to feel the pain of betrayal again, either. That's how Finn died. He bled to death.

I've been fighting the allure of death for a long time.

After Finn, I was lost, and my parents were lost as well. They were supposed to guide me, to care for me, but they couldn't. I climbed out of bed in the mornings. I ate the food that was placed in front of me. When someone smiled at me, I tried to smile back.

It was all unreal. I was fake and my life was make-believe and my happiness was pretend.

Mother returned to us, but I could never forget how she returned and what she found.

She insisted that we sleep in the same room for the first year, and all through the night she would reach over and touch me, as if to convince herself that I was still breathing.

But if I didn't forgive her, if I held tight to my anger, then I didn't have to look too closely at my own guilt. And then, with April, I learned to change myself into a different Araby. I never forgot the misery inside, but I found ways to lose consciousness. I sit up, gripping the ivory handle of the knife. I imagine letting all that warmth, the blood, flow out of me.

Finn got sick after a man came to our cellar to speak with Father about the masks. I suspect the germs crawled off his lank brown hair and infested everything. Including my brother. Finn became covered with bruises and sores, but he held my hand, and never cried. I sat beside him, night and day. I didn't always wear my mask. Father insisted that I should, but we weren't accustomed to masks yet and I didn't want Finn to regain consciousness and be unable to recognize me.

The prince's guards came for Father. They wanted him to explain how the mask worked. To demonstrate the properties of his invention.

"I'll return as soon as I can," Father told me. "Finn will pull through this. I've given him something to help his body fight off the contagion. Keep him very warm."

I wasn't afraid when Father left. Finn and I had spent many hours alone in the cellar while Father worked. But I couldn't let go of Finn's hand, so I didn't follow him up the stairs and bar the door.

Finn woke once, and I spooned soup into his mouth. He smiled up at me, and I remembered what Father said and felt a spark of hope.

"This is good soup," Finn said. It probably wasn't. I had just emptied various cans and bottles into the pot.

Father was gone all night. I put coal in the stove. I made breakfast. I read to Finn from an illustrated adventure book that Mother had given him for Christmas. And then the men came down the creaking stairs, into our home.

They were big, strong, with faces that were blank and stupid, like the corpse collectors who were hired to clean the streets later. They didn't ask for my parents, so I knew something was wrong. They showed me a paper but only held it out for a moment, not long enough for me to decipher the cramped writing.

"We're clearing out contagion," they said. "Cleansing the city so that some of us might live." They gestured to Finn. "He may as well be dead."

I stared at them, frozen.

The larger man stepped forward, and I threw myself over my twin brother.

"My father says that he is getting better," I cried. "It is just a matter of time."

One of the men picked me up and threw me against the wall. Tins of preserved food rained down around me. They didn't believe me. They didn't know who Father was or how Finn, unlike all the other dying people, could get better.

The man who hadn't thrown me said to the other, "Leave her alone, she's just a girl."

"She's been living down here, breathing the same air as the boy."

"Then we come back and kill her."

I didn't see them press the knife into Finn. I don't know if he was aware of it. They did what they had come to do and then clomped up the stairs and out of the cellar.

Blood soaked the blankets. But then he moved his hand. Ignoring the wet stickiness, I held him. I forced myself to look, even though I didn't want to see. I didn't want to see what was inside a person, my own brother. Later I wished that I hadn't. I've had nightmares about it most every night for the last three years. With or without drugs.

There was no stopping the bleeding. I've thought about it a lot, wondering if, had I been wiser, I could have staunched it or sewed him up. But I don't believe it would have been possible. The men knew their business. I held him until evening. That's when Mother returned. He was already dead.

"We can't let your father know," she said. "Not now, not ever. He has to believe that there is still some goodness in this world. Do you hear me?" I never considered that her fear might be of Father. But now I think of the way he spoke to me at the university. His hopelessness.

I helped Mother carry Finn up the stairs, after she had cleaned the blood from his face, kissed his forehead, and wrapped him in our tattered blankets. We were cold that night. They were our only blankets. His body was the first the corpse collectors took that day. He fell to the floor of the cart with a hollow clunk. Father may still believe that Finn died of the contagion. I don't know.

In this dank cell beneath the burning city, I hold the knife for a long time, mesmerized by the sharpness of it. By the possibilities. But in the end, isn't it more of a betrayal of Finn if I throw my life away? I hate that it was Will who made me realize this.

CHAPTER
TWENTY-FIVE

HOURS LATER THE REVEREND MALCONTENT opens the door of my cell and gestures for me to come. The jaunty angle of the red scarf at his throat is at odds with his grim expression.

"Follow me," he says.

When I look into his eyes, I see a feverish sort of intelligence, and it frightens me. I rest my hand against the rough stone wall and wonder whether I should refuse to go.

"We've received word that Prince Prospero is going to flood this section of the tunnels."

I follow him.

"What's happening in the city?" I ask.

"Sinners are dying."

I'm guessing that everyone is dying. Our eyes meet. I look away first.

"The Red Death is just a disease," I mutter. Though nothing, not since the first inhabitant of the city came down with the contagion, has ever really been just a disease.

"All plagues are the work of the devil," he says. But he's not really paying attention; he's scanning the tunnels ahead of us.

Reverend Malcontent adjusts his scarf, and beneath it I see deep scar tissue. Someone slashed his throat. And suddenly, looking at his fair hair that is going gray, I know who he is. Who he was.

The vial that Father gave me is cold in my pocket, the knife cool against my ankle. We walk slowly. Reverend Malcontent takes slow, measured steps, hiding his limp. It reminds me of Elliott, and thinking of Elliott hurts.

"Your children believe that the prince murdered you."

He touches the scarf at his neck. I should be terrified of him, but I'm numb, and I don't feel frightened, even though I know that I should.

"I had children a long time ago. But I lost everything."

I look at him with revulsion. I'm the one mourning his children.

"How did you survive?" I ask. The stones of the corridor are smooth and easy on my slick-soled boots. I can't think what else to do, so I ask questions, forcing myself to walk slowly, to wait for a chance to escape.

"My brother had me thrown out into the streets with

the diseased corpses. I lay in the cart for two days. My tongue swelled until it filled my mouth, and the pain was terrible. I prayed like no man has ever prayed before. A crocodile waddled up to me. It looked me in the eyes, and I saw a certain wisdom there. No crocodiles lived here before the plague, you realize. They are God's emissaries."

I would ask him why God sent us crocodiles instead of curing our illnesses, but he's obviously mad.

"My prayers were answered by the diseased swamp dwellers. They pulled me out of the muck and healed me. They taught me their religion. Eventually I taught them mine." He cups his hands in front of his face like he is praying, but his eyes are open and bright. "God wanted them to worship me."

If someone like Reverend Malcontent had taken Finn, what would I have done to get him back? Who could I have betrayed? I allow myself to forgive Will, just a little bit. He did what he had to do. But I don't think I will ever trust him again.

The reverend leads me around a pile of rubble. I glance up. Elliott told me that some of the passages were collapsing, but the roof of this one seems intact.

We've walked a long way. I struggle to find some sense of direction, to search for any markings on the walls. It smells damp and moldy here.

"Did Elliott know?"

"Elliott was worthless. It's his sister who will help

me." April is still alive? That's something. If I can find her . . .

"Why did you give up on Elliott?"

"Firstborn sons are always in high demand as sacrifices. Haven't you read the Bible?"

"I haven't."

The passage twists, and we follow the curve of the wall.

"Elliott fell in love with science. It didn't bother me to kill him. Your father has been keeping the sinners alive through devilry and science. It is time for all of them to die."

"You blew up the ship," I say. "Why?"

"We needed a grand gesture, to get the people's attention."

He did it for no good reason. I look at him with complete loathing. Like the prince, he is a murderer, and both of them are searching for my father.

A man approaches from an adjacent tunnel. "Our men aren't protected from the Red Death," he tells the reverend. "Not like they are from the contagion. Some of them are dying."

The reverend takes his hand from my arm. This could be my only chance to get away from him.

"Those who are worthy are protected," the Reverend says. "If they are dying, they aren't devout enough." His voice is rising. The other man cowers.

I dash to the nearest opening, only to discover that

it is a stairway that leads down into deeper darkness. It's warmer in there, and the darkness seems absolute. I feel my way to the bottom of the stairs and realize that the chamber I've stumbled upon is filled with people, standing upright, silent, and still. There is a light suddenly, a torch to my left.

No one is wearing masks.

The man closest to me has a rash snaking up the left side of his face, like a tattoo of some sort of vine. It is raw and oozing pus.

I stumble back. They are all infected.

We are in a vast underground room, a storage area or warehouse. In the flickering light I see that the walls are adorned with carvings that look like religious figures, saints twisted with agony. Statues line the walls. It seems the reverend has spent a good amount of time stripping relics from our abandoned places of worship.

I make eye contact with a boy who might be a year or two younger than me. His eyes look sad, and he mouths the words, "I'm sorry."

Fear rushes through me. I have to get out of here.

The people are moving now, turning, surrounding me. I gasp. Is it possible for so many people to survive, to be carriers? Were all of them living in the marshes?

A man has stepped directly in front of me. His eyes are covered with pus.

He reaches his hand out to touch me.

"You are completely clean?" he asks, his voice rasping.

His eyes crawl over my exposed arms and legs. Over my throat where the neckline of this ridiculous dress plunges down.

"Yes," I whisper.

Another man steps forward and pushes the first out of the way. I wince at his oozing hands. The others shift, restless. They are breathing hard, exhaling and inhaling. The air in this room is moist and heavy, and I am surrounded.

"I'll let you keep wearing your mask," one of the men says.

I want to laugh. I didn't keep myself sane with a vow. I didn't reject the caresses and kisses that I desperately wanted from Will to end up here, like this. The knife is in my boot. I whip it out and hold it in front of me, confident. But there are too many of them. And they are armed with knives and cudgels. Some of them have muskets. *This* is Malcontent's army. Taking a deep breath, I scream as loudly as I can.

The circle of bodies shifts. I look for the boy with the sad eyes—maybe he'll help me. But he is gone.

I hear a commotion at the top of the stairs.

"Araby?" It's April's voice.

"It's the saint's daughter," one of the men mutters.

"April?" My voice is small. It hurts to inhale.

"Tell her to go away," a man says as he reaches for me.

His diseased hands are on my waist, and I imagine the contagion seeping through his skin and running in rivulets down my dress. I only have so much dress; eventually he will touch my skin. I scream again, louder this time.

Someone grabs me under my arms and pulls me into the crowd. Away from April. Away from the stairs and the clean air above. I want to fight, but I don't want to touch anyone or anything. I gag. My knife clatters to the floor.

"Let her go." The command is obvious, though her voice is quiet. She reminds me of Elliott. "Let her go or you will burn in hell, sooner rather than later."

Unexpectedly, the hands fall away. I hit the floor hard.

"Araby," April says, "up the stairs, now." I don't hesitate.

She's standing at the top of the stairs in her silly sequined corset, holding a musket. "Come with me," she says. "Father will have a safe place for us. For our own good."

When we reach him, the reverend, who is smiling, sweeps us into a wider tunnel that has been bricked off on one end and takes the gun from April.

"You've ruined your dress, but your hair looks fabulous," she says. She laughs. "I am speaking to you, of course, not Father. His hair looks awful."

The look he gives her is not loving, or kind.

"Sit here." The reverend gestures to a spot on the floor. I see quickly why he has chosen this location. He takes a pair of manacles from his pocket, snaps one side around my wrist and the other to a metal pipe that runs the length of the wall. "Stay put," he says. Then he chuckles to himself.

"Don't hurt her," April says. "You can always convert her. Think of how impressed the people will be that you've converted the scientist's daughter."

The reverend ignores her. And then she says, with complete and absolute certainty, "Elliott loved her."

I stop breathing. After everything, how can this be what makes me cry?

Reverend Malcontent crosses the room in three quick steps, pulls the mask from her face, and throws it to the ground. He brings his foot down on the porcelain and crushes it into the stone floor. April and I stare in complete horror.

"Now I can be sure you are trusting only in God," he says.

I expect him to smash my mask as well, but he ignores me and walks out of the room.

April puts her hand to her face, frowning . . . and then she pulls a small mirror from her pocket.

"Is this lipstick too red?" she asks. I move my head a tiny bit. She must think I mean no. "Good, because one family should only have so many crazies, and I'm not going to compound these sins by wearing lipstick that is too red."

I laugh. I can't help myself.

"It all comes back to the original crazy, of course.

Uncle Prospero. My father wasn't crazy until his throat was slashed and he was thrown into the body cart. That would drive anyone insane." She looks at me like she wants me to agree. I nod slowly.

"He is not the father you remember," I begin.

She smooths her hair. "That man lived for five years among those poor rotting people without a mask, and he never got the disease."

"Maybe you won't either."

"No," she says. "I'm pretty sure that I will." She holds up my father's journal. "Malcontent values this, so I guess we'd better take it with us." She places the book in her makeup bag. It's a testament to the size of the bag that it goes in easily.

"April—"

"Shh." She puts a finger to her lips. From the corridor outside this room comes the sound of marching feet. "His army."

"I don't understand how there can be so many."

She shrugs.

The footsteps gradually fade away.

"Didn't he leave guards? Surely—"

"Father doesn't think I will leave. Because . . ." She blinks a couple of times, like she does before she lies to her mother. "Because people are murdering each other in the city and he's offered me his protection." She pulls a pin from her hair and kneels in front of me. "Be still. The city is going to burn." The lock pops open.

She cocks her head, listening. The echoes of the last footsteps have faded. She pushes the door open, and we stand looking out into the tunnel.

"Which way?" she asks.

I look one way and then the other, like a child about to cross the street for the first time.

Water is swirling around our ankles, dark and cold. The prince is flooding the tunnel, like the reverend predicted.

"That way," I say.

We begin to walk, quickly, against the flowing water. We need to get out of here.

"Remember when I told you that Elliott liked books better than girls? I didn't know he'd end up besotted—" Her voice breaks, and she tries to suppress a sob. "He had a place . . . he was working on some secret project."

The mask factory . . . Kent, who seems involved with everything . . . the balloon.

"I know how we're getting out of the city," I say. "We should take the next tunnel to the right and then climb up to the street as soon as we can." My voice sounds sure, but I'm not completely certain of any of this.

Water rushes down the corridor in a steady flow. We have to lift our feet higher than normal to walk, and it's exhausting. I suspect this passage isn't flooding yet because there are lower passages, and the water is finding its way there.

We pass one perpendicular passage and then another.

The water swirls around our ankles. We can keep going this way. It's probably safer than fighting through the mob on the street.

"So the Reverend Malcontent plans to send an army of the diseased to take over the city?" I ask.

"They want stone buildings and running water. You can't blame them. Though, if you think about it, that's all going slowly to hell. Crumbling. And the water"—she splashes it against the wall to prove her point—"tastes like swamp muck. Maybe they'll be happy in their houses in the city. No one else is."

The water is freezing cold, and I can't see much of anything.

"Was Elliott very upset when he realized that I was gone?" I ask, trying to distract myself from the cold and my horror.

"He was frantic. He thought one of the prince's spies had taken you. He threw one of those old men against the wall and knocked over a bookcase." She sighs. "Don't feel too terrible. If he's alive, you'll be the one who saved him. He saw you in the crowd and started down the gangplank. It's possible—"

Her words are interrupted by a splash from behind us. Not water hitting the walls, but something bigger. Is someone following us? April and I hold very still, but I hear nothing, and now the water has risen to our knees.

"It's not flowing down to the lower passages fast

enough. Do you think we should climb up yet?" April asks.

"Let's keep moving until we find a ladder," I say.

The floor of the passage rumbles, and as we turn the corner we see a wall of dark water roaring toward us. My face hits bricks, and my mask makes a sound like bones cracking. Elliott's ring slips down to the edge of my finger. I make a desperate fist because I don't want to lose it.

The water settles at our waists, but the current is stronger. A vortex swirls around my body, and I can't help imagining being sucked into the darkness of the corridors below.

"Araby!" April points to a ladder. I grab wildly, and when my hand touches metal, I wrap my fist around a rung and hold on, even as the water pushes me into the wall again.

April climbs quickly. I'm a few rungs below her.

"Come on, Araby," she commands.

But I can't. I'm frozen, and something is nudging my ankles. Something has crept from a dark, abandoned corner and is swimming in the water beside me.

A body floats past. Maybe it touched me; maybe that's what I felt.

And then there's a noise from above, and a face looks down, silhouetted in a circle of afternoon light.

"Hey there, you need to get out!" a boy's high-pitched voice calls.

I stare up, surprised.

The large metal screws that hold this ladder in place must have come loose, and the ladder makes a horrible discordant squeal as the metal twists. I can feel it bending beneath my feet even as I reach for the next rung.

We will only make it to the top if one of us takes the boy's hand. But he is diseased. And we both know never to touch someone who is diseased. Pus drips from a sore on his arm and drops into the water. I can see the fear on April's face, revulsion bordering on panic.

She has no mask to protect her, and he's clearly part of her father's army. He's one of the enemy.

I don't want to take his hand either.

The left side of the ladder pulls from the wall with a loud screech.

Closing my eyes, I reach up past April. The ladder is moving now, shaking with the current, but the boy has both of my hands. Something tears through my shoulder. It could be the metal of the ladder, spearing me as it rips away from the wall. It could be a crocodile, ready to devour me.

April wraps her arms around my waist.

Our only hope is this boy. We are so heavy with our wet skirts, we will drag him down with us. . . .

But he is surprisingly strong. He pulls me to street level, and I let go of his hand, clawing at the cement around the mouth of the tunnel. I'm on the sidewalk, and April is beside me. A corpse is close enough that if I reach out

I could touch it. A man's body, with blood on his cheeks.

I turn to warn April so she won't look directly at it. Seeing her without a mask, surrounded by corpses, makes me want to cry. How did this happen to us?

April grabs my shoulder, and I almost scream with the pain. "Oh, God, you're bleeding all over. This is going to scar." She whimpers. "You're never going to be able to wear a backless dress again."

Suddenly we hear screaming from inside one of the buildings. I struggle to my feet and put my hand out to April.

"Thank you," I say to the boy. He has a gently sweet face, and he's young. I realize that he's the boy from below, in the tunnel. "You saved our lives."

He's staring at my mask. I put my hand to it. The main part is intact, but I feel a cracked place on the inside.

"I didn't know," he says, staring at his hands. He thought we were diseased, like him. "You're hurt," he says. A sore beneath his eye bursts, and pus runs unchecked down his face. April makes a sound.

"I'm sorry," he says. "We don't cover the sores because fabric makes them itch."

"So you aren't dying?" April asks him. "You're one of the lucky ones. . . ." She trails off. Who knows if the lucky ones are the people who live or the ones who die quickly? April and I lean against each other. My shoulder is burning.

"I've had it since I was nine," he says. "In the last year it's gotten worse."

"Does it hurt?" April asks.

I want to tell her to leave him alone. She's never been the least bit interested before. Musket fire echoes from the buildings on either side of the street before he can answer her.

"We have to go," April says.

The boy watches us.

"Do you have someplace to go?" I ask.

He shakes his head. "Our homes out in the marsh were destroyed. I don't want to go back in there." He gestures to the tunnels.

I wipe at my arm, surprised when I see that my hand is dripping blood.

"Araby, it's deep. We have to find something." April sounds distressed.

She tears at her skirt, but it's made of stiff pieces of lace. Lace isn't going to staunch the bleeding. "We need something to use as a bandage."

My dress is made from emerald-green mesh, and the idea of pressing it to the wound, which throbs and burns at the same time, is unthinkable. The dead man's shirt might be absorbent enough to use as a bandage. But his clothing is probably crawling with germs. The boy has a cotton sash wrapped around his waist. He unties it slowly.

"You can use this if you want." He holds it out,

offering it to me. April looks at the sash for a long moment.

"April, I don't feel so well." My hands are shaking.

"Stay with us, Araby," she says as the world wavers around me. And then she presses the cloth against the heat of the wound.

She puts her arms around me and drags me toward a heavy wooden door. The boy pushes it open, and we all stumble into a dim room, April still pressing the sash against the gash in my back.

"I can tie that," he says. "If you don't mind me touching you."

"I don't mind. . . ." I falter. "I don't want to die." In my mind I'm back in the garden at the top of the Akkadian Towers, and I'm saying it to Elliott. Or maybe in the balloon, saying it to Will. I don't want to die.

"What's your name?" I ask the boy.

"Thom," he says. I nod and sway on my feet as I do.

A burning smell hangs in the air.

"She's going to pass out," the boy says. But I don't think I will.

"Here." April hands me her flask. I drink everything, and then it falls from my fingers, clinking against the tiles.

"Enough sitting around," I hear myself say. "Let's go."

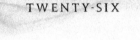

CHAPTER
TWENTY-SIX

APRIL PICKS UP THE FLASK. I'M GLAD, BECAUSE I feel too dizzy. I would have left it on the ground.

Then she completely shocks me. She turns to Thom and asks, "Do you want to come with us?"

"What are you doing?" I whisper to her.

"We can't just leave him here," she says.

I stare at her, and she blinks a couple of times, as if the afternoon sunlight is too bright.

"He can't be more than twelve years old. We can't leave him alone. If we decide he's too contagious, we can leave him someplace safe."

She doesn't have a mask. Everyone is too contagious.

April puts her arm around me, careful not to touch the side that is wounded.

Thom moves to support me from the other side, but April says, "No. I can hold her.

The alcohol in my stomach burns. My wound begins to itch. I tell myself that I am imagining it. I am not infected. But maybe April is. There are red bumps traveling from the base of her hand to her elbow. "April . . ." I say. "Why did your father leave you with me?"

"What?"

"Why did your father trust you to keep me prisoner?"

"I'm his daughter."

I laugh. Actually laugh. "Tell me the truth."

"I don't want to talk about it." There are tears in her eyes.

"Fine. I won't walk with you. I'll just bleed to death." I reach back, threatening to pull the bandage from my shoulder. Then I look her in the eyes and try to soften the threat with a quiet "Please?"

"He infected me," she says in a flat voice.

I gasp. "With . . . ?"

"Not the Red Death. The contagion." We both glance at Thom. At the glistening bruises running the length of his face. "Father claims that he has the antidote. If I do everything he says, he'll give it to me."

"But you left."

She shrugs.

"He was going to do the same thing to you. That's what he meant by converting you."

"April, if he has an antidote . . ."

"I couldn't just let him have you."

I pull the vial from my pocket. "Drink half of this."

"What is it?"

"Just drink it."

April takes three delicate sips, emptying the vial exactly halfway, and hands it to me. My arm is too numb to put the vial back in my pocket, so I put it into the bodice of my dress. I have to save it for someone who can make a bigger difference than me.

Thom looks at my wound. "I can't think what would have ripped your shoulder like that. It looks like something took a bite out of you. . . ." His voice trails away. "Oh."

"The water was too cold for crocodiles." I sound silly, even to myself.

"We have to get out," April says.

"There's no getting out of the city. Reverend's God soldiers are surrounding it, blocking all the roads," Thom says, shaking his head apologetically.

God soldiers? We have to get to that balloon.

"We're heading for the Morgue," I tell them.

It's much like the beginning of the last epidemic. Groups of people pass us, some with suitcases, some carrying the bodies of loved ones. At one point an old man stumbles into our path, shakes his fist in the air, and dies instantly, bleeding crimson tears. We step over his body. I am afraid that none of us will make it out.

And equally afraid that someone will get to the balloon before we do.

The city is sticky and humid. My wound won't stop

bleeding. How long until I bleed to death, like Finn? Maybe this was meant to happen. April is holding me, and the boy wants to help, but he isn't sure if he should touch me, so he's just walking beside me.

The Morgue is several streets away. An abandoned textile factory stands directly in front of us. The street splits, and either way we will be the same distance from the Morgue. But I pull to the left. It feels better, going this way.

Two men come out through a side door, carrying a box between them. I recognize one of them. I tell myself that it can't be him. There are other men who walk that arrogantly. Other men with fair hair.

But perhaps some other man, turning toward us, wouldn't stumble and stop.

He is wearing his mask, for once. He's not dead after all, and maybe, just maybe, he's done taking unnecessary risks. A blue-and-red woven scarf is tied and knotted about his throat.

"That scarf is hideous," April mutters. But there's a deeper emotion in her voice, something she doesn't want any of us to see.

"Elliott." My voice comes out a whisper.

His face is pink and raw, and there are bandages on his hands and arms.

I take two steps forward, about to throw myself at Elliott, but he leans away from me, putting his side of the chest between us.

"Good, you're here," Kent says. "Now we can go."

April rushes forward, and Elliott drops the chest and pulls her close for a moment. His eyes, as he looks at me over her shoulder, are cold.

I open my mouth to say something, to apologize, but a gust of wind throws a flurry of papers at us. One gets caught in my skirts, and I reach to brush it away.

It's a political pamphlet. And there is a picture of my father, crudely drawn with a caption.

Wanted for crimes against humanity.

Phineas Worth, scientist, wanted for setting loose a deadly plague and killing at least half of the people on Earth.

The words swim in front of my eyes, and I struggle to make sense of them. Half the people on Earth. This is optimistic. Father says the death toll was too huge for us to comprehend. I put a hand to the wall of the building to steady myself. Was this what Mother knew? That Father destroyed humanity before he saved it? No wonder she was afraid of him losing hope.

"How could he have——" I gasp.

"Araby, it probably isn't true," April says. "But if it is, we can't help who our fathers are, or what they do." April squeezes my arm. The one that isn't bleeding. Elliott scans the street behind us. His eyes, when they meet mine, remain wary.

"Hey, kid, can you help me with this chest of

supplies?" Kent calls to Thom, giving Elliott a pointed look.

The paper in my hand flutters as the wind picks up again.

"We have to go," Kent insists.

"I hate the idea of leaving now." Elliott frowns. "This new affliction is bad, and Malcontent is encouraging the chaos. If my uncle won't do anything, then maybe—"

"Malcontent isn't alone, Elliott. He has an army and they have weapons," April cuts in.

"And *your* army isn't ready," Kent says. "We don't have enough masks to give away yet. We don't even know how to protect against this new contagion."

"But there is no one to keep order in the city."

"That does not mean that you can do it by yourself," Kent snaps. He seems to know Elliott's plan better than anyone. "We're going to take this box of supplies to the roof of the Morgue. My interest here is in saving my work. And myself. I'd love to take all of you with me, especially since Elliott financed most of the inventions I'm saving."

He slaps Elliott on the back, and Elliott winces. Then Kent gestures to Thom, and they begin carrying the box toward the building.

"Where did Malcontent get an army?" Elliott asks. At one time I would have enjoyed Elliott's bewilderment, but that time has passed.

"The swamp," April says. "Hundreds of men."

"Hundreds?" He motions for April to follow Kent and Thom.

"Araby is hurt," April tells him.

"Aren't we all?"

April puts her arm around me again. I take two steps, and now Elliott can see my back.

"How bad is it?" he asks as we walk.

"She's lost a lot of blood."

The music pulsing from the first floor of the Morgue is a reminder of Will and his betrayal, and my own betrayal.

"Elliott," I gasp.

When he turns, his eyes aren't as cold as before.

"Yes, darling?" The words are ironic, but his tone is not.

I don't know what to say. I'm still holding the flyer. I hold it out to him, but he looks away, as if he can't stand to look at it and at me at the same time.

"Let it go, Araby," April says gently.

But I can't. My shoulder is on fire, I'm exhausted, and I can't remember the last time I ate. And here is this awful thing, these . . . lies . . . about my father.

I stuff the flyer into my sleeve. Just like I did with the plans for the masks. So long ago.

"We should hurry," I say in a low voice. Kent and Thom have disappeared into the club, with the box between them.

"It doesn't matter now," April says. "Look."

The balloon is floating up and away.

"Damn it!" Elliott mutters. "That's going to attract every wretch in the city. What is Kent thinking?"

We hear footsteps approaching. Many people, men, marching together through the street.

"Run," April says, putting every bit of horror that she has ever felt for the disease into that one word.

We do.

In the lobby of the Morgue, people are standing around holding drinks. Their expressions register distaste as we stagger in.

"You have to pay at the door," someone says. Elliott punches him in the face. And then we are off at a run again, going through the door to the stairs. By the second flight, I'm flagging. Elliott scoops me up, pulling me close to his chest. I know that it hurts him, but I can't walk another step, so asking him to put me down is out of the question. I wrap my arms around his neck and hold on as tightly as I can.

"We have to get out of here," Elliott says under his breath as he climbs. "The city is all going to hell. Burning and murder. We can do something about this, but not if we're dead."

CHAPTER
TWENTY-SEVEN

MIRACULOUSLY, I'M STILL CONSCIOUS WHEN WE reach the roof.

The enormous beige tarp has been pulled back, and the thing that was under it is exposed. It's some sort of ship. Not a ship for navigating waterways, though. It is attached to an elongated balloon and floating about a foot above the roof. An airship. It looks very similar to a water-going vessel, complete with several portholes that show there are rooms inside. Like a ship, it has two decks.

"We have to go!" Kent shouts from the front of the lower deck. "We have to go *now!*"

"I thought you were dead." Elliott's voice is muffled by my hair. He carries me across the roof and up a set of wooden stairs. April is right behind us.

Once we're on the deck, he sets me on my feet. We stand and stare at each other. Then he strips the mask off my face.

Before I can blink, or slap him or scream, his mask is off, and he's kissing me, right there in front of April and Kent and the boy, Thom. I reach up to put my arms around his neck, but I can't. I ignore the pain and concentrate on the kissing. I haven't known how to do it for that long.

"And I didn't think anything could be more distasteful than that scarf," April says.

Elliott lets me go, and then, as I try to find my footing without his arms around me, he hands me my mask and turns to fold the wooden stairs. The ship is rising.

"Can you steer, Elliott?" Kent is working a set of controls.

Elliott pulls me along as he goes to a steering wheel at the front of the craft. He puts one hand on the wheel. His other is twined with mine. I'm not sure what's happening between us. It's enough, right now, that we are both alive.

"Oh, hell," Elliott says.

I look over the side of the airship, expecting to see an army on the roof.

Instead I see Will, running across the roof, carrying Henry. Elise is lagging behind them.

"What do we do?" Kent asks. The ship is rising, and we're already out of Will's reach.

"Throw down the ladder," Elliott says.

I see a man with a musket behind Will and the children, and then two more. One of them shoots up at us; others follow, brandishing knives.

"We can't throw down the ladder," Kent says. Men are pouring onto the roof from stairways at either end of the building. "If enough of them jump on it, we'll capsize."

"We can't leave them to die," I say quietly. Will sacrificed me, but it was because he loves them more.

"I don't want to!" Kent says. "Will and I have been friends since we were boys. I just don't know how to save them."

"Is what we are doing more important than their lives?" April asks.

"Yes," Elliott says. "We can save countless lives."

Will has reached the center of the roof, directly below us, and the ruffians are pouring out of the stairwell. All he has to defend himself is a knife.

"They're Malcontent's men," Thom says. "Those men are killers."

Elliott looks at me and sighs. He gestures for Thom to hold the steering wheel, then tosses the rope ladder down. It lands at Will's feet. He grabs it and steadies it for Elise to climb up then drops his knife and follows, with Henry against his chest.

"We have to move," Kent tells Elliott. "I'm taking us higher!"

We rise fast. But not so fast that two men don't jump onto the ladder, climbing more quickly than Will and Elise. A third leaps on as the ladder dangles above him. The others watch us rise into the sky.

Suddenly Elise stops climbing. Will tries to push

her on, but she is frozen with fear and Henry is locked around Will's neck.

"Hell, damn, hell." Elliott grabs a musket. I stumble to the wooden barrier at the edge of the deck.

"Give me that. I'm a better shot than you." April takes the musket and aims. The way it's pointed, toward Will and the children, scares me. But then she shoots, and one of the men falls from the ladder and lands below. He's moving, but his legs are twisted beneath him. His death is just a matter of time.

The men have inched upward. "I can't shoot now. They're too close to the children," April says.

I kneel and call to Elise. "Can you climb to me?"

"No," she says. Her face, peering up at me, is colorless.

"Go to Araby." Will's voice is strained. He's been holding himself and Henry for too long.

"Elise," I say, "you have to do this. For me. For your brothers. They can't hold on much longer, and they can't climb past you." A tear trickles down her face, but she doesn't move.

"I'll climb down and get her."

"You can't climb." I'm surprised by Elliott's voice from behind me. "Your shoulder—"

"I can do what I have to do."

Wind is moving through my hair, and the flimsy rope ladder whips back and forth. I won't be able to climb down fast enough.

"Pull up the ladder," I say. "It's the only way."

Elliott pulls at the ladder and then pumps the handle of the winch. After only a few feet, the rope frays against the wood of the ship.

"Too heavy," he gasps.

I lie flat on the deck and reach my good arm down to Elise. She's closer now, at least. I grit my teeth and ignore the pain.

A gust of wind shakes the ship, and she screams.

"You have to take my hand," I tell her. "Please. Trust me."

Elise reaches one small hand toward me. She's shaking. I grab her hand with both of mine.

"Put your foot on the next rung."

A second musket shot deafens me, and then the ladder swings wildly as one of the men drops off it.

Elise won't let go of my hand, and I'm sliding forward, but then someone is rolling the ladder up and grabbing both of us.

I pull her away from the edge, even as Will and Henry climb to safety.

Out of the corner of my eye, I see an unfamiliar man scrabbling onto the deck. And then Elliott hits him with the butt of the musket. The man crumples. Elliott hits him again and then drags him away.

Will is so close that if I put out my hand, I would touch him.

"Thank you." Will breaks the silence.

I don't know what to say. April too is silent.

"She wouldn't have climbed to anyone else." Will says,

searching my face with his dark eyes. I look down at the deck.

"Araby?" Just yesterday he tried to convince me that there was still good in the world. Then he betrayed me, and now the city is burning below us.

"I guess fear of heights runs in the family," I say finally.

He laughs without humor.

Elliott comes out of the cabin. "I'll question the prisoner when he wakes up," he says grimly. He hands Will several blankets. "Try to keep the children still," Elliott says, "Otherwise they'll be in danger of falling."

April settles onto another part of the deck, near Thom. "It's better if he's not breathing on the children." She sits on the deck, not beside the boy, but close enough that he isn't completely alone.

A gust of wind hits the ship, and we tip to the side.

"I'm going to the upper deck," Elliott says. "Come with me?" he asks softly.

I go with him.

"The city," I breathe. It looks terrible. Water flows through the streets in some places, gushes up from the tunnels in others. People are fighting in the streets, and everywhere people are fleeing.

"Where are they going?"

"My uncle is having a party," Elliott says. "His biggest event ever."

I laugh. "So the city is in ruins and the prince is holding a party?" I wonder if it will be a masked ball.

"He's gathering all the clean upper-class citizens who can make the journey. They say he'll let exactly one thousand people in. Then he'll seal the doors. "

"What of the Red Death?" I ask, finally.

"He thinks he can hide from it."

"That's crazy."

"Maybe. Maybe he's finally gone insane. Or maybe he knows something we don't know."

I shake my head, not sure what I know any longer. If my father killed all of those people, then he killed Finn, too. So many deaths, and now there's the Red Death. . . . I still have the vial.

I remove it from my bodice with shaking fingers. Elliott watches with interest.

"That's a fascinating place to store items." The wind whips his scarf back and forth.

I uncap the vial with my teeth. Father told me to drink half and give half to the person I care about most. Half of it is left. I hand it to Elliott. He puts it to his lips.

I find it endearing that he is willing to drink it without questioning me, but I'm light-headed and blurt out, "My father gave it to me. He told me to give it to the person I cared about most."

I watch his face, waiting for his reaction. I remember the depth of emotion I glimpsed when we were on the prince's boat. He's hiding whatever he feels.

He lowers the vial.

"You drank the other half?"

"No. I gave it to April."

He holds it out to me.

"Your father wanted you to drink it."

"Elliott, you told me that the reason you wanted my help was that I didn't care. You drink it. Go back and save my mother. Kill the prince, and Reverend Malcontent, and anyone else who . . . needs killing. Save the city. I probably won't get the sickness; my mask is intact."

He puts it to my lips.

"I'm going to do all those things. But I need a reason to do them."

"No," I say, because this isn't how I planned my act of selflessness. But when I open my mouth to say the word, he tips the vial, and I have no choice but to swallow the contents.

I sit, miserably, on the deck of the ship.

"What happens next?" I ask.

"We have two clear choices," he says. "We can go looking for other people, or we can join my uncle's party."

"My mother will be there, won't she?"

The castle is a dark blob to the west. A steady stream of carriages lines the road.

"There's a third option," Elliott says. "But it's crazy."

"Tell me."

He holds the empty vial between two fingers. "We go back into the city and find the only man who can help us make sense of all this."

We look down at the chaos that is the city. Burning and

flooding and diseased. And then there is a great cracking sound and we see one of the Akkadian Towers—not the one where we lived, but the unfinished one—cracking and falling. My building is obviously on fire.

"Oh, no." I grip the wood railing. Some part of me still believed that I could return there, that my parents would greet me.

"I'm sorry," he says. He reaches to put his arm around me, but then pulls back. "Perhaps we should have someone stitch that up."

"Will can do it." I sigh.

"Let's go below and ask him. I don't want you to die."

"That's the nicest thing you've ever said to me."

His eyes meet mine, and I remember that he told me once that he was falling in love with me. I might finally believe him. He touches my shoulder with his singed fingertips, and I lean my head against him, so tired. But there are things that he has to know.

"April has the contagion."

He stiffens. "What?"

"The Reverend Malcontent infected her on purpose. We could all die."

"Not if we can find your father." The flyer rustles in the wind. I remove it from my sleeve, clutching it tightly. "They say that he had a vaccine. And that the night your brother died, he cursed humanity and threw it into the harbor."

"Who says that?"

"Kent's father. He worked with yours—"

"He doesn't know anything. Finn didn't die at night."

But perhaps Father found out about Finn's death in the evening. I don't know anymore. Why would a father curse all of humanity when he still had a living child?

"We must find your father. But first we have to recover, make plans. We'll camp for a few days, regroup."

I can see the tops of trees at the edge of the city, an oasis that we might just be able to reach.

"Going back into the city will be dangerous," I whisper. But it's what I want to do. We'll find Father first, and then Mother.

Elliott lights a match. "Don't tell Kent. We aren't supposed to smoke onboard. The hydrogen."

Something explodes far below us. Not a result of Elliott's match. I hope.

There's a sound behind us, and April joins us on the upper deck. She settles between us, pulling her knees to her chest.

She takes my hand. I squeeze hers without thinking about the contagion. She has it. And we're here together. Elliott takes her other hand, meeting my eyes from above his mask. He lets go of her hand and puts his arm around her. I smile.

When I close my eyes, everything is dark and silent. I feel as weightless as the ship.

The charcoal sky has begun to spit a cold rain as we rumble along, out of the city, and into the wilderness beyond.

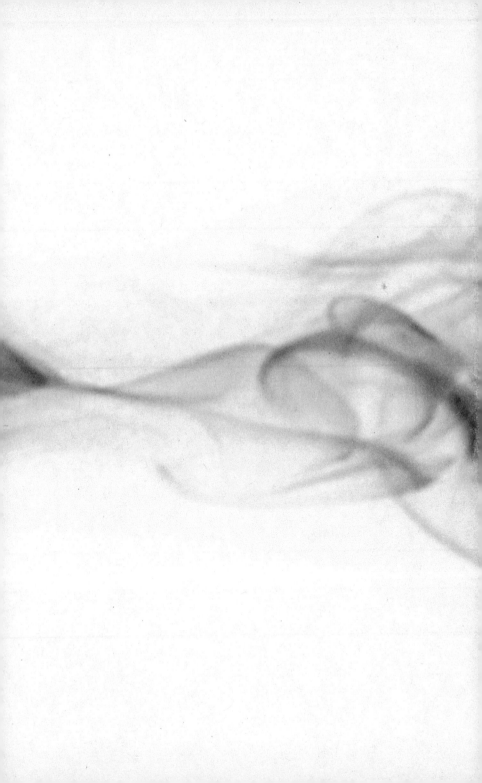

ACKNOWLEDGMENTS

I would like to thank:

The Musers, who both keep me sane and keep me company in insanity.

Suzanne Young and Amanda K. Morgan, who were with me through every step of this adventure.

Kurt Hampe, who never minded looking up information about airships, and for being part of my real-life critique group, along with Katie McGarry, Colette Ballard, and Bill Wolfe.

Lee Faith, who doesn't mind my constant preoccupation when I'm writing.

Ezra and Noel, for making me happy every single day.

My mom, for reading me so many books and then for taking Ezra and Noel on oh-so-many grandma excursions so I could write my own books.

Kellie, Carrie, Laura, Judy, and Doug, because sometimes you have to quit writing and go out for a few hours.

My agent, Michael Bourret, for general awesomeness and for answering emails at the speed of light.

My editor, Martha Mihalick, for drawing little hearts all around the love scenes. Oh, and for making this book better than I ever imagined it could be.

And my students, who keep me from getting too old and out of touch, with special thanks to Elizabeth Maddox and Joye Walton.